THE BYCATCH PRINCIPLE

THE

BYCATCH

PRINCIPLE

Kath Morgan

Hermitage Press

CORNWALL

Published in Great Britain 2023
Hermitage Press Limited, Cornwall
hermitagepress.org

First Edition

Paperback edition: ISBN 9781739453510
Electronic edition: ISBN 9781739453527

A CIP catalogue record for this book is available from the British Library
Cover art: Laura Clayton

Printed and bound by
TJ Books, Padstow, Cornwall

Content Warning

This story contains content that might be troubling to some readers, including, but not limited to, references to self-harm, suicide and underage sex, depictions of alcoholism, scenes of violence and instances of strong language. Please be mindful of these, as well as other possible triggers, and consult the dedicated page at the end of this book for a list of organisations that provide additional support, should you feel you need this.

CHAPTER ONE

Had I wanted to kill him, or had he left me with no choice? That's what Miss Beryl wants to know as she settles herself onto the garden wall next to me. It matters to them, this stuff, cos it's all about 'intention' and 'motivation' and ticking all those boxes on all those forms. Truth is, I don't know what they want from me anymore. After six years in this place, I don't know much about anything.

On the far side of the garden zone, two magpies kick up tufts of vegetation and thrust out their chests; they duck and weave and stab the air with their sharp beaks. I let my gaze travel past rows of newly planted cabbages and winter-skeletal bamboo sticks, until it comes to rest on a four-metre high brick wall. Beyond that wall lies mile after mile of open moorland, wild and free. At night, I dream about my legs pounding across it, making a break for freedom. But the problem is, when you run you get chased, and even in my dreams they always catch me.

'Adam's a dick,' I mutter.

1

Miss Beryl fiddles with the curls at the back of her neck. 'How can I help you, David, if you won't let me know what's going on with you? I'm not a mind reader.' She pauses. 'I thought we could talk to each other, you and me?'

She got a point. Of all the counsellors in here, Miss Beryl's the only one who ever really talks *to* me rather than *at* me. She sometimes tells me personal stuff, stuff that makes me feel like a human being rather than a project. Two years ago, or it might've been three, I found her in the vegetable garden, crying, eyes puffy as cheese balls. When I asked her what the matter was, she told me she'd just got diagnosed with some really grim cancer. I must've looked at her like she was about to drop dead right that minute or something, cos she blew her nose and started on about how there were all sorts of things they could do these days, miracles they could perform. And here she is, years later, thinner but still intact, so she must've been right. Afterwards, she'd begged me not to repeat a word to anybody and hurried away. I've never told a soul. Not that I can trust her. I'd be a fool to trust any of them.

'Tell me what happened this morning,' she pushes. 'I'm … it's important.'

I stare up at the sky and sigh. The usual shit with Wilson happened, that's what. We had circle time, like we do every Friday morning. Wilson was being a prat, like he is every day of the week. Freaky Adam was being an even bigger prat, if that's possible.

'Nothing special,' I say. 'Just another fun-filled day in the unit.'

As I squint my eyes against the sun, it occurs to me I'm not being totally honest. There *was* something not quite right about this morning's session. Mr Wilson had been out of order even by his own usual low standard. His behaviour had been ... off, if you know what I mean. I squeeze my eyes shut, focus on the soft warmth of the sun on my eyelids, and think back.

I'd been sat in my usual seat in the circle, and I'd been thinking about how, despite all his other failings, I had to admire Wilson's honesty. While some of the other counsellors in here tried to pretty things up by introducing a stab of colour here and there, or tossing in a few soft cushions, Wilson's room is as sparse as his soul. Nothing to see but sanitised white; no furniture except the functional circle of chairs we were all sat on; not a single solitary ornament, cos he wouldn't want one of us using them as a weapon, would he? In Wilson's room, what you see is what you get, I got to give him that.

We'd got about ten minutes into the session when Wilson strode across the circle and pressed the soft leather speakeasy into my hand. Speakeasy: that's Wilson's little joke, that is. Feet shuffled and wooden chair legs scraped against cracked lino as sixteen pairs of eyes locked onto my face. My fingers pinched the worn leather ball and plucked at the stitching as I turned the speakeasy over and over in my hands until sweat greased my palm.

'Speak up, David,' Wilson said from where he'd resettled into his black leather throne. 'Young Michael here is upset about what happened with his mother. Difficult mothers, hmm?'

I stole a glance at Fat Michael, who isn't fat and who arrived just a few weeks ago. He wears this deerstalker type hat, like some Yank, though you can tell from his accent he's from Manchester or someplace like that. We all know why he wears it. We all know why he likes the thick, furry ear flaps that bury half his face. But the hat don't hide his hands or the red puckered flesh trailing up his arms. It don't hide the flakes of skin that drop off whenever he reaches under the hat to scratch, which he's forever doing.

I focused on the blue and red, leather clad ball in my lap and concentrated until the faint buzzing started up in the back of my head, *bzzz, bzzz, bzzz,* like a bee in my brain. It's a trick I learnt back on the estate. Whenever the local louts would follow me, shouting stuff, I'd build up this buzzing in my brain so loud it'd drown out whatever they were saying; stuff about my mum mostly.

'You know the rules, David,' Wilson purred. 'We're waiting.'

Rule number one: give them nothing you don't got to.

I ignored him. Concentrated harder. *Bzzz.* I stared down at the ball in my hand, picked at the frayed stitching, tried and tried to build up the buzzing in my head.

It didn't work.

All round the circle, the other boys flicked their gazes back and forth between me and Wilson, waiting to see who'd crack first. The buzzing inside my head stuttered – then died. Everything came at me, crystal clear. The white walls sweated with the heavy breath of sixteen boys, who sat, feet flat to the floor, hands in laps, eyes watching.

'Screw you,' I said, and I let the ball drop from my lap onto the floor, where it trundled to the dead centre of the circle and lay there.

The room fell silent.

Across the circle, Oliver gave me a look that was a mix of sympathy and admiration. He smiled, a brief twitch of his lips. I didn't smile back. I wasn't keen on the sneer forming on Wilson's face, and when his long fingers reached out and grasped the speakeasy, my ears filled with the sound of my own lungs inhaling, expelling. His soft voice pushed through. 'Does anybody else care to comment?'

The speakeasy was on the move. It travelled from hand to hand around the circle, passed untouched across my lap, came to rest in the soft white hands of Freaky Adam. I fixed my gaze on the red circles on the inside of Freaky Adam's wrists. They look like love bites, but every boy in here knows that's not what they are.

'I think—' Freaky Adam began.

Wilson put up a hand. 'Adam, remember our rule about our legs during circle time, hmm? Bodies open, please. Feet on floor.'

If looks could kill, the one Freaky Adam gave Wilson would have earned him his place in here, and for a millisecond – no more – I almost felt fond of the freak. I was willing him to kick off, but then he went and did as he was told, uncrossed his legs and planted the soles of his feet with an exaggerated slap on the lino. He stared at the floor and stroked the indent on his left wrist. It's like that when they wire you up; bits of your body itch for hours afterwards.

'Thank you, Adam.' Wilson smiled like he meant it. 'Now, what did you want to say to David?'

The circle waited.

Freaky Adam sat up straight, held the speakeasy in the air between finger and thumb and twisted it this way and that like he was checking out some rare diamond, relishing his moment in the spotlight, loving watching me squirm.

'Well now,' he drawled, 'David's own mother's idea of a tenth birthday present was parcelling him off to this dump, so I'm not convinced he's fit to be giving anybody advice on how to handle mothers.'

He tossed the speakeasy into the air and snatched it, and before I could stop it, an image of my mum flashed into my head – face twisted and red, the lines around her mouth stretched white. Nearly six years ago, last time I saw her. I shook the image away and tried to focus.

'Aw, what's the matter, David?' Freaky Adam grinned. 'Does thinking about mummy make you wanna cry?' He played his finger up and down on his lips, making a blubbing sound.

'That's out of order,' Oliver cried. 'Mr Wilson, tell him, he shouldn't—'

Freaky Adam shook the ball high in his fist. '*I've* got the speakeasy so *you* better shut up.'

Wilson held up his palms and gestured for everyone to calm down. 'Oliver,' he said, 'remember the rules, hmm? Adam has the speakeasy.'

'But—'

'Rules are rules, Oliver,' Wilson had said, 'and breaking them has consequences.'

Oliver had folded his arms across his chest and stared at his knees.

When I open my eyes, Miss Beryl is still watching me, this pained look on her face. I blink up at the sunlight. Wilson might be a total asshole, but he *is* a stickler for the rules, and the rules of circle time dictate that you should always be constructive, should only speak if you got something useful to say. On what planet could Freaky Adam blubbing his lips at me be considered constructive? Yet Wilson had let it pass. Encouraged it even, now that I think about it.

Miss Beryl leans in close. 'Mr Wilson says—'

'If you're going to listen to Mr Wilson, Miss, then you might as well shoot me now. You know he hates me, right?'

'Of course he doesn't hate you, David. He just … He's just doing his job, that's all. We all are.'

She doesn't even sound like she believes that herself. I stare at my hands in my lap, focus on remembering.

'The problem with David,' Freaky Adam had gone on, 'is he thinks he smells better than the rest of us.' The fat, white flesh of Adam's neck had wobbled as he'd pointed a flabby finger at me, cocky as you like. 'Mr In-te-llec-tual, with his head always stuck in a book.'

And what had Wilson done? He'd nodded, encouraging Freaky Adam to go further. The other boys had been watching, waiting to see how far I could be pushed. I'd given up trying to tune them out. Sweat pricked at the back of my neck. I'd warned Freaky Adam to lay off or else. And the thing was, everybody there knew I'd warned him.

'As for his father,' Freaky Adam droned on, 'no, don't even get me guessing at what kind of lowlife might have spawned him.'

I dug my nails into my palms and tried to let the words slide over me without finding their mark, but Freaky Adam knew which buttons to push. I'd never really thought about who my father might be before I came into the unit, but a zillion counselling sessions later and it was impossible to pretend that not having a father didn't bother me, cos everybody's got one somewhere, don't they?

'We're all agreed that his mother's nowt but an old alky, yeah?' Freaky Adam belly laughed and looked right at me. 'So imagine what kind of bloke would knock her up in the first place?'

A loud roar erupted from somewhere deep within me and I flew across the circle, blood pumping in my head. Wilson's hand groped under his chair for the alarm button fixed there, and I knew I only had seconds, so I grabbed Freaky Adam's throat before he got chance to scream. His nails flailed and a hot scratch burnt my cheek, but I got my knee between his knees and shoved it high. His screams came then all right. His big, fat, red, wet, sticky, spitty mouth opened wide and let rip. I released one hand from his throat, grabbed the speakeasy from his lap, and shoved it into his gaping gob. His eyes bulged as I forced the round leather ball deeper and deeper into his throat. The heel of my free hand pinned his head in place. My knee jerked again and again into his groin, and he was still screaming, only now, no sound came out.

A chant erupted into the room as the other boys clambered onto their chairs yelling, 'Kill him, kill him, kill him.'

If I pressed much harder for much longer then I just might, but if I backed off, I'd be dead meat. The orderlies should've arrived already. Freaky Adam's face had turned all purple. The speakeasy split. Thousands of polystyrene beads poured out of Freaky Adam's mouth, over his chin and into his neck, ribbons of animated dribble. Where were the orderlies?

And then I felt them: hands on my arms, my head, my neck, my T-shirt. A needle scratched my arm. Knowing better than to give them an excuse to turn it into a fight, I released my grip and let Freaky Adam slide to the floor. My own limbs grew limp.

As the orderlies dragged me backwards, I caught a glimpse of Oliver's face, skin all tight across his cheeks, mouth open wide in a vague 'Nooo'. It was then that I'd clocked Wilson's triumphant smirk and had wondered what I'd done.

Thick hands had lifted me by my elbows and propelled me from the room, just as the drugs kicked in. I'd felt like I was drowning.

And now Miss Beryl wants to know what I was thinking, what I was feeling, what I was *intending*. I shrug and say, 'What difference does it make?'

She hesitates, stares up at the sky for a moment and closes her eyes. 'Last week, when I asked you why you punched Adam in the toilet block, you said you did it because you felt like it, that you just wanted to.' She turns and looks directly at me. 'Was that true, or were you being glib? Please don't lie to me, David.'

I hesitate. Truth is, I don't know if I did it cos he left me no choice, or if I did it cos I *wanted* to hurt him, cos I *wanted* to grind his face into the floor. Saying that out loud isn't likely to do me any favours, so I mock yawn and say instead, 'I told you, he asked for it.'

'Asked for it how?'

I sigh. The reason I lamped Adam one last week was cos he'd shoved Oliver's head down the bog, but I can hardly tell Miss Beryl that, can I? Snitches don't fare too well in here.

I shrug. 'Just did, that's all.'

'You're going to have to trust me on this, David. I'm trying to help you.'

Trust her? Oh, believe me, I want to, I really do. But, like I say, I'd be a fool to trust any of them.

I focus hard on the dirt under my nails, the thin lines criss-crossing my palm ... *bzzz* ... and before long, I got Miss Beryl's words zoned out. Her mouth is moving but I'm only catching snatches of words between the buzzing. *Sorry ... bzzz ... intention ... bzzz ... mother ...* I hold out, and eventually her mouth stops moving, her head starts shaking. She's lost and she knows it.

I stand up. 'Can I go back to CSU now, Miss?'

'David—'

'Lunch'll stop serving in five and I got nothing more to say, Miss.'

She stops fiddling with her hair and stands too, red in the face. 'Fine. Have it your way. But you need to take this as a warning, David. A last chance. Whatever's going on with you, you need to get that temper of yours under control and start talking to me properly, or I'm not going to be able to help you anymore. Do you hear me?'

'So can I go now?'

She thumps back down onto the wall, and with a look I can't quite read, signals to the orderly that I can leave.

I feel her eyes watching me as a I walk away.

CHAPTER TWO

For some reason, breakfast in the Care and Separation Unit always knocks spots off the soggy offerings of the main dining room. Maybe it's got something to do with the condemned man being treated to a slap-up last meal. I try not to think about that as I shove a third rasher of hot bacon onto my sandwich-in-the-making, squirt on more ketchup, slap on the top layer of thickly buttered bread, and bite.

Liquid oozes out of the sides of my mouth and I scrape my finger up my chin, then lick. That's the other reason why breakfast always tastes so much better in CSU: privacy, or something that passes for it anyway. I eat every scrap, messy as you like.

The duty orderly leans in to take my empty plate, then drops it into a bowl on the trolley next to the row of pills and sterilised needles. 'Miss Beryl has arranged for you to have an hour in the pool, from eleven on,' he says. 'Mr

Carson will supervise. First you have a meeting with Dr Carl.'

I make a show of downing my omega-3 and calcium tabs and smile sweetly up at the orderly. I don't say anything – can't have them thinking they can manipulate me – but inside I'm tap-dancing. I don't know why the others don't get themselves sectioned more often. Once the initial drug blast that accompanies you in here wears off, CSU is great. For a start, a swimming session at eleven in the morning means I'll be getting the whole pool to myself again, and the fact that Miss Beryl's managed to swing it for me tells me she's still on my side. Well, as much as anybody's going to be. Okay, I got Dr Carl to get through first, but I got to do that anyway and sometimes I even enjoy those sessions. Here in the unit, you got to make your own entertainment.

Dr Carl's room is tiny and all mellow yellow and plump cushions, making out like he really cares. He don't fool me. One time, way back, he left the door to the next cubicle open, and I spied a white-clothed trolley-bed with single handcuffs fixed to each corner. Wires dangled from the ceiling. When he saw me looking, he kicked the door shut, but I can't un-see it. On top of that, Dr Carl must be the most repulsive looking shrink that ever lived. But – and it's a big BUT – the man has the voice of an angel. Listening to Dr Carl's voice is like being bathed in sweet, thick honey. If he ever decides to switch career, he should try his hand at hypnotism or maybe phone sex or something like that. Or he could rent himself out as a visitor at hospitals: soothing the injured, caressing the comatose with his silky tongue.

'I'm not going to talk about what happened with Adam,' Dr Carl croons. 'You still need time to process that before we can usefully explore the emotions surrounding it. Let's focus on what happened last week instead, shall we?'

I shrug, which in the unit is tantamount to a signed statement of co-operation.

'Let's talk about the feelings you experience when you light a fire, David. Specifically, afterwards, once the deed is done. What do you feel? Anger? Sadness? Frustration?'

No point in telling him I don't get off on lighting fires, that I only did it a couple of times to wind them up. That's not what Dr Carl wants to hear. He scrutinises me, searching for telltale signs of a response: a flickering of pupils, a clenching of fingers. Sometimes, I give them what they want. Sometimes not. Either way, I like it to be my choice, not theirs. That's the aim of the game. I might drop Dr Carl a crumb or two if he comes up with anything interesting. For now, I try to keep my face straight, my body dead still, but I suspect the very fact I'm doing this gives me away. They're not totally stupid, these people.

Dr Carl twiddles his beard. 'For some people, when they've got a good blaze going, they feel afraid of what might happen.' He eyes me over his clipboard. 'Now, this might be in terms of what damage their fire might do, or it could be in terms of what might happen to them if they're caught. Can you describe …'

His soothing tones drizzle over my head, and, with the combination of a full belly and the after-effects of the drugs, my mind grows hazy. I got to fight just to keep my eyes open.

'… people feel a kind of tingling in their hands, or, for some, in their crotch even. Do you ever feel this way, David?'

Dr Carl's voice has hit a high note. As he talks, his fat lips writhe up and down, in and out, like mating slugs.

I sit up straighter.

'A really good blaze can be an exciting thing, you know, particularly if you're responsible for it – its creator, so to speak.' Dr Carl hesitates, pats a tissue across his beaded forehead. 'For certain people, the sight of flames shooting forth, the heat, the noise, the sheer potential of the thing … well, it can be exciting in a whole myriad of ways. It can get some people all wound up, all fired-up so to speak, in a sexual way. It's not that uncommon. Is this how it is for you, David?'

On Dr Carl's face, the slugs curl up like love spoons between his whiskers. His eyes crease around the edges. He reminds me of somebody. His nose twitches.

Santa Claus! Dr Carl is Father Christmas.

Ha. Okay then, a present for Dr Carl. A little gift to make the good doctor happy.

I hang my head and give a minuscule nod.

The air in the tight little room is suddenly charged with expectancy. Dr Carl stiffens, hunches over and scribbles on his pad.

More questions follow, but I'm all done. They'll get nothing else out of me today. Besides, I'm gagging for a swim.

I fill my lungs with air and thrash against the resisting water, pummel it into subservience until all that's left is me and the rhythmic movements of my body: mind empty, memory blank. In water I am King of the World. I don't stop swimming until I hear Carson shout, 'Time's up, David,' then I pull myself into a sitting position on the edge of the pool and fight to get my breath back.

Carson hangs back and allows me this couple of minutes to come down from the buzz of my swim. Earlier, he'd offered to time my lengths for me. *No thanks.* Don't know about you, but when I'm swimming, I don't want anybody else in my head, don't want anything reminding me of where I am. For one whole hour at a stretch, I get to be free. Sod the timings.

I haul myself to my feet and head through the short tunnel that leads to the changing rooms, followed closely by Carson. Whenever Miss Beryl arranges these solo sessions for me, I take my time showering and dressing, cos with the other boys off doing their yard exercises, I don't need to watch my back. I hear a bench somewhere behind me creak as Carson sits on it, but that's fine. Whatever else Carson might be – and your guess is as good as mine – he's no perv. He stays put on the bench while I go through to the showers and slap soap around. I linger, eyes closed, and let the powerful jets thrash my face, my neck, my shoulders.

'Get a crack on,' Carson yells through the open doorway.

I turn off the water and bite back my irritation, cos Carson's okay, really. To me, he's just part and parcel of life at the unit, coming and going and sticking his nose in, but not too much. It was Carson who brought me in here six years ago, my ten-year-old arse sandwiched in the back of a black saloon between him and some silent type whose name I never learnt. A thin scar in the corner of Carson's lips forces his face into this permanent smile that never quite reaches his eyes, though he gives it out friendly enough. All I remember of that whole journey is that scar and the soft jangle of his boot chains every time we hit a bump in the road. Those same chains jangle and echo in the vast empty space of the changing rooms as he walks across to the exit and leans, arms folded, against the wall. I've known him long enough to know when something's off, and he's definitely been off all week. Probably girl trouble.

Once I'm dressed, he chucks a plastic water bottle at me and gives me this lopsided grin, which you'd probably think is just him being friendly, but fact is, thanks to the lip scar, his real grin's not a pretty sight. 'You're a tough kid to help, David Jessop. You know that?'

What the hell does that mean? I almost ask him but catch myself. What's the point? No one in here gives me answers. Just questions. Endless sodding questions.

'Help?' I say. 'Don't make me laugh.'

I head back to CSU and turn into the reading room, which is all blinding white walls and rubber-edged furniture. I let my fingers trail a row of book spines. CSU is where they bring you on your first day in the unit, a chance to settle in before coming face to face with the bunch of freaks you're going to be locked up with. I read somewhere that your average freak thinks their own behaviour is perfectly normal, though they can recognise freakishness in others easily enough. Everyone in here probably thinks they're the normal one. Me included. The thought catches hold in me for a moment. Had I been trying to kill Freaky Adam?

My fingers locate a book I started during my last stint in here, a tale of boats and bullies and boys who should, frankly, know better. I take it and flop into a beanbag. The duty orderly, whose job it is to tail my every move, settles himself onto the sofa with a soft creak of rubber and a crackle of newspaper. I lose myself in my book in an effort to drag out the delusion of freedom I've carried back with me from the pool.

'Visitor,' the orderly says, breaking the spell.

Under the rules of CSU, a 'patient' is allowed a short daily visit from a friend. Nobody except Oliver ever volunteers to visit me. Sure enough, the skinny little runt is standing in the open doorway. I nod at him to pull up a beanbag, then put aside my book, drag across the chessboard and start setting up the pieces. Oliver shakes his head at the board and my antenna pricks up. Oliver never not wants to play chess, even though he's crap and always loses.

The orderly turns his attention back to his paper, not a bit interested in whatever me and Oliver got to say. Mostly we just bang on about books – cool characters, cool bits of action – until the attending orderly's eyes glaze over and they stop paying attention to us. None of these meatheads are exactly bookworms.

Oliver plucks at the beanbag beneath him. 'They wouldn't let me come to see you yesterday. I ... you know ... wanted to.'

'You all right?'

'Yeah, course.'

He don't look all right. His eyes are red, his face milk-white, and he stinks of sweat, the kind that's got a vinegary edge to it. I look away. I much prefer being in CSU to being in the main unit, but with me out of the way, Oliver becomes fair game.

'Someone had a go at you?' I ask.

'No. I mean, yes. I mean, you know, I'm fine.' Oliver shrugs. 'Freaky Adam's not though. His neck's all purple and his voice sounds croaky. He's going around boasting how he's going to, you know, sort you out.'

'Not a chance.'

'That's what I said.'

'You should learn to keep your mouth shut. He'll have you in a blink.'

'I wish you weren't, you know, stuck in here.' Oliver reaches up a hand and swipes a flop of fringe out of his face, then slips a finger inside his mouth and draws out a folded piece of pink paper.

The orderly's newspaper rustles, and the flash of pink vanishes into the folds of Oliver's T-shirt. The orderly shoots a look across the room. If he bothered to get to his feet and take a proper look at Oliver's face, he wouldn't need telling twice that something's up.

I throw Oliver a warning look and change the subject. 'So, what's happening out there? Did you get down to the pool yesterday? Yeah? What time did you make? You beat my record yet?'

Oliver blinks. 'Twenty-eight twelve.'

'Not bad.'

'Nowhere near as good as, you know, you.'

'Might get faster if you spent more time practising and less pretending you need the loo just to get out of it.'

Oliver's cheeks flush pink as he reaches across for my book. 'What you reading? Let me have it. Oh, I've read this one. Bit rubbish.' His voice sounds tight. 'I hate that bit when he's, you know, gonna take off and leave his friend behind. He hasn't even told him. He's just gonna leave.'

The book lies open in Oliver's lap. As he flicks through the pages, the storyline runs through my head. Nobody takes off anywhere. I stare at Oliver, who opens his eyes wide and holds my gaze.

Sensing something, the orderly lowers his newspaper and peers across at us. How do they do that? It's like they got psychic powers or something.

I take a deep breath and rattle on about the ins and outs of the plot and the way the boy in the story keeps putting his foot in it and getting everyone into trouble. When I'm sure the orderly is no longer listening, I look pointedly from his newspaper to Oliver's T-shirt and back again.

'What did you think about the way it turned out then?' I ask.

Oliver yawns and scratches his chest. 'Chapter seven is, you know, interesting.'

He hands the book back to me and I flick through to chapter seven, where I find a pink Post-it plastered in Oliver's scribble.

'I wos helping Matron in the kitchen and I hurd
Miss Beryl say come Monday he'll be gon it wos
abowt U. She sownded pissd blamd Wilson.
Wot's going on UR not leeving R U'

Leaving?

The word lodges deep in the pit of my stomach.

I rub the Post-it note flat and read it again. Leaving could mean one of two things. Either I been a good boy and they've decided I'm not a dangerous thug anymore and I'm being released. Or I been a bad boy and they've given up trying to fix me and are sending me for 'transfer'. None of us knows what transfer involves exactly, but whenever it happens, this weird atmosphere hangs about the place for a week or so afterward, like somebody died or something. Miss Beryl's like a weathervane, so we all know whether it's been a release or a transfer just by watching her mood: skippy and light means a release, low and slow means a transfer.

I double-check that the orderly isn't paying us any attention and rack my brains for the right thing to say. 'See what you mean about chapter seven,' I manage eventually, keeping my voice light and steady. 'Like this bit here, when the boy says he had no idea any of that was going on, don't got a clue what they're on about, but he knows it don't feel good.'

'That's just rubbish.' Oliver pinches the material of the beanbag in his fist and looks ready to cry.

I clear my throat and hide my shaking hands in my lap. 'I don't see what he can do about it. Not like he gets much

22

of a say in anything, is it? If that's the story, then that's the story.'

'Then it's a, you know, stupid story.' Tears fill Oliver's eyes.

An hour after Oliver gets shunted back to the residential zone, Miss Beryl comes in smelling of White Linen.

'How long am I in here for this time, Miss?' I ask before she's even had chance to sit down.

'I've had another word with Mr Carson,' she says. She lowers herself carefully onto the beanbag that Oliver had vacated earlier and fiddles with the curls escaping from her bun. Low and slow.

My stomach tightens.

'He's agreed to supervise you in the pool tomorrow morning, too. Would you like that?'

'How long?'

'The usual, an hour or so.'

'I meant how long am I in here for?'

'Are you ready to talk to me yet? About what happened with Adam?'

'Why can no one in here ever just answer a straight question?' I punch the beanbag into shape and sit up straighter.

Beryl's hands fidget and fiddle with her bun. 'You could have killed him. You do realise that, don't you? Is that what you intended?'

I shrug. 'You're the ones keep telling me I got issues. What d'you expect?'

'Did you lose your temper,' her gaze is sharp, focused on my face, 'or were you just trying to prove some point? Was that it, David? Talk to me, will you? If you don't give me something I can use to—'

'To what?' Her perfume is clogging my airways, making it hard to breathe. 'You all been talking about me again in those meetings of yours, Miss?'

She looks everywhere except my face as she tucks a curl back into place. 'I promise you, David, I'm only trying to help.'

I leap to my feet and lean across her, my mouth close to her ear. 'Where are they sending me?'

'Sending you? I don't know what …' She tries to get to her feet, but she struggles to get up from these beanbags at the best of times and I'm standing right over her, blocking her way. I know how to induce fear – the unit has taught me that much. I screw up my face to keep out the thought that here I am, intimidating a sick old lady, and what does that say about me, about who I am?

'Liar,' I hiss, disappointed by the fear on her face that tells me she's so ready to think the worst of me.

'No, I—'

'I know you know. Where are they sending—'

'Back off, David.' The orderly appears next to me. 'Don't make me tell you twice.'

Is that shame I see in Miss Beryl's eyes as the orderly helps her to her feet? It's true then, what Oliver heard about me going away. But I'm not going home. I'm being transferred.

I turn and flop back onto my beanbag and pretend to read as though nothing's happened – that drives them nuts – but I can't read. The buzzing is in my head, and the only words that float in front of my eyes are 'come Monday he'll be gon'. Tomorrow will be Sunday. The day after that, I'm finally getting out of here. That should be a good thing, right? But the question gnawing at my guts is where the hell are they sending me?

Monday morning rolls around and I wake to find Carson standing in my bedroom with a silver briefcase in one hand, a suitcase in the other, and that stupid grin that's not a grin on his face.

I fight to keep my voice level. 'Where are you taking me?'

He throws the suitcase onto my bed. 'Start packing.'

CHAPTER THREE

Above my head the reading light flickers. I reach up to twiddle the knob. There are no windows back here, nothing to distract me from the drone of the engine pulsating in my stomach. Carson sits next to me, his cowboy boots planted on the floor next to his briefcase, which is silver to match his boot chains.

I focus on the line of fancy stitching trailed across the boot nearest to me, but it don't help. I think about the world flashing by, right there on the other side of this thin metal panel, but that don't help either. I might be out of the unit, but all I can see is the look in Miss Beryl's eyes this morning as Carson led me out of the back gate. I clench my fists and try to quash the burn of acid in my throat.

'Rickleson, pull over.' Carson grips the shelf fitted into the grille that separates us from the driver.

'No can do.' Rickleson sips strong coffee from one of those big plastic cups with a lid on. The stink claws at my guts. 'Give him a sick bag.'

Heat sweeps up my neck and across my cheeks. My chest heaves.

Carson draws away from me. 'Here, David, use this bag … Oh, shit.'

I want to laugh at the disgust on Carson's face – nice shot – but another hot surge overtakes me.

'Damn it, pull over,' Carson shouts through the grille.

'But they said—'

'Pull over right now or I'll come through there and smash your head through that fucking windscreen. Don't think I won't.'

The van slows, swerves left, then bumps along until it shudders to a stop. Carson slaps a handcuff on my wrist, attaches the other end to his own wrist, then slides open the door.

Out on the grassy verge, sharp air slices through my thin jacket. I bend over double, and hurl. I press my free hand onto my knee to balance myself. Cars speed past: flashes of silver, red, white. Blasts of air rock the van where it stands on the narrow strip of tarmac and scrubby grass verge. Carson rubs at his left boot with a handkerchief. Despite the deafening roar of traffic and the vomit burning in my throat, I grin.

Rickleson takes his life in his hands and hops down from the front seat of the van, clutching a pack of wet wipes in one hand and his coffee in the other. He comes around the back of the van and stands there, slurping through the cup's teat like a man-sized baby, which is enough to set me off on a fresh bout of hurling.

Carson steps back and shoves me as far away from him as the cuffs allow. 'God damn it, David.'

Rickleson paces the thin stretch of tarmac, jittery and sweating. I don't know what he thinks he's got to be whining about; I'm the one chucking my guts up here.

'We're not supposed to stop, Carson. You know the rules. That's why we carry our own food and piss in a bottle. Hurry him up. I can't afford to lose my job, not with my boy starting college. You should see the bloody fees, enough to bankrupt us.'

Carson scrubs the sides of his cowboy boots on the grass verge. The handcuff cuts into my wrist with every jerk, and I wince when he turns towards Rickleson, taking my arm with him.

'Talking about breaking rules, Joe, maybe I should take a sniff of that coffee of yours? Look at the state of you. You even fit to drive?'

Rickleson thrusts the cup at Carson. 'Be my guest. It's just coffee. I don't drink on the job.'

Carson ignores the offered cup. 'Wouldn't be the first time, Joe.'

'That was … Look, I'm dry, okay.' Rickleson plucks a wet wipe from the pack and offers the rest to Carson, who glares and rubs the soles of his boots on the ground like a bull about to charge.

For a moment, they've forgotten all about me.

I spit into the grass and check out my surroundings. Four lanes of traffic, two in each direction, stand between me and escape. Engines whine, loud in their freedom. Around my wrist, the metal cuff cuts into my skin.

Not a chance.

'I haven't touched a drop for six months.' Rickleson waves the wet wipes at Carson like a white flag.

'Yeah, okay, relax.' Carson accepts the peace offering and nods at the van. 'Nobody can see him back here.' He shoves the wet wipes at me. 'Clean up.'

'And hurry up,' Rickleson whines. 'We've got hours to go yet.'

A soft breeze soothes my cheeks.

'Let's go,' Rickleson orders the second I've wiped the vomit from my hands and chin.

The thought of climbing back into that mobile coffin holds about as much appeal as giving Fat Michael a head massage. I lean over and make as if I'm going to hurl again, every part of me aware that, where they're taking me, I might never get to see the outside world again. I find myself cataloguing everything I can see and feel in case it's for the last time: grass, prickly hedges, cool air, bright blue sky, pockets of clouds, a scattering of daisies. In the distance, I see a clump of trees, a small flock of sheep, a wind turbine spinning its white blades, a clump of trees huddled together like they're holding their own circle time session. I say their names quietly under my breath – sheep, turbine, trees – afraid I'll forget what they look like, what they're called. I turn my face towards the sun and feel its warmth on my cheeks and imagine for a moment that I'm free.

My arm is yanked forward as Carson heads back to the van. Once we're both inside, he releases the cuffs and yanks seat straps into place. The engine turns over.

I squeeze my eyes shut and conjure up Mum's face. I don't ever want to forget her face. The image is clear and fresh, and I let out a long breath. If I throw up again, I'll aim for Carson's lap. I focus on his boots as the engine drones on and on and the last of the daylight fades into dusk as the minutes slip by.

The last time I was in a car with Carson was the day he took me in. That journey had ended in a sweeping driveway, hedges blazing under fat pink flowers and green fields rolling away into nothing but other shades of green. More green than I'd seen in my whole life. A pair of stone lions had guarded the grey mansion that towered above us. I'd been easily impressed back then and had seen what they wanted me to see: a posh boarding school. It looked like the sort of place rich parents would send their swotty kids to. Oh, the irony.

I allow the rhythm of the engine to enter my bones. Try to relax. Drift in and out of sleep. Try not to think.

'Shit.' Carson's voice jerks me out of a deep sleep.

The van is swerving sideways, zigzagging back and forth, setting off a concert of horns and flashing headlights that light up the inside, which has grown almost dark while I slept.

For a moment, we straighten, and Carson yells at Rickleson to pull over. Then we swerve again.

Carson tears at the partition. He grabs his silver briefcase and bashes at the grille. The briefcase is strong, made of aluminium, and the partition collapses into the driver's cab. Carson rams the case through and forces his head and one arm into the gap, but his barn-like shoulders are too wide. What the hell? Does he think having a scrap with Rickleson is a sound plan right now?

Then he backs up out of the hole, red in the face. 'You try,' he says, and releases my harness and yanks me to my feet.

'Get your fucking hands off me.'

'Grab the wheel.' He pushes me towards the open partition.

'Screw you.' I swing my arms wide and my knuckles crunch into something hard.

Carson slaps a hand across his bloodied nose and growls through his fingers, 'For Christ's sake, David, he's having a heart attack.'

I glance through the gap and see that Rickleson's head is thrown backwards. His hands clutch at his chest. His eyes are rolled up into his head and he's having some sort of seizure, arms jerking. Then he stops. His jaw hangs slack.

Horns blare. The van swerves into a skid. Rights itself again.

Shit.

I ram my shoulders through the partition gap, fingers stretching for the wheel, closing on it. Just as I'm getting there, Rickleson's shoulders slap into the seat back, knocking my hands aside.

Everything goes slow but lightning fast at the same time. We cross the hard shoulder. Metal screeches against metal. Wheels bump. The van plummets off the road and downhill. My ribs are being crushed against the partition shelf, knocking the breath out of me. I struggle to back up, but my shoulders are stuck. They're freaking well stuck.

Carson shouts my name, but it sounds warped, and anyway, I can't answer cos my voice is being squeezed out of me. Hands grab my feet and pull. I scream. Kick out. My head fizzes like a bottle of pop being shaken. I crane my neck around. Carson's opening the door in the side of the van.

'Wait.' It comes out as a squeak.

'Too late,' he shouts.

'No. Please. Wait.'

The son-of-a-bitch jumps.

I kick and writhe. The door slams shut. The van picks up speed and bounces. Faster. Harder. My ribs are being battered clean out of me.

Then everything goes still.

We're flying.

It's okay. It's going to be okay.

The van drops, leaving half my stomach behind.

We smash into something that splashes. My head whacks the roof. The shelf punches into my chest, then rips out of the partition. The grip on my shoulders relaxes, hurling me into a nosedive, and then, I'm lying across Rickleson's lap.

A scream bubbles up inside me as I scramble for the passenger seat. Something dribbles down my cheek. I touch a hand to my face. Blood.

Churning water masks half the windscreen like we're in some kind of giant carwash. Everything spins. We're bouncing along the surface of a wide river, hurtling downstream.

Windscreen wipers swish. Headlights, sidelights, hazard-lights, all flash in time to the repetitive blast of the horn.

We're floating.

I breathe. We're floating on the surface, like a boat. We're okay. Someone will hear us, will see us, will get us out. Carson knows I'm in here.

With my hands pressed to the glass, I shout, 'Help. Help us.'

I glance across at Rickleson, whose head dangles to one side thwacking the window with every dip and bounce. Fish-flat eyes stare blankly back at me, and I realise I'm sitting next to a freaking corpse.

My screams grow louder. 'I'm here. Please. Help.'

I can hardly hear my words over the blaring horn. The van bounces one last time, high, high, high, taking what's left of my stomach with it. Then it sinks below the surface, and the world disappears.

A hollow *thunk* echoes beneath me and resonates in my chest as we touch bottom and scrape to a halt. The pale beam of the headlights picks out a murky riverbed.

I grope for the door handle. Yank. Shove. It's like there's a ten-ton elephant on the other side, shoving back. My hands search out the electric window button. Nails scratch against plastic.

The lights blink out. The horn dies. I'm plunged into gloom.

I tug and prod and claw at the button.

Nothing.

Water is pouring in under doors, through heating vents, around windows. I grope around the floor for Carson's briefcase, then pull back my arms and smash it into the window, over and over.

Not even a crack.

Water pushes in on me. Up my legs. Past my waist. Across my chest. Cold. So freaking cold. I scramble higher in my seat trying to get away but there's nowhere to go. The water's coming over me.

Rickleson is still strapped into his seat. The rising water crawls up his face and pours into his gaping mouth. I hear a high-pitched shriek and realise it's coming from my own mouth. His thinning hair lifts and fans out on the surface for a second or two before he disappears, leaving me all alone.

I press my cheek to the ceiling and gulp at the remaining six-inch band of air before water fills my ears and covers my head.

I'm under. I'm freaking well under.

But instead of panic, I suddenly feel calm as you like. This is where I like to be, isn't it? Submerged in water, cut off from the world. I could stay here. I could stay here forever. A welcome buzz starts up in my head.

Rickleson's face lurches out of the gloom and bobs in front of my nose like a Halloween mask. I pull back and instinctively grab the door handle and shove my shoulder against the frame.

It moves. It moves!

Two more good thrusts, and a gap appears.

I squeeze through the gap and I'm rising. My feet kick off from the roof of the van, propelling me upwards. I don't look back. My nails claw at the current as if they can tear holes in it, and just as I think I got to open my mouth and let the water in, freezing air burns into my lungs and I'm coughing and choking on it.

From somewhere to the left of me, lights flicker. My clothes twist around my limbs, threatening to drag me back under. I fight my way out of the jacket and kick off the plimsolls. Cold stings my feet and hands, sharp tingles that send my blood into a frenzy and make me gasp for breath.

Upstream, a crowd has gathered. Headlights and torches shine in my direction but their beams waver and fall short of where I surfaced. The river tugs me away from the lights and I fight against it, arms thrashing towards the wobbling lines of white.

Dead in front of me, something pops onto the surface and near gives me a heart attack of my own: Carson's briefcase. I grab it and hold on like you would a kickboard. My legs beat the water. Beat the current. Move towards the lights.

Then I remember: Carson is somewhere in that crowd.

Other things come back to me too. The look of triumph on Wilson's face. 'Come Monday he'll be gon'. Miss Beryl's eyes: first fear, then guilt, then something else. Something that might've been grief.

Behind me, black water churns in a widening channel.

Ahead of me, beams of light scour the surface.

I stop thrashing and let the river drag me away from the lights, away from any hope of rescue.

When I reach a point from which there's no turning back, I grit my teeth, take a deep breath, and kick out for what I hope is the far bank.

CHAPTER FOUR

I been in Camden for hours now and I'm getting used to the chaos and the smells: the aromas of fried onion, curry and kebab mingles with the stench of bodies and petrol. All around me, people shout and swear, buskers blast out music, traffic trundles past. I no longer jump clean out of my pants every time a car brakes or a horn honks, but the sheer number of people still makes my nerves jangle. I hunch up against the wall of the closed library behind me and clutch my cardboard cup. I'd be happier crawling into a dark corner where nobody can see me, but I need coins cos I need food, and this is the safest way I can think of to make that happen.

When the truck driver I hitched a ride with first dropped me off on the outskirts of London, every bone in my body had ached to head home. But if they do figure out that I got out of that river alive and come looking for me, then the first place they'll look is Mum's.

I mumble, 'Thanks,' as a coin lands with a soft clink in my cup. Black stiletto heels clatter as the woman who tossed it sweeps on past. Nobody wants to make eye contact with the homeless, which works just fine for me. Some bloke in a suit comes marching along next. I bite down on my lip, reminding myself that he don't really see me. I thrust my cup into the air and shake it while keeping my face tilted low. He ignores me and stalks on by, leaving only the stink of his aftershave. My belly rumbles as the other smells of Camden make me salivate and take me back to life-before-the-unit.

Every few weeks, for as long as I can remember, Mum would wake up sober and smiling and take me on the tube to Mrs Beanie's Deli, ten minutes away from where she grew up. She'd push a handful of coins onto the counter and ask for 'a large jar of pickled walnuts please'.

'If it wasn't for you, Miss Jessop, I'd stop stocking these,' Mrs Beanie would say. 'Nobody but you eats them nowadays.'

'My father used to love them,' Mum would answer.

Old Mrs Beanie would smile and say, 'I know, luv. I remember him well.'

It was always the same conversation, and I do mean exactly the same – our own version of Groundhog Day – but I didn't mind so long as she was happy. We'd catch three tubes back home and get stuck in. My mouth waters now at the thought of those pickled walnuts. I peer at the coins in my cardboard cup. I got no idea how much pickled walnuts cost but decide to hang out for one more donation before checking it out.

A woman with a long woollen coat in reds, browns and purples is coming along my side of the pavement. She looks kind. I stick out my arm and shake my hand. She stops and drops something substantial feeling into my cup.

Without lifting my face to hers, I mumble, 'Thank you.'

It's not just cos I don't want to be recognised that I avoid her gaze. Why would anybody here recognise me anyway? It's cos I'm embarrassed, asking total strangers for money. I'd much rather steal my food, but I daren't risk getting caught.

A glance into my cup reveals a chunk of coins wrapped in a note, which causes my eyes to fill up. I knew she'd be generous, that one, but I'd been ready to be disappointed. Where I been, it's easy to forget people can be kind just for the sake of it. I tip the coins into my hand and close my fist over them. Food.

Mrs Beanie's Deli should be two streets off the other side of the tube station, so I head in that direction, but when I reach the red-brick building where the deli used to be, I find a psychedelic tattoo studio and body piercing shop instead.

Damn. Burger it is then.

And, to be fair, it's some burger. If eating food in the CSU had tasted of freedom, this is something else. With an additional slice of cheese and bacon, plus a bag of chips, it's taken up a fair whack of my collection money, but in return it's feeding my soul as well as my body. Sitting on the edge of the canal towpath, biting into this food, I feel like a real human being for the first time in years.

I lean back against the brickwork, close my eyes and allow myself half an hour of dozing and pretending that all is well in my world. Just half an hour, then I'll get back to the begging as much money as I can before nightfall. I don't need much. It had been easy enough to nick clothes and an old dog blanket off a washing line after I'd dragged myself out of the river and walked towards the nearest lights. I never did get how people can leave their clothes on the washing line overnight and expect to find them still there come morning. Back when I lived with Mum, other people's washing lines and unlocked porches were the only thing that kept me in half decent clothing and footwear.

I huddle deeper into my layers of stolen gear: jeans a size too big but okay, a black zip-up hoodie that's nice and thick and plenty warm enough for the daytime, and a pair of Diesels that knocks spots off any pair of trainers I ever owned. I've stashed a couple of T-shirts, along with Carson's briefcase, wrapped in the dog blanket and hidden behind a bush in a woodland near the swimming place out on Hampstead Heath, where Mum would take me on a rare good day. Apparently, she used to go there with her dad all the time. I been fretting all day that someone might find it, but I can't risk carrying that briefcase with me. Imagine the police if they saw a case like that in the hands of a supposed street kid like me. Their antennae would go wild.

I finish my burger and make my way back to the street where I'd been begging, hopeful of more coins, but some bundle of blankets has taken my spot and I don't challenge him for it. It'll be dark soon, and Camden is famous for more than its arty weekend market and pickled walnuts. I remember Mum telling me there had to be more drug pushers and all-round dodgy types to be found in the streets around here than anywhere else on the planet, except maybe New York. 'You stay close and watch yourself,' she'd warn me, like she was Miss Respectable herself. From what I already seen today that situation hasn't changed much. I count out my remaining coins and look across to a hardware store on the other side of the road. I need a screwdriver and a torch. With a bit of luck, I'll have enough left over for another burger.

Ten minutes later, clutching the screwdriver up my right sleeve and cursing the price of the torch in my pocket, I start walking.

When the sun drops behind the multi-coloured buildings, the night air grows chilly. I yank the smelly dog blanket off the briefcase and drape it round my shoulders, trying to ignore the hunger pangs gnawing at my gut. I finger the outline of the screwdriver. There's probably nothing more exciting than Carson's packed lunch in that briefcase, and if that's the case then the sooner I get to it the better. But I got to admit there's no shutting up this little voice inside my head whispering that whatever's inside there just might be a whole lot more interesting than a stale sandwich.

At last the sun drops out of sight and the increased darkness under the trees gives me some sense of security. I grope around for the briefcase handle and drag it onto my lap. Sitting with my back against a tree trunk, I force the screwdriver into the lock of the briefcase like a lever. The lock creaks and grates but holds firm. My hand slips and the screwdriver slices my thumb like a bit of bacon. Goddammit.

Another ten minutes of grunting and cursing, and the lever suddenly shifts downward and the lock hits the trunk of the tree opposite me with a loud clang. I catch my breath and freeze. When nothing happens, I ease open the case and shine my torch inside.

No lunch, more's the pity, cos my stomach is nagging away and not liking being ignored. No mega stash of cash either, like there would be in the movies. At the bottom of the otherwise empty case lies a plastic folder, and in that plastic folder sits a buff file.

With a weird mix of disappointment and dread, I lift the folder, lay it on my lap and shine my torch at the name, *my name*, typed in bold on the front cover, next to the words 'HIGHLY CONFIDENTIAL'.

CHAPTER FIVE

I flick off the torch and sit in total darkness, my heart thudding in my chest. These are my private notes, the ones only the counsellors ever get to see. I scan the trees to check no one's watching, then slip the file out of the folder.

When my heart rate slows to something like normal, I switch on the torch and double-check nobody's lurking in the shadows. All clear. Hands shaking, I turn the front cover.

```
Clinical History – David Jessop – Summary of
Contents of Document H1DJ436


PRIOR HISTORY:
1.    Single parent family
2.    Mother alcohol dependent
3.    Neglect (of subject)
4.    Emotional and physical abuse (of subject)
5.    Poor academic performance
```

6.   Persistent truanting
7.   Gang affiliation
8.   Bullying at school (by subject)
9.   Violent tendencies (by subject)
10.   Obsession with fire (by subject)
11.   Late bed-wetting

I home in on the words 'prior history'. A quick flick through the other pages makes it clear this refers to before I went into the unit, back when I was living at home with Mum. I scroll down the list and find myself nodding along right until I reach:

7. Gang affiliation

Well, that's a load of crap. I never been in a gang in my life, never even had what you'd call a mate until Oliver. 'Loner boy' was one of a whole range of things the other boys on the estate used to shout at me. How can you be a loner if you're in a gang?

8. Bullying at school (by subject)

That's the first I ever heard about me bullying anyone at school. Where'd they get this rubbish from? The few scrapes I did get into at school were in self-defence, when I was the one being bullied. I'm not a bully, I … The image of me standing over Miss Beryl as she struggled to get up from that beanbag pops into my head, but I shake it away. That was different. She was keeping stuff from me, and I wasn't going to hurt her, was I? And it wasn't 'prior' to the unit, was it? The thought rankles and I move on.

9. Violent tendencies (by subject)

Well, okay, if this is talking about my history since I been in the unit, then that's probably fair enough. Threatening violence is how I survive, how I don't become a victim like Oliver. In fact, the vast majority of the violence I've committed has been about protecting Oliver's skinny arse. The boys in there are predators; you can't show weakness. But before the unit? No way.

10. Obsession with fire (by subject)

Again, I might've played along with their stupid obsession at the unit – my last session with Dr Carl wasn't the first time I've let him believe that fire really does it for me – but before the unit? What are they on about? I scan down to the last one on the list.

11. Late bed-wetting

I'm opening my mouth to mumble 'what a crock' when a memory comes flying at me so hard I nearly duck. I'd been six years old, and I'd wet the bed. Mum would've gone mental if she found out, so I tried to dry the sheet in front of the living room fire. The whole thing went up in flames. Mum was passed out cold and wouldn't wake up, so I crawled into bed next to her. I just lay there with smoke curling down from the ceiling, choking me, but I couldn't leave her. A neighbour had called the fire-brigade.

It was an accident. I was only six. I can't believe they're using some little kid mistake against me, making out like I'm obsessed, dangerous. Is this what Mum thinks too? Is that why she hasn't been to see me in all this time?

I shake my head. No. Nobody at the unit ever gets any visitors. It's a rule, so you got a better chance of healing quickly or some such rubbish. I remember laughing when I first found out, cos I thought it would serve her right if she weren't allowed to come. Later again, that changed. Now, I bat the thought away.

But the thought won't budge.

I scan the list again. There would've been records about the fire, so they could've found out about that easily enough, but no one except Mum could've told them about the bed-wetting that went on until I was nine. Mum don't like doctors and she hated my school. Me and her were the only two who knew about those soggy sheets, and I know I didn't tell them, which means she must've. What kind of mother does that to her own son? I laugh and answer my own question. My kind of mother, that's who. The kind of mother who spends half her life in a drunken stupor and the other half wishing she'd never had you. I clench my fists, close my eyes and force myself to breath steadily.

A scuffling sound behind me gets my heart racing. I swing the torch towards the noise and the beam catches the long wiry tail of a mouse or vole or something like that as it disappears into the underbrush.

Taking a deep breath, I turn back to the file and flip to the next page.

Diagnosed   with   early-onset   conduct disorder.

Huh? I got no idea what that even means let alone any of the drivel written underneath it. I turn to the next page.

CLINICAL CARE HISTORY:
Subject records a PCL-R rating of 32, well within range for psychopathy, DSPD. High CU traits are evidenced. Subject meets the criteria for the homicidal triad. Subject has failed to respond to long-term cognitive behavioural therapy combined with a diet rich in omega-3 fatty acids and calcium. No notable increase in the orbitofrontal region or the amygdala evidenced.

I might not got a clue what half of this even means, but it don't take a genius to get the gist of what they're saying. They're saying I'm some kind of psycho. *Homicidal triad?* Homicide means murder, right? Who'd I murder? I picture my hands around Freaky Adam's neck, shoving that ball down his throat, choking the life out of him. I pull the blanket tighter around my shoulders as the night air dampens. I let him go, didn't I? A little voice in my head whispers, 'yeah, but only when the orderlies arrived'. I shake that thought away. The point is, I didn't kill him, did I? I haven't killed anybody else either, and you can't go around calling somebody a murderer unless they've actually murdered someone. Even I know that. So what's this 'homicidal triad' stuff all about?

Failed to respond? Respond how? To what? I bite back my irritation and read on.

SUMMARY:

The subject was diagnosed as a PSK in June 2022 and despite nearly six years of intervention therapy he continues to pose a significant danger to society.

I lay the paper in my lap, then turn my torch off and sit in the dark letting it sink in. I've failed to respond. I'm dangerous. I'm a 'PSK'. I force a quiet laugh. According to the file in my lap, I'm a PSK, but the joke is that I don't even know what that means. I'm guessing it's not good. I play with possibilities:

Plays with Swords and Knives.

Pushes, Steals and Kills.

Psychotic Stupid Kid.

I'm trying to make a joke of it but my breathing sounds deafening in my own head and feels raw in my lungs. Maybe I do know. Maybe I just don't want to know.

I flick the torch back on and turn to the next section.

SUPPORTING EVIDENCE:

This part of the file is thick, stuffed full of meeting notes, reviews, and graphs and tables that I don't understand. It's basically all the stuff that's happened – or that's supposedly happened – since I first arrived at the unit six years ago. The list of lies is so long I could be reading a novel that's all about me, only it's not, not really. There's just enough truth in there to make the made-up bits sound real.

There's this one bit about a fire I supposedly started in the bogs about a year ago. It's true that there was a fire, but it wasn't me who started it. Freaky Adam did that. Okay, so I saw him do it and I didn't report him. A fire alarm meant that everybody got to pile out into the courtyard and hang around in the fresh air waiting for the all-clear, and like I say, anything to break up the boredom. But according to the sheet in my lap, I later admitted to Wilson that it was me who set the fire in the first place. That. Never. Happened.

Another bit that jumps out at me is the bit about the time Freaky Adam – him again – shoved Oliver's head down the bog. According to Wilson, during our weekly one-to-one sessions, I admitted it was me who nearly drowned Oliver, and that's a joke on two counts.

Count one: I didn't do it.

Count two: the level of conversation in my one-to-ones with Wilson has never got beyond 'come in' and 'see you tomorrow', and none of those words came from me. I never speak. He sits there waiting for me to speak. That's what we do. It's like we're locked in some pointless competition to see who'll crack first.

Yet here I am, reading about how we had all these conversations, and about how I confided all this stuff in him. I think back to Miss Beryl in the garden asking me about what happened that day. I thought she knew what had gone down but if she'd read Wilson's report, then she would've thought it was me all along. Attacking Adam over nothing. Attacking Oliver, my only friend. No wonder she thought I was losing it big time.

I plough on through, and towards the end of this section come to last week's circle-time session and my fight with Freaky Adam. Seems I've since admitted that I was one hundred percent hell-bent on committing murder, and again I admitted this to – my gaze flicks down to the signature – yep, to Wilson.

My breathing comes harder. Wilson's set me up. He deliberately let Freaky Adam wind me up until I had no choice but to silence him. He's lied about me over and over in his session notes. But why? It makes absolutely no sense.

I read on, hoping to find something that will explain the inexplicable, but the rest of the file contains loads of medical stuff that I don't understand. There are two pictures of brain scans, presumably mine, with handwritten notes that say things like 'PET scan shows low activity in prefrontal cortex and the amygdala; some lesions to amygdala'. I don't know what it means but 'lesions' don't sound like a good word to me.

There are several pages of what look like lie detector readings, which must be the results of all those tests they keep running on us, when they stick wires to our arms and heads and then flash lights and bang things to see how we'll react. I can't make sense of the wiggly lines but the note next to them says 'subject shows low sensitivity to fear'. Is that a good thing or a bad thing?

I thumb through the pictures of me in my primary school play, in my primary school classroom, in assembly, in the playground, in the library. It makes me feel sick remembering how I thought I was all safe in Mrs Moon's classroom, with her colourful walls and star charts, but all along she must've been spying on me. Why?

I'm relieved to reach the last page, but not for long.

CONCLUSION:

In conclusion, David has not responded to long-term intervention, and it is our opinion that he should now be transferred to the permanent residency unit. No further treatment is considered likely to be effective. Our findings are that the subject is, and remains, a potential serial killer.

The trees around me lurch sideways and I drop the torch. Its bright little beam picks out a blurred line of leaves and broken twigs.

PSK. Potential serial killer.

I'm not just any old killer. I'm a serial killer. I'm a PSK. Jack the Ripper, Ted Bundy, Hannibal Lecter – they were serial killers. Monsters. Fiends. The stuff of nightmares.

That's me? There got to be a mistake somewhere, don't there?

One word flashes into my mind: *potential.*

'Potential serial killer' must mean that even though I haven't killed anybody yet, they're saying I got the potential to do it, and that's why I was in there. How can that even happen? How is that not against the law? Everybody's got the potential to do anything, don't they?

Then the other bit sinks in: *permanent residency unit.* They were locking me up for good – as in, forever – and all cos I've apparently got some sort of freaking *potential?*

Everything churns around and around in my head. I'm a freak. A monster. That's what they're saying.

Are they right? Are they lying about me or am I lying to myself? I could've killed Freaky Adam, couldn't I, if the orderlies hadn't come? But had I wanted to? At one point, yes, I think I did. Maybe that's what they see in me, and I just don't see it in myself yet.

Does Miss Beryl think that about me? I recall the look of fear on her face when I towered over her. I clutch my head in my hands and groan.

Then I remember that Wilson has lied about me, over and over. That much I'm sure about. I grab hold of that thought and hang on tight. Retrieving the torch, I re-read his notes, and punch the air with triumph when I spot it. He *is* lying, and I can prove it.

At the time that Oliver was attacked in the bogs, I remember that I was having a private swimming session that Miss Beryl had arranged as a thank you for helping her in the garden. I remember it clearly cos I'd felt guilty for leaving him on his own. There'll be a record of it somewhere. Evidence. If I can prove he's lying about that, then … but I can't, can I? And who would care anyway? They were going to lock me up, throw away the key. Maybe whatever lies Wilson told about me made things look worse than they were, but maybe they didn't really change anything? Maybe I'd still be diagnosed as a PSK. Maybe that's just who I am.

I shine the torch around the trees before stacking the papers back into the briefcase and crawling under my blanket, which feels way too thin. I curl up between the tree roots in a foetal position. My head aches and my whole body shivers. The blanket helps keep out the worst of the cold but the bulk of it seems to be coming from inside of me. I never felt so empty.

I must've somehow managed to fall asleep, cos the next thing I know, I'm waking up and I can smell smoke. I shove the blanket off my head and stare out into the dark, adrenaline pumping. Low laughter rumbles through the trees. The smoke is coming from a small fire contained in a metal bucket placed on the ground several metres away from where I'm hidden by the brush. There was no bucket there when I went to sleep, I'm certain of it.

Trying not to make a sound, I ease myself up into a crouch, ready for flight. The orange glow from the fire has revealed the figures of two men, dressed in thick layers of coats and wrapped in blankets: one sits, one stands, and both are glugging out of bottles. Heart racing, I search the surrounding trees for an escape route. No way I can get out of here without those two hearing or seeing me. I force myself to stay rock still. If they're not already drunk, then they pretty soon will be, and I know from experience that'll make me faster than them.

I settle in to wait.

When my eyes come properly into focus, I see what they're putting into the fire. My heart sinks.

They already know I'm here.

CHAPTER SIX

At the T-junction, I tug my hood down over my face as a white van trundles past and at last a gap appears in the traffic. I quick-step across the road and hesitate at the park gates.

What am I doing here?

I been asking myself that for hours now and I'm not all that keen on the answers coming through, cos if Mum told the unit all that stuff about me, then it's her fault I got locked up, and that thought is messing with my head. Six freaking years. For all that time, I been wondering how she's coping, hoping she's okay. Wondering if she misses me, if she's scared cos she can't come and visit me. But it looks like it's her fault I was in there in the first place. Did she really do that, my own mother? And if she did, why?

Thanks to those homeless blokes over in Camden, I don't even got the papers to confront her with anymore. They had a point, mind – eye for an eye and all that. I'd nicked the guy's sleeping spot, so he nicked my case and used the paper for fuel. Keeping some homeless guy warm is probably the best use for that pack of lies anyway. They were all right, those two, once I'd stopped bricking it and got talking to them. The ginger-bearded one chucked me a load of fried chicken that'd been thrown out by some restaurant. Tasted bloody good for leftovers.

I press my forehead against the cold metal railings that surround the park. All I got to do is cross the gardens and I'll be back on the street where I grew up, the street where I been presuming all this time that Mum still lives.

What if she's moved?

How has it never occurred to me before now that she might not even be here? The thought shakes me, but at the same time, this nagging voice inside my head is telling me this is a bad idea. I should take off, get out of London, go somewhere nobody will ever find me. But the fact is, I can't. I got to see Mum, got to know what she really believes. She's still my mum and I don't got anyone else. Maybe the real reason I'm here is cos I think she's going to throw open her arms and welcome me home and make everything good again. Okay, maybe not *good* – and definitely not *again* – but better. I'll settle for better.

My gaze falls on the patch of park where flat grass turns into a rocky hill, and despite the anger clogging up my chest I smile for the first time in days.

I'd been seven years old, scrambling about on top of the mound. King of the World: arms raised, fists clenched in triumph. Mum was smoking, sat on a stone bench way down below. And not in that manic way she sometimes has about her, but like she had all the time in the world just to be there in the park, with me. She waved. I grinned, waved back, and lost my balance. I tumbled, foot across ear, elbows cracking, and crashed into a white boulder on the edge of the rockery.

Mum was on me in seconds, hurling me into her lap, hands patting my face and shoulders. 'Where does it hurt? Oh, baby, where does it hurt?' Tears welled up in her eyes, fat, round ones. 'Please be all right, Davey.'

'I'm okay,' I said, and I meant it, even though the doctor later announced like it was something to be proud of, that I'd sprained an ankle and broken my arm.

'Jesus, you scared me.' Mum stroked the side of my head. Her bitten fingernails scraped my ear. She leant back and stared right into my face. 'Don't ever frighten me like that again, do you hear me?'

'I won't,' I'd promised and, despite the stabbing pain in my arm, I remember feeling happy. Or something that could pass for it anyway.

I slip in through the park gate, hands in pockets, head down. A couple of Goths gnaw at each other's faces and ignore me as I pass them. I'm just a kid in a hoodie, invisible. I flick a side glance their way, checking them out. Don't get me wrong, I'm no pervert, but I never kissed a girl, nothing near it.

In my life-before-the-unit, I hung out in this park masses, mostly when I should've been in school. I ignore the words 'persistent truanting' as they flicker through my head. Loads of kids nick off school. Don't make them serial killers.

As parks go, it's a bit of a dump, but there are loads of bushes to hide in and it offers an easy escape from the Tippingdon Estate with all its graffiti and crackheads. Even better are the woods that stretch out from the back of the estate. When I wasn't in here, I was in there, hiding out in my special place, burying my treasures in my secret box, setting traps for intruders.

A quick scan of the area comes up all clear, so I step two paces to my right, drop onto all fours and tunnel into the undergrowth. Branches snag and scratch at my face as I belly-crawl towards the railings. I reach the edge and shove broken twigs and stones aside until I'm in what could pass for a comfortable position. Through the narrow gap between two leafy branches, I got a clear view of my old street, Underwood Close: a long stretch of tower blocks and their poky windows and steel doors. On one end of each block, an open stairway zig-zags up to uncovered balconies. I count the doors on the nearest tower: four floors up and five flats to the right and there it is – home.

The curtains are closed. Is she there? Is she sleeping?

To one side of the tower blocks, the car park sparkles with shattered glass and twisted beer cans. Four parked cars: two battered Mondeos, a white van and a silver Mini. All empty. In the surrounding streets, an old woman hobbles along the pavement and a bald bloke with two dogs in tow heads into the woods behind our tower block. I could probably reach the flat without being seen, so long as no one's staking the place out. But what then? Does she even know I'm out? Would she care?

I lie in the same spot for another half hour. Watching. Waiting. No police hammer at Mum's door, no anoraks lurk in the alleyways, there's no glint of binoculars poking out from a window. Cold seeps through my clothes until my legs hurt and my back aches. I scour every window again. Nothing. So what am I waiting for?

I shift position. Since they dragged me off to the unit, I've not seen or heard from Mum, not once, not even a Christmas card. At first, I'd been glad. Sod her. Later, of course, the penny dropped, and I stopped being mad at her for not visiting. Now it seems she'd actually agreed to help them. Maybe she even contacted them first, told them she thought I was a PSK, asked them to investigate.

The bald bloke with the dogs comes back out of the woods and a second dog-walker heads towards the park gates. My heart sinks. It's my pain-in-the-arse ex-neighbour, barmy old Mr Brockerton. Ex-army and built like a bull, old Brockerton's mission was to always be on my case, nagging at me to do this, to not do that, snitching to Mum about me. Him and her were always nattering together. Not in a lovey-dovey way or anything, more like he was her grandad or something. Thinking about it now, he was probably her only friend. She was always popping round to his, helping him out with shopping and that. If she has moved, he might know where to.

He ambles along the path, this terrier-type mutt trotting at his heels.

I press my body closer to the ground and clamp my eyes shut, waiting for him to pass by. The branches by my feet rustle and part, near giving me a heart attack as the yellow-stained mongrel pushes through. When it spots me, it snarls. I shake a hand at it – shoo. The mutt eyeballs me, growls, and arches its back ready to take a crap. On the other side of the bushes, old Brockerton whistles and wheezes.

'Bertie. Bertie boy. Come here.'

'Do one, Bertie,' I hiss.

The whites of the dog's eyes flash. It sniffs the air and shuffles its rump in a semi-circle. Squats again. A walking stick whacks the outer bushes.

'Bertie, you little git. Come here.'

The walking stick thwacks and wallops. A pair of legs appears through the leaves. Bertie strains harder. I bare my teeth at him and draw back my lips in a silent snarl. That's worked on a couple of the boys in the unit, but this mutt just laughs and keeps on straining.

Huge hands force branches aside. 'Bertie, you'd better get your arse out here or …'

I grab a sharp stick and jab it into Bertie's fat butt. The little beast yelps and shoots forward. There's an almighty racket as old Brockerton crashes back onto the footpath.

'Bertie, you little bastard. Just you bloody wait.'

I grin. Nothing much has changed around here.

I'm still grinning when the rustling and cursing gives way to silence and I turn my attention back to the street. There's a car right next to the fence, so close I can smell the hot engine. How could I not hear it pull up? An arm appears at the passenger window. Fingers flick. Something lands inside the railing, narrowly missing my ear. A cigar butt, glowing red, stinking. I scrape soil over it and peer along the car's sleek black body. An arm, thick with dark hair, rests on the open window. Stumpy fingers drum out a rhythm: *ta-drum, ta-drum, ta-drum-drum-drum*. I edge backward until I'm rock certain that a pair of eyes turning this way won't see me. A door opens on the other side of the car.

'Ask them if there's been any change in her routine these last few days,' the voice belonging to the arm says. 'Find out if she's home, if she's alone. And don't take all day.'

Heels click against tarmac as somebody gets out. 'We shouldn't have wasted all that time hanging around down there,' the owner of the heels says, and my stomach clenches into a knot. I know that voice. Feet shuffle and scrape and I catch the faint rattle of chains.

'You're not paid to think, Carson. And so long as he's paying for our time, it's his to waste.'

Paying for our time? Are they talking about Wilson? Has Wilson sent them here to bring me back? I shake my head. No: no way Wilson is bossing Carson around and hiring people to do his bidding. He's a creep and a liar but he's no mastermind.

'We needed to be there,' the voice goes on, 'in case the briefcase survived. Or worse, the boy's body turned up.'

'Yeah, well, all we did was lose a day. I told you, the way that kid swims there's no chance he drowned. And that briefcase is probably buried in mud on the riverbed.'

'That briefcase could fuck us all up, so you better pray it doesn't float up somewhere. Do yourself a favour, yeah? Stick to following orders and leave the thinking to me.'

Carson laughs. 'You're the boss, Drummond.'

'Damn right I am.' *Ta-drum, ta-drum, ta-drum-drum-drum.*

I bite hard on my lip to hold back a groan. The file, the very thing I could apparently use against them, is gone. Ashes, every freaking sheet of it.

The two men fall silent and my own breathing sounds deafening in my ears.

'What do we do if she's in?' Carson says eventually.

'We get it over with,' the man called Drummond says.

Over with?

'We should wait until we find him,' Carson says. 'Just in case.'

'We've done nothing but bloody wait. If he'd let me deal with this properly in the first place, we wouldn't be in this mess now.'

A car door clicks shut. 'The mother knows nothing,' Carson says. 'Christ, she barely knows her own name most days from the sound of it. She's no threat.'

I clench my fist, bite down on my knuckles and concentrate on catching their every word.

'Loose ends have a way of turning into noose ends. She might not have been a threat before, but if she's seen the boy, spoken to him, or … We can't risk it.' The fingers keep on drumming: *ta-drum, ta-drum, ta-drum-drum-drum.*

Carson grunts.

'Everyone's expendable, Carson,' Drummond says. 'You and me included.'

Carson's boots jangle and scrape against the tarmac. 'What if she's not home?'

'Then we wait. She never goes far.'

Suddenly, everything I read in those papers, all Wilson's lies, that bloody briefcase – none of it matters a rat's arse. I want to throw up. They're talking about Mum – my mum – using words like expendable, calling her a loose end. Who the hell is Carson anyway? My gaze traces up to the closed curtains in our flat. Please don't let her be in. Please.

'Get on with it then,' Drummond says.

Carson strides off, chains rattling, and hot bile rises in my throat. I force it back down and bite harder on my fist.

But instead of heading to the flats as I expected, Carson crosses the car park and makes a beeline for the white van. When he reaches it, the side door slides open, and he clambers in. What the ...? I duck even lower, and mentally run through my movements since I got here. If the place has been staked out this whole time, how likely is it that I been spotted? Not very, I decide. Even if they did look in this direction, the bush here is pretty thick and they'd be hard put to see me. I let myself breathe.

The van door shuts behind Carson, and it's just an empty white van again.

The hand in the window keeps drumming: *ta-drum, ta-drum, ta-drum-drum-drum.*

Questions scream through my head. What should've they taken care of properly in the first place? What are they going to do to Mum? What's she got to do with anything anyway? Why do they want to find me badly enough to stake out Mum's flat? What the hell is going on and who the hell am I?

I stare up at Mum's window until my eyes pop, but there's no sign of life. Whatever anger I been feeling about her gets buried under an avalanche of fear. Don't be home. Don't be sleeping it off. Be out. Please.

Ta-drum, ta-drum, ta-drum-drum-drum.

The van door opens again, then slams shut behind Carson, who strides back over to the saloon window.

'She's not home. Goes out every Wednesday. Took off about an hour ago. Won't get back until dark, maybe morning. Nothing out of routine. Nobody's been here.'

I close my eyes and let my head drop onto my arms, let the soil swallow the sound of my breath as it escapes me. She's not home, she's not home, she's not home.

'I said we should have given those guys a call before dragging our arses over here,' Carson says.

'Sure,' Drummond says. 'You do know that those guys over there make a career out of tapping calls and recording evidence, yes? You really want to have a telephone conversation with them about this?'

'Yeah, yeah, don't get your knickers in a twist.'

'Did they say anything else? She had any phone calls?'

'Nope.' Carson sighs. 'I'll go check out the flat then, shall I?'

The man called Drummond leans out the window and looks up at the tower block. Closely cropped black hair sprouts around a central bald patch. I glimpse pit-black eyes, bad skin, thin lips. I know that face. It belongs to the silent man who was in the car when Carson took me into the unit six long years ago.

'We'll go together,' he says.

'I've been in this game a long time,' Carson says. 'I don't need babysitting.'

Game? What game? Who the hell *is* Carson?

'We'll go together.'

'For fuck's sake.'

'Get in.'

Carson clambers into the driving seat and the saloon pulls across the street into the car park. Both men get out. Carson might be dressed in his usual plaid shirt and jeans, but the one called Drummond looks like some spook straight off the telly: smart suit, confident walk, shiny black shoes.

I wait as they head up the open stairway and saunter along the balcony. It takes them maybe thirty seconds to pick the lock and slip inside. For a few seconds longer, I lie there, fighting for breath. All I been thinking about till now is finding Mum, having it out with her then running to … Well, I hadn't got that far to be honest. But now? Now all I can think about is stopping these two whatever-they-are's from finding her first. I got to keep her safe, keep us both safe. I push backwards out of the bushes and scramble to my feet, hitting the path at a run. I'm nearly at the far end of the park when I hear somebody yell my name.

'David!'

I keep running but look back over my shoulder and see old Brockerton being dragged along a side path by his mangy mutt.

'Hold on,' he shouts.

Fat chance. I leg it out of the park gate and into West Street. A bus is pulling into the bus stop fifty metres ahead of me. I drag my hood over my head and pick up speed.

'Wait,' I yell, and for once the universe listens. I toss the last dregs of my begging coins into the ticket dispenser and throw myself onto the back seat.

The bus pulls out and joins a queue of traffic that's crawling onwards so slowly I swear old Brockerton could overtake us any second. I want to scream at the driver to hurry up, but I'm not totally stupid.

I got to get to Mum before Drummond and Carson do, and I got an advantage cos I know where she is. Drummond said today is Wednesday. There's only one place where my mum will be on a Wednesday afternoon. I slump into an empty seat at the back of the bus, lean my head against the headrest, and will the bus to go faster.

CHAPTER SEVEN

I turn into Eastgate Cemetery, a place where dead people hang out, and a place I know well. The cemetery is made up of different sections, each laid out in a sort of valley of its own. On the hill I'm heading for, an old oak tree towers over its surroundings and guards the non-religious section. Just beyond that oak, over the other side of the ridge, stands the wooden cross that marks my grandad's grave with nothing more than a name and a date: Arthur Jessop, 1962–2010.

I take a shortcut across the Catholic section, where crows perch on headstones, brazen as you like. My feet skid on rotten leaves and down I go, landing butt-first on polished black marble. There's an ocean of shiny marble in this section. I rub my wrist and glance up at the name of the corpse rotting beneath me. Patrick Harrington.

With this being the Catholic section, gold lettering lists the names of Patrick Harrington's multitude of children, his grandchildren, his great-grandchildren, his beloved wife. At the top of the list, there's a picture of a man with a hollowed-out face. The deceased, presumably. 'Creepy,' I mutter, though I secretly envy Catholics and Muslims and all that. Imagine having all those relatives looking out for one another. And who've I got? My mum. That's it. That's my entire family. And she's apparently expendable.

I prop myself up against the headstone of Patrick Harrington's grave, close my eyes for a moment and let the cold of the marble seep into my back as I steady my breathing. When I'm back on my feet, I bend down and grab a couple of roses from the overflowing pot in the centre of the grave. 'Sorry, Mr Harrington,' I mutter, and I take a deep breath and head for the swaying oak on the hill.

When I reach it, I press myself into its trunk like an old friend, surprised by how emotional I feel. The bark is rough against my cheek. I reach up and trace my fingers along the outline of my name, hacked in with my penknife in another life. My head swims with images of the past, the countless Wednesdays I spent hanging out here, bored out of my skull while Mum banged on about her perfect life with her perfect Daddy and how good it all was before I came along and spoilt things.

I push away from the oak and crawl like an action movie commando to the top of the ridge, reminding myself it's Mum I'm expecting to see, not Attila the Hun. But I still count to ten before I peer over.

My eyes scan the grass, the path, the gravel, the wooden cross. The only sign of her is a bunch of fresh carnations laid in their wrapping on my grandfather's grave.

Panic squeezes my chest. I'm too late. She's been and gone already. Maybe she don't stop here for so long these days. Maybe she's on her way home, where Carson and Drummond are waiting to show her exactly what they mean by expendable. All the energy slides out of me and I bury my face in the grass and fight to gather my scrambled thoughts. If she's on her way back home already, there's no way I can get to her before them. My fist clenches around the stolen roses. Thorns stab into my palms. The pain is good, helps me to focus.

Carson said she'd left the flat about an hour before me. It's possible that she's been and gone from the cemetery already, but he also said she probably wouldn't get back before dark. She could be at the Bull and Cock. We used to stop there most weeks on the way back. Sometimes we'd end up staying there all night. It never shuts, the Bull and Cock. Of course. That's where she'll be. Relief pours through me, and I lie there for a moment just letting it sink in.

I'm about to push to my feet when a flicker of movement catches my eye. I freeze. Mum is picking her way along the cemetery path, carrying a vase in both hands.

Even from this distance there's no hiding the fact that the yellow mac she's wearing is cheap and nasty. Her feet wobble in equally nasty high-heeled boots. Blood thumps in my ears and it's a good thing I'm lying down cos my legs suddenly feel jellylike. The word 'Mum' bubbles up inside me and I slap a hand over my mouth to stop it escaping.

As she cuts between two rows of graves, her heels sink into the grass. She stumbles and curses, a long string of expletives, and the bubble dies in my throat. I squeeze my eyes shut tight, desperate to see her but unable to bear it too.

When I open my eyes again, she's looking straight at me.

I spring to my feet, gaze locked onto hers. I want to say something, but when I open my mouth to speak it's like trying to talk while chewing on boiled eggs. Even if I could form some sort of speech, all the words I ever wanted to say to her have been erased from my head, leaving a blank screen in their place.

The vase hits the grass with a thump and water splashes her boots. 'Davey?'

I've forgotten how to breathe.

How can this be the woman who haunts my dreams, sometimes kind, sometimes cold, sometimes raging, lashing out, terrifying. She's tiny, this woman. Frail. A sparrow of a woman. Has she shrunk? Do people do that?

I don't move.

She don't move.

Something about the way she's standing puts me in mind of those wild animals in the documentaries, the ones who thought all they were doing was enjoying a bit of sunshine and chewing grass but then suddenly find they've walked right into a trap. She looks ready to bolt at the first sign of trouble.

'Hi,' I say eventually, surprised that it comes out sounding all right, not all strangled and raw like it felt on the inside.

Mum don't make any move towards me, but she don't run either. 'They told me I'd never see you again,' she says, and it sounds like an accusation. Her voice is tight, and I wonder how much she's had to drink. I wonder too who 'they' are. Carson? Drummond? Someone else?

'They were wrong then, weren't they?' I don't take my eyes off her face, and what I see there makes me feel sick inside. I see fear. She's scared. Of me.

Maybe she's right to be afraid, but that don't stop it from hurting. My guts ache as I wait for her to speak again, to say something that will tell me how she really feels about me being here.

'They should have told me,' she says. 'They should have told me you were coming. I could have … I would have …'

'They didn't know.' I pause. 'They don't know.'

I watch for her reaction. The muscles around her jaw clench tight.

'Then how—'

'There was an accident. The van I was in crashed into a river. We were trapped underwater.' As I say the words, a picture of Rickleson's hair lifting on the rising water flicks into my head. 'The driver didn't make it.'

Mum's hand flies to her mouth and she takes two steps towards me. 'Are you hurt?'

I shrug. 'I got lucky.'

There's still enough distance between us to make flight possible. For me? For her?

'Would've you cared if I hadn't?' I say, aware that I sound like a petulant child.

'Of course I would.'

She comes closer, almost within reaching distance. I take a step back and realise I'm not afraid of what *she* might do; I'm afraid of the anger I can feel creeping back into me.

'I know you told them stuff about me, Mum. Stuff that got me into trouble, like wetting the bed.' I watch her face as I say it, but I can't read her.

She shocks me by suddenly walking right up close and putting one hand on each of my shoulders until I got no choice but to look into her face. 'You're the only thing that keeps me going, Davey, the only reason I've had to keep going.'

I want to believe her, I want the anger to go away, but I shake her hands off my shoulders and step back another pace. 'Six years, Mum!'

She turns her face away and squints up at the pale blue sky above us. Over her shoulders, the graves of strangers stretch into the distance, including my grandfather's.

'It's my fault you were ill,' she says quietly. 'You only did what you did because one way and another I screwed you up, and I didn't even notice what was happening because I was ...' She trails off and rubs her eyes.

I resent the surge of guilt that passes through me at the sight of the bitten nails and the chewed skin at the tips of her fingers. 'Drunk,' I say, and it sounds mean. 'You were drunk, Mum.'

She nods. 'I'm a drunk. I screwed you up, and I'm sorry. You were a good boy and I screwed you up. You'll never know how much I regret that.' She roughly rubs her face and pushes back her hair. 'I just wanted you to be fixed.'

Before I can answer her, she turns and walks towards my grandfather's grave, scooping up the vase on her way. She kneels on the grass in a posture I remember so well, snipping stems and balling up the plastic waste in her fist. I stand there like a spare part, something I also remember so well. A small part of me wants to say, 'I'm sorry, too,' but an even bigger part of me can't.

'Are you?' she says, without turning to look at me, her hands fussing with the carnations.

'Am I what?' I ask, wondering if she's learnt to read minds.

'Better. Fixed.' She places the vase in the middle of her father's grave and pats the ground around it, a well-rehearsed ritual.

I take a deep breath, walk over and sit on the ground beside her. 'Here.' I hand her my stolen roses.

Something I can't read flickers in her eyes. She accepts the roses and adds them to the vase. 'It's not like I had any choice in it,' she says quietly. She reaches into her bag, withdraws a packet of Lambert and Butler and lights up.

I stare up at the branches of the oak as they groan and creak in the breeze.

'Look at me, Davey,' she says.

I look.

'Tell me what you see. Honestly.'

Her eyes are blotchy and red. The make-up creased into the lines of her face looks days old. Her hair's like some sad, greasy Barbie's. I catch the scent of sweat and stale piss.

I shrug. 'You look all right.'

'You always were a terrible liar,' she says with a small laugh. Her breath is rank with whisky and cigarettes. 'I'm a walking disaster, Davey. I can barely look after myself, never mind a child.'

'In case you haven't noticed, I'm not a child anymore.'

'No, you're not, are you?' She puffs on her cigarette. 'Have you forgotten how things were, Davey?'

It's my turn to laugh. 'There aren't enough shrinks in the world for that, Mum.'

She catches my eye and we both flick a smile, and for a moment she's my mum again.

Daylight is fading. The vase tilts at an angle on the gravel between us, her carnations, my stolen roses. Mum sucks the last of the nicotine out of her cigarette, rubs the butt in the dirt and drops it into an old Marmite jar. I'd forgotten that about her, the way she's always got some kind of butt-pot to hand. She might be an alky and a crazy heavy smoker, my mum, but she's no litter lout.

'I've always loved you, Davey,' she says. 'It's all my fault, not yours. You were a good boy before I broke you.'

'What's so broken about me, Mum?' My voice cracks. 'I don't understand. I don't remember being that bad.'

She shakes her head and looks away.

'Mum. Tell me. Please. What is it that's wrong with me?'

'I can't do this, Davey.' She pulls out another cigarette. 'Do what?'

'Play games.' She takes a drag on the fag. 'It's not like you don't know.'

'Mum,' I reach out a hand and lay it on her arm, the way she used to do to me when she really needed me to listen to her. 'Please, tell me what I did. I don't remember. Please. I just need to hear you say it. Maybe that'll help me remember.'

She narrows her eyes then nods and reaches into her bag. Pulls out a bottle of whisky.

'Okay, Davey.' She takes a glug, then another. She looks tired and sad and hopeless. 'If that's how you want to play it, okay.'

CHAPTER EIGHT

My stomach is clenched so tight it hurts. Mum takes another glug from the bottle before lifting her chin and murmuring, 'Kamal.'

I wonder if I misheard her. 'Kamal?'

'Kamal Chakrabarti.'

Kamal Chakrabarti was in the year below me in school. When I was in Year 5 and he was in Year 4, he drowned.

'Right,' I say. 'What about him?'

'You wanted to hear me say it, and I've said it.' She lifts the bottle to her lips and swallows, eyeing me all the while. 'Does it help you remember?'

Shortly before I was taken into the unit, I'd been walking across the canal bridge on my way home from school when Kamal fell into the black, oily water. He couldn't swim for toffee, and when he went down for the third time, I flung myself over the bridge railing and into the freezing black liquid. I dived and dived but it took too long to find him, and when I did find him and pull him to the surface, he wasn't breathing anymore. Kamal's dad was this big-wig football player for West Ham United, so my picture was splashed all over the papers. A reporter from the *London Evening Standard* came to the flat and interviewed me. I was hailed as some sort of local hero, so how does that make me broken?

I prod and push at Mum with questions, until she tells me how two detectives had come to see her and told her how I had murdered Kamal in cold blood. They explained how lucky I was that there wouldn't be any trial cos I was young, and I'd owned up to what I'd done and wanted to make amends, so I'd be taken care of. Just not by her anymore.

'They said I confessed?'

She looks at me oddly, but nods.

My insides have turned to mush, and for a moment I wonder if it could be true. Did I kill Kamal? I can tell from Mum's face that she believes it, and she's my own mother, so maybe it is true. A sparrow lands on the wooden cross and cocks its head at me as if to say, well, did you?

I shake my head and straighten my shoulders. Rubbish. I remember every detail of that day, seeing him fall, diving down, searching, diving again. His flaccid face, limp body, blue lips. I tried to save him.

'Is that why they banged me up then?'

Tears roll down Mum's face. 'His poor mother.'

I don't know how I hadn't seen the connection before. It was only a week or so after Kamal died that Carson had turned up and taken me away. But why had they suddenly decided I was a killer? And why had nobody at the unit ever mentioned Kamal to me?

Mum sits cross-legged, face smeared with drying tears, the bottle going up and down, up and down. The sparrow watches her from its perch on the cross.

'They said I'd broken you,' she says quietly. 'That it's my fault you're the way you are.'

'And how am I, Mum?' I ask, my voice cracking.

She wrinkles her nose as if searching for the right word. 'They said you've got something called … conduct disorder.'

My insides lurch. That's the name they used in my file, the name I don't yet know the meaning of. It's the little spattering of truths that make a lie work. I think back to Carson in the car park: 'His mother knows nothing'. I look at her sitting there, dishevelled, weak, ignorant. The anger I thought I'd put away comes creeping back.

'Do you know what conduct disorder means, Mum?' I ask.

She waves a hand, dismissive, and the sound of the liquid slipping down her throat fills my ears. 'It means you're broken, doesn't it?'

The anger builds in me. She's had six whole years to find out. Six years to get a lawyer and fight for me. Six years to do something, anything, other than wallow in self-pity. A low throb rumbles in my head and the sparrow flaps into the air and finds a more distant branch, higher in the oak. Wise sparrow.

Mum leans towards me. God, the stench of her. It was a mistake coming here, a stupid mistake.

'You were always in trouble, Davey: missing school, nicking stuff.' She points the bottle at me. 'That's what made it so easy for them to take you off me.'

Part of me sighs with relief. It's all my fault then? Good, at least I know where I am now, at least I know what I'm dealing with. This is the Mum I remember. Self-pitying, criticising, mean. Any minute now and she'll start getting downright nasty. I realise that the sparrow has gone from the tree. Time I wasn't here either. Being here don't make sense anymore. I can't save Mum. Not from them, not from herself.

'I can't imagine where you get your temper from,' she slurs with no sense of self-awareness whatsoever. 'You don't get it from your grandfather, I know that.' She nods to herself and takes another swig, and I can see exactly where this conversation is heading, but I'm not ten years old anymore and I'm not going to let her get away it.

'So, Mum,' I say, 'where *do* I get this bad blood of mine from? If not from your side of the family, then …?'

She eyes me sideways.

'Come on, I'd like to know. Really. I would.'

The bottle hovers in mid-air. 'Shut up, Davey.'

'Any clues, or were you too drunk to remember him?'

'I'm warning you, Davey.' She raises her arm.

'What? You going to slap me?' I thrust my face forward and offer her my cheek. 'Go ahead, but it's only fair to warn *you*, Mum, that I'm a lot bigger than the last time you tried that crap, and I don't take that shit lying down anymore.'

Her arm drops to her side.

I scramble to my feet. 'Bye, Mum. It's been … Well, you know.'

'Davey … I —'

'You said it all before, Mum. You got nothing to say I'm interested in hearing.' I turn to go.

'Wait!'

I turn back. 'What?'

She turns her wrists over and thrusts them towards me like a gift. 'After they took you away, I tried to die,' she says. 'See?'

Scars lie white against her already vampire-pale flesh. As I stare at them, they blur, one into the other, and whirl around in my head. I thump back down to a sitting position.

When Oliver first arrived at the unit, he'd been even paler than he is these days, and that's saying something. My first thought back then was what a pathetic little squirt he was. Then I noticed the scars covering his wrists and the purple bruises circling his neck. It looked like someone had tried really hard to kill him. One day, long after we'd become friends, Wilson cornered Oliver into confessing to the circle that he'd done all that stuff to himself. I still remember the shock, like a punch in the guts – the idea that somebody would do that to themselves. No matter how bad it got inside the unit, I never, not for one minute, considered suicide.

'I didn't want to go on,' Mum is saying now. 'Not without you.'

Something inside me breaks. I curl up into a ball – a tight, safe ball – right there on the ground. I close my eyes.

White scars swirl around the inside of my head like pieces of string, choking me. I'm tired. I'm so freaking tired.

Mum drags my head into her lap, and I let her. She strokes her hands through my hair, and I let her. I wait for her stories to come. I know how it'll go. It'll go how it always goes. For starters, happy memories, her Daddy-Dearest stories. For mains, her Poor-Lucy stories. And for dessert? Well, that's what I think of as her Damn-you-Davey stories. Same old, same old.

The rhythm of her voice slides over me. She's no Dr Carl but it'll do. I'll just lie here and sleep. Jesus, how I long for sleep. I try to let the buzzing take over, try to zone out, and I nearly manage it but then I realise something. This isn't the same old, same old at all. She's saying something new, talking about stuff I never heard before.

I shake off sleep and listen.

'For my fifteenth birthday,' Mum clears her throat, 'your grandfather took me on a trip to the Lake District, just the two of us, or so I thought.'

She hesitates for so long I think she might've gone into one of her trances. I wait, and eventually she starts up again.

'When we got to the hotel, this woman he knew from back home turned up. Jeannie, her name was. They made out like it was a coincidence but how stupid did they think I was?'

She throws back her head and swigs whisky.

Again, I wait. If there's one thing the unit's managed to drum into me, it's how to wait. She wipes her mouth with the back of her hand and shoves the bottle aside. If she didn't already have my full attention, that would've done it. Whatever this is, it's serious.

'After my mother died, my father – your grandfather – doted on me. I became his whole life, and then along comes this woman and suddenly he's lying to me.' Her fingers pluck the petals off of a carnation and I get a flash of Fat Michael peeling flakes of skin off his arms and letting them float to the floor. He got his head kicked in more than once for that, but he still kept on doing it. I never could figure out if that was brave or just plain stupid. I shake the memory away. Something important is happening and I got to concentrate. Mum's eyes have glazed over like she's watching the past unfold on some secret screen in front of her.

'You were telling me about your holiday,' I prod.

'It's all mixed up together.'

'What is?'

'The truth.'

'The truth?'

She shivers. It's twilight now, the hour for laying ghosts. I unzip my hoodie and lay it around Mum's shoulders. She tugs it tight around her neck and starts talking and talking.

Her father had wanted them to take a picnic up Helvellyn, which apparently is some sort of hill above one of the lakes. She sulked and cried and said she didn't want to go on any bloody picnic, but he put his foot down for the first time ever and made her go. I can't help thinking that maybe if my sainted grandfather had put his foot down a whole lot sooner and a whole lot more often, Mum might not have turned into such a talented sulker in the first place; cos if she got any talent at all, sulking would be it.

'I purposely decked myself out in this tiny red skirt,' she says. 'No tights, and these shoes with long narrow toes, all the rage back then.' Her lips flick in and out of a smile. 'My feet were on fire.'

I can't help smiling, too, at the image this conjures up. Grandad Arthur trying to impress his date and act like all was normal, and Mum gagging for a moan but not able to say anything cos she wasn't talking to them, and had anyway shot herself in her own foot, neat as nuts.

After the walk, they stopped off at an old-fashioned pub, which was all tankards and log burners, just the sort of thing she'd love these days but hated back then apparently. Mostly the place was stuffed with people Grandad Arthur's age or older, except for in the poolroom, where a much younger crowd were messing around. Laughing. Loud. She'd never seen so many pairs of designer jeans and woolly jumpers.

'I felt like a right idiot, dressed like I was. My feet were full of blisters, and what did my Daddy and Jeannie want to do? Go and visit some bloody cave at the bottom of the garden.'

She point-blank refused to go with them. So they left her there, on her own, warning her not to move until they got back, which went down like a bucket of cold sick.

'One of the boys from the poolroom came over,' she says. 'Started chatting to me. He was gorgeous. Made me laugh, you know?'

I realise that no, I don't know. I never seen Mum having a flirt and a laugh with anyone, or laughing at someone else's jokes. How sad is that? I never seen her have a good time either, so when she goes on to tell me how the birthday boy had invited her to his eighteenth birthday bash in a holiday cottage just up the road, I'm sort of rooting for her to go, which she did.

'I thought serve Daddy right,' she says. 'Let him worry.'

Fair enough, I think.

The crowd at the party grew and grew, with people arriving in flash cars, bringing more and more booze. At some point, someone asked her about her age, and she lied and said seventeen. I would've done the same. Not that I ever been invited to a party, mind. Can you imagine it, a party at the unit?

She's still talking and I force myself to tune back in to her, and my breath catches in my throat when she explains how she'd only ever had a few sips of alcopop at Christmas before that day, but when they offered her a glass of tequila, she'd taken it. And then another and another.

Is that why she's telling me all this, cos that was the start of her drinking? I sit up and pull back from her a fraction. Being in a sulk isn't exactly a solid reason for blowing your whole life up, is it? If she expects any sympathy for that, she's going to be disappointed.

She stares at the horizon. 'Me and the boy whose birthday it was got talking, got dancing, and then ... We were both drunk.' Her head is bent forward, her hair hiding her face. 'It shouldn't have happened.'

I resist shoving my hands over my ears. I got to hear this. I bite my tongue and force myself to watch and listen.

'Afterwards, he fell asleep, and I grabbed my shoes and sneaked off,' she says, her eyes closed, her mouth moving.

She'd walked back to the hotel and hadn't even reached their holiday suite when her father flung the door open, looking deranged. She'd run into her room and tried to close the door, but he'd chased her, demanding to know where the hell she'd been, what the hell she thought she was playing at. He'd already called the police and reported her missing, even though she'd only been gone a few hours.

'I flung myself face down on the bed, trying to get away from him, but he kept on and on. "Don't you dare ignore me, young lady. Where have you been?" He kept prodding me, shouting, demanding answers until I couldn't think straight.'

I want to feel sorry for her, but I can't. It's Grandad Arthur's got my sympathy right now. All this, just cos she was in a sulk about not wanting to go on a sodding picnic. She had a father who loved her, who took her on holiday to celebrate her birthday, for God's sake. When'd she ever celebrate my birthday? Poor little Lucy, eh?

'Do you have any idea what you've put us through?' he'd yelled, and she'd lifted her head and spotted Jeannie standing in the doorway. The woman was everywhere. At the hotel, on their walk, in the pub, and now even in their hotel suite. She realised that 'us' didn't mean her and her Daddy anymore. 'Us' meant him and Jeannie. She'd felt sick, furious, confused. Her father was still fuming, going on and on about how he'd always put her first, always taken care of his little girl, and this was how she repaid him. For once, me and Grandad Arthur are on the same page.

'So I told him,' she says so quietly I got to strain to hear.

'Told him what?' I ask, though I'm not sure I want to know.

She puts the cigarette between her lips and tries three times to ignite her lighter. I want to snatch it off her, show her how it's done, but I'm not feeling inclined to help her, so I don't. She gives up and takes the cigarette out of her mouth.

'I told him,' she repeats. 'And in his eyes, I saw a light go out.' She shudders. 'I think I killed him, there and then.'

'For God's sake, Mum. Told him what?'

Tears spill out of her, like her whole face is leaking, not just her eyes. 'I told him I'd been raped. I told him it was all his fault.'

'But you said—'

'I just wanted to hurt him. And I did. Oh, god, I did.' She clutches her stomach and moans, a long, deep sound that makes every pore of my skin prickle.

I can't speak, which is probably just as well.

She pulls a pack of tissues out of her bag and blows her nose. Takes a long shuddering breath and carries on spilling. I want to stop her. I need her to go on.

Grandad Arthur had hauled her off to the police station, where they wanted to run tests, gather evidence. She'd tried to take it back, she says. Tried to tell them it was a lie, but it was too late. She was underage, and her Daddy was going to make the bastard pay.

'I refused to let them do any tests,' she says. 'Daddy was furious, but that was the only way I could stop it. I never meant for it to go so far.'

I listen. Say nothing. She talks on.

The police had found the boy, and he denied having sex with her. Case closed. Her father had cried openly, right there in the police station, a thing that shocked her more than anything else.

'I broke him, too,' she says.

She stares at the cigarette in her hand, like she don't remember what it is or how it got there. 'We came back to London but nothing was the same. Daddy couldn't look at me. We just bumped around the house like two strangers. Jeannie came and went and tried to be nice but ...' she shrugs. 'Then we discovered I was pregnant, and he flipped.'

A loud buzzing flares up in my head but I still hear enough to learn that the news that she was pregnant confirmed statutory rape, and my DNA would prove who was guilty.

'Let him deny it now,' her father had screamed down the phone at the police.

They came around and took a statement, but they wouldn't disclose any information about the boy. Two days later, they announced that they wouldn't be pressing charges.

'Daddy just lost it,' she breathes, clutching her chest.

He set off for the Lakes to find the house, to find the boy. Three days later, his car turned up in Ullswater. They found alcohol in his blood. He'd driven straight off the road.

A fresh waft of cigarette smoke chokes me, but not half as much as her next words do.

'So there I was. Fifteen years old and pregnant. And instead of my Daddy, I got you.' She knocks back a long, slow glug of whisky. 'So, now you know.'

Now I know.

CHAPTER NINE

I shift onto my side and cramp shoots through my back. My brain can't seem to focus. I'm lying on a bench. Wooden seat. Metal frame. Cardboard on top of me like I'm some hobo. Not that I got anything to be snobby about cos this is my third night of sleeping rough, but I'm not planning on making a career of it. I read somewhere once that the word hobo comes from 'homeward bound'. Am I though, homeward bound? Home seems to have slipped into the abyss the minute I came seeking it.

Sleep reclaims me and in the chaotic bubbles in my head, Rickleson sips coffee and drifts deeper and deeper under the sea. Fish gnaw at his face.

'It's only me.' Mum's voice drags me back into the light. She's behind the bench, leaning over to peer at me, a lighted fag in her hand. Her mac's rumpled and dirty, her hair matted. 'You okay, Davey?'

I sit up. Mistake. The cramp hits again. Over Mum's shoulder, rows of old but tidy gravestones stutter into focus. At the thought of Grandad's grave, memories of last night, of what Mum did, come hurtling round the corner of my mind. I got what I wanted, didn't I? To know.

So, what do I know?

Well, I know nobody wanted me. Not my mother, not my father, not my grandad. Oh, and I'm a potential serial killer. Mustn't forget that. Whoever said knowledge is power has never had a week like this one. I got all this knowledge now and all I feel is sick. But there's no going back, cos you can't un-know a thing.

But you can tame your thoughts, get them under some sort of control. That's one of the little tricks Miss Beryl taught me. I gather all the shitty thoughts into a bundle, shove the whole lot to the back of my head and seal them up in a mental vault to be dealt with later.

'We got to get out of here,' I say, pushing off the cardboard blanket.

'Buses start running in half an hour.' Mum stubs out her fag and drops the butt into the Marmite jar.

It's weird, you'd think she'd be hung-over and whiney this morning, or weak with shame, but instead she seems stronger. It's like she woke up with a clean slate, all reborn and full of self-confidence. Isn't that what all those circle-time sessions at the unit were supposed to be about? Downloading. Unburdening. Cleansing. They always left me feeling contaminated.

A drop of rain lands on my nose as a low bank of cloud blocks out the struggling morning sun. A chill wind kicks up and whips around our legs. Mum shudders and hugs herself.

I close my eyes and slam the vault doors, try to focus on what needs to be done. Up until today it was simple: get out of the water alive; get warm and dry; get away from Carson; find Mum. Nice straightforward goals, what the teachers at the unit called SMART objectives: Specific, Measurable, Attainable, Realistic, Time-appropriate. But now I don't got a clue what to do. I need a goal, cos as objectives go, even I can see that 'stay alive and away from Carson and Drummond' aren't SMART goals. How will I know when I've achieved them? How will I know when I'm safe? I glance at Mum. Her eyes are closed. She's humming softly to herself. How can I keep *her* safe?

'Mum? We got to figure out what to do, where to go. Mum?'

She opens her eyes and smiles. It's a wide, carefree smile, and I can't help wondering if she's got a bee in her brain buzzing away too, zoning out all the crap.

'I'll go home,' she says, 'just as soon as the buses start running.'

'We can't,' I remind her.

Her smile vanishes, and I'm almost feeling sorry for her when her words sink in: '*I'll* go home' not '*we'll* go home'.

From the roads surrounding the cemetery, a steady drone of traffic is building up. Morning rush hour. London is kick-starting a new day and we got nowhere to go. The thought of living on the streets makes my head throb harder. From my experience so far, sleeping rough don't involve a whole heap of sleeping. And Mum? How long would she survive on the streets? I'd give her five minutes.

But the streets are all I got to offer.

'You got to know someone,' I say. 'You lived in London your whole life.'

She shakes her head and sticks out her chin in that childish way she does when she don't want to listen. It takes another ten minutes of interrogation to get her to offer anything up.

'Well, there is someone ... But I don't know if ... No ...' She shakes her head again.

'Who? For God's sake, Mum, we're not drowning in options here. Who is it?'

She hesitates a moment longer, then says, 'Jeannie. The woman my father was seeing.'

I blink. 'I thought you hated her?'

'I hated my father liking her; that's not the same thing. She was kind to me when ... you know.'

Her face glows a deep pink and in my head a hundred accusations try to break free but now's not the time. I shove them back into their vaults and bolt the doors.

'You think she'd help us now?'

'She'd help *me*, I think.'

Again with the 'me'. I glance up at the darkening sky and sigh. 'Where does she live?'

'She used to have a house in Islington. I guess she still might.'

'Are you sure we can we trust her?'

She hesitates, just for a fraction of a second but it's enough.

'Yes,' she says. 'I can trust her.'

At the Angel tube station, the platform is packed. There must be some sort of gig on today, cos a bunch of the boarding passengers got on these black T-shirts with the same white-lettered slogan printed across their chests: 'Save Our Sick Society – Vote Yes'. As we push our way off the train, through the crush of bodies piling into the open doors, an old man shouts out, 'Save it for who, ya bunch of fascists?' There's a scuffle. The old guy is shoved to the back of the platform and some bloke near me says, 'Stupid old fart,' and laughs.

Me and Mum force a pathway through, fighting against the tide. The crowd gets sucked into the train, leaving us washed up and dazed on a near-empty platform. I trail behind Mum, who weaves through the station, head down, feet moving fast.

Within minutes we emerge, blinking, into daylight. The rain's finally packed it in and stabs of sun pierce the grey sky. Our wet clothes steam. When we turn a corner, the drone of traffic disappears and Mum stops so abruptly I bang right into her.

'This is it. This is the street.'

A grand, sweeping crescent with houses curved along one side. They're town houses but they're dead posh ones, three storeys high, each one a different colour of the rainbow. Along the inside bit of the curve, high railings cut off a bank of greenery. Between branches, I glimpse a canal and I blink away the image of Kamal's blotchy face as they pulled the blanket over his head.

Mum's hand sneaks into mine. She's buttoned up her coat all wrong. I undo it and start again. The pavement stretches in a semi-circle before us. 'Come on.' I half lead, half drag her along the street until she draws to a halt in front of a cream-and-black house. Window boxes spew red and yellow tulips into the sun. Stone steps lead both above and below the street. The gate is latched.

'This is the one,' she whispers.

I'm thinking that maybe Mum was right about what she'd said back at the graveyard. Maybe this is a stupid idea. But if we got any other options, any at all, I don't know what they are.

I lift the latch.

Mum's trembling and won't look at me, but she lets me take her arm and together we walk through the gate. There's this fancy knocker on the gleaming front door, a carved bear's head that rears up at us like a challenge. I grab the bear's neck in my grubby fist and slam. *Bang.* From inside the house, we hear the echoes: *bang, bang, bang.* Mum is still grasping my hand.

Footsteps. We brace ourselves. The door swings open.

A plump woman, around the same age as Miss Beryl, blocks the doorway. She's round in that granny kind of way, wearing these multi-coloured slacks and a smock top. She's splattered in paint and clutching an oily cloth. From somewhere behind her comes a deep-throated bark.

'Can I help you?'

I glance at Mum but her face is giving away zilch.

'We're looking for someone who used to live here,' I say.

'Oh?' The woman wipes yellow paint spots off the chunky watch that she's wearing and squints at us.

'Her name's Jeannie. You know her?'

Suspicion clouds her eyes. 'And who are you?'

'Hello, Jeannie,' Mum says.

The woman blinks, squints closer at Mum. 'Lucy? Dear God, Lucy, is that you?'

Mum and the woman stare at each other like a couple of imbeciles.

'Sorry. Whatever am I thinking?' Jeannie flaps her hands. 'Come in, come in. Look at you, you're frozen.'

Mum's shivering like a bubonic plague victim. I take her elbow and push her in ahead of me. Jeannie ushers us through a ginormous black-and-white tiled hallway. Mum's heels clatter loudly on the tiled floor as we're led through to the back of the house, where this Rottweiler forces its way past Jeannie and comes to inspect us. Well, it comes to inspect *me;* Mum's already followed Jeannie into the kitchen and I'm left alone out in the corridor playing at statues while a wet nose sniffs me all over. Then the beast rears up, slaps a paw on each of my shoulders, and shoves its humongous face into mine.

He's got this head the size of a small country. Drool drips onto my neck. It's like being on a date with the devil, with us staring into each other's eyes waiting to see who'll go to hell first. The mutt tilts its head and sticks out a huge tongue, catching me full in the kisser. A whimper escapes me.

I lose, and the dog knows it.

Jeannie sticks her head back out of the kitchen door and laughs. 'Don't worry about Jack Daniels. He's my neighbour's dog. Soft as butter, aren't you, Jack?'

The head resting on my shoulder is hard as rock. Try spreading that on your toast, I think.

'Down, Jack,' Jeannie says.

His tail wagging, Jack Daniels drops onto all fours, and I wipe my face with my sleeve. Gross.

'You're a friend for life now,' Jeannie says, then she clocks my face. 'Right then, I'll put him out, shall I? My neighbour, Florrie, only works mornings. He can let himself back into his own garden through the fence.'

I wait until she's followed through on that promise before I make any move towards the kitchen.

After the stark order of the unit, where everything's got a strictly designated place, Jeannie's kitchen comes as a shock. Clutter covers every surface: pots dangle from the ceiling; not one of the chairs matches; dozens of paintings cling to the wood-panelled walls, every single one at a skewed angle; animal figures inhabit every speck of shelf space.

'Right then, please, sit down.' Jeannie indicates a massive table, wooden bench running along one side, a jumble of chairs scattered along the other.

Mum slips onto the bench and struggles to unbutton her mac. I pick the wicker chair opposite her and shuck off my hoodie. She folds her hands on the tabletop and sits up straight. I copy her. I don't know how I'm expected to behave in this posh house.

Jeannie looks from Mum to me and back again, her face quizzical.

'I'm David,' I say. 'Lucy's son.'

Jeannie's gaze flicks from Mum to me then back to Mum, then she nods and says briskly, 'Right then, what would you both like to drink?'

Mum's gaze flicks across to a drinks cabinet propped between a tall, red fridge and one of those old dresser things you display plates on. It can't be much after ten in the morning.

I clear my throat loudly. 'We'll take tea, won't we, Mum?'

A tray appears: masses of scones, a jar of jam, a pot of cream, a teapot. Those scones look so freaking good I'm practically drooling here, but I don't touch them. In the unit you wait for your food to be divvied out fairly first. Or unfairly, depending on who's doing the divvying. Either way, you wait.

Several millennia later, Jeannie eases her backside onto the stool at the end of the table, between me and Mum. She picks up a scone, slaps jam on one half, cream on the other, and presses them together.

'Help yourself,' she says.

Why didn't she say so sooner? I take a big helping of everything and fall on it like a hyena devouring a corpse. Mum don't touch any. There's only one thing she wants and it's not food.

'I'd given up hope of ever finding you, Lucy. I can't believe you're actually here.'

Mum shrugs and sips her tea like a sulky teenager, constantly glancing at the drinks cabinet. I force out a smile and point to an oil painting of a family of bears messing about on a riverbank. 'You do that?' When Jeannie turns away to look, I kick Mum under the table and give her a glare. She kicks me back.

'Oh, I wish.' Jeannie plucks the painting from the wall and hands it to me. 'Quite brilliant, isn't it?'

I only asked about the painting as a distraction tactic, but the minute I got the metre-wide frame in my hands and I'm taking a proper look, I swear I'm blown away. My fingers trace the rough texture of oil on canvas. You can actually feel the cool water soothing and calming you, and the sheer ferocity in the mother bear's jaw could teach Freaky Adam a thing or two.

'A friend of mine did it.' Jeannie puts the painting back on the wall at a ridiculous angle.

'It's great.'

'Yes, he's such a talented young man.' She smiles. 'Lucy—'

'How about that one?' I point to a cartoon sketch of a donkey in a tutu, but she don't fall for it a second time.

'That's one of mine. Lucy, where have you been? I've wondered so many times.'

Sulking or not, Mum can't resist the chance to revel in a bit of self-pity. I get stuck into another scone while she gives Jeannie the whole sorry story. I don't need to listen; I heard it often enough. Jeannie's staring at Mum with this pained look on her face. 'But what happened to the money your father left you?'

'There wasn't any. It's as much as I can do to pay the rent most weeks.'

'But Arthur was a wealthy man, Lucy, and he left everything to you. None of it went to … Well,' Jeannie busies herself stacking the plates and clattering the cutlery into a pile on top, 'he wasn't the type to leave it all to a cat's home, was he?'

My warning antenna pops into life. What's she not saying? Who else might my grandfather have left money to?

'You were his precious little girl, and I know he would have provided well for you,' Jeannie says. 'This isn't right.'

'Sounds about right to me,' I say, sick to death of hearing about how fabulous Arthur-bloody-Jessop was. 'I can see the headline now: "Drunk driver, lucky not to kill anyone other than himself, leaves only child in debt". What's not to believe?'

I don't *see* the slap coming, but I feel it all right when it does.

'Lucy! Are you all right, David?'

I rub a hand to my cheek and nod. I asked for that. I sit in silence while Jeannie and Mum talk on, Mum wallowing in self-pity and Jeannie trying to comfort her. 'It's pointless, all this blaming and fault-finding. You're Arthur's daughter, Lucy, and I loved your father, and he loved you. Taking care of you was the last thing I could have done for him.'

Mum sticks her chin out. 'So why didn't you?'

Jeannie looks confused. 'I tried, but with you refusing to see me, there was nothing I could do, even with my late husband's influential connections. It was your choice to make.'

Mum shakes her head back and forth. 'But I wanted to stay here, I felt safe here. They just took me away when you were out shopping and told me *you* didn't want to see *me* again.'

Jeannie frowns. 'That's not true.'

Mum's face looks pained. 'You abandoned me,' she whispers.

'No, I—'

I say, 'Well, if anyone should know what that feels like, Mum, I should, shouldn't I?'

Mum turns her stare on me, and it's like she's seeing it from my point of view for the very first time. She leans in, grips my arm tight enough to hurt and pulls me close. 'I'm sorry, Davey. I'm sorry.'

Her breath is hot on the side of my neck, and she wraps her arms around me until my head is on her chest, the beating of her heart so loud in my ear that suddenly I don't care about the stink of stale whisky or fags or B.O. I clamp my eyes shut and bury myself in the warmth of her – King of the World – and the rest of the room disappears.

We stay clamped together like that for an ice-age, and when I open my eyes again, Jeannie's gone.

CHAPTER TEN

If rule number one is tell them nothing, then rule number two is trust no one. Jeannie's been giving it out friendly enough but ... The side door stands ajar.

'Wait here,' I murmur to Mum.

She nods, slumps on the bench and closes her eyes.

The side door leads to a conservatory. On the other side of the glass panes a thick grey sky glowers overhead. The walls are CSU-white, but a ginormous canvas, carved with bold slashes of colour, breaks the monotony. A newspaper lies abandoned on an armchair. Rain falls softly on a cramped garden where bamboo and sculptures of creatures – tiger, dog, stork – fight for space. From the other side of a door, I hear mumbling. I ease the door open and step through.

I'm back in the black-and-white entrance hall. Jeannie is sitting on a red velvet stool, facing away from me. On the table next to her there's a black telephone base, one of those old-fashioned jobs. Her legs are crossed. Her left foot swings back and forth. She's stroking a tabby cat. What's wrong with this picture? The hairs on the back of my neck leap to attention.

'Yes, they're here. You can come and get them.'

What was I thinking of, coming here, trusting this stranger to help us? I rush forward and swipe the phone out of her hand. The cat flies into the air with a yowl. Jeannie leaps to her feet. Her lips part. I drop the phone and clamp my hand over her mouth. She squeals and thrashes. Something sharp traces a hot trail across my cheek and I'm back in circle time with Freaky Adam, trying to shut him up. I push harder than I mean to, pinning her to the wall, but she's no sixteen-year-old psychopath and she looks fit to faint.

'Stop fighting and I'll let you go,' I hiss.

The thought punches around my head, are they right about me? Is this how a PSK carries on? No wonder I saw fear in Miss Beryl's eyes. She got to be about the same age as this Jeannie – I know she celebrated her sixtieth a couple of years ago with a month off to go on a cruise – so this is the second time this week I've put the frighteners on an old woman. I relax my grip. Jeannie stops struggling.

'Don't scream or do anything stupid,' I tell her.

She nods. Slowly, I remove my hands and she slides down to her knees and leans against the wall, rubbing her neck. Her breathing comes out ragged.

'Who were you talking to?' I ask quietly, my gaze flicking back and forth between her and the front door.

'My gallery.'

'You were setting us up.' Any minute now and that door could come crashing open.

'No.'

'I heard you tell them to come and get us.'

Her eyebrows crease together, then separate. 'No. I said they could come and get *them*. Paintings. For my exhibition.'

Paintings? I grab up the phone and punch 'redial'. 'You better not be screwing with me.'

The phone rings three times. 'Paladino Gallery ... Hello?'

I hit the off button and lift a hand to my face. It comes away red.

'Sorry,' Jeannie says. 'This watch is burred. The sharp bit must have caught you.'

She's apologising to me. What's she playing at now?

'Why did you sneak off like that?' I snap.

'I wasn't *sneaking* anywhere.' She sounds indignant. 'This is *my* house. I thought you two could use a bit of privacy. I was being considerate.'

'I thought you were—'

'What? You thought I was what?' She's breathing easier now. 'David ... Is Lucy in some sort of trouble?'

I crouch down till I'm level with her and look her right in the eye. I see nothing there to fear but I'd be a fool not to be wary. I'd also be a fool not to see that no matter what she thinks of me – and I suspect not a lot – she does care about Mum. Mind you, she don't know her as well as I do, so that might not last.

'Yes,' I say. 'Big trouble.'

'And you?'

I straighten up and hold out a hand to help her to her feet.

'Davey! What are you doing?' Mum is standing in the hallway behind me, a look of sheer horror on her face. I'm suddenly aware of the blood on my hands, the red mark on Jeannie's cheek where I gagged her, the cut on my face. If she sees me like this, how I really am, the King of the World will be lost forever. I open my mouth to protest, but fact is, I don't got any defence.

Jeannie's saying something. Her lips move but her words buzz around my head and fail to land. Then the fog clears.

'… and David helped me find it, see.' She holds up a gold hoop earring. 'It had rolled under the telephone table.'

'But his face—'

'My cat,' Jeannie gestures to the tabby cowering on the windowsill, half-hidden by the curtain. 'Snagged him with her claw, I'm afraid; savage little beast with strangers.'

Mum looks at me and I nod dumbly. Her gaze darts between me and Jeannie, who keeps on smiling and clasps her hands together.

'Right then. Now don't take this the wrong way, Lucy, but you need to freshen up. I've got a wardrobe full of clothes that will more or less fit you. And while you're doing that, David and I can wash up and get some lunch sorted. All right?'

The last question is for me. Nothing for it but to nod again.

When Mum walks off ahead of us, Jeannie hisses in my ear, 'You and I need to talk, young man. I think it's high time you told me what you're doing here. Don't you?'

Fat chance, I think, and before I follow her back into the kitchen, I cross over to the front door, latch it, pop on the chain and slide the top and bottom bolts across. Just in case.

Back in the kitchen, Jeannie dabs disinfectant on my cheek. 'So, are you going to tell me what's going on?'

I gaze up at the ceiling. Rule number one, give them nothing you don't got to, right?

'You said that Lucy is in trouble. Why did you come here? Who did you think I was phoning?' After an age of getting nowhere, she changes tactic. 'I want to help you, if I can.'

'You can't.'

'How do you know if you don't try me? To you I might look like an ancient old crone who doesn't know anything about anything, but my late husband was pretty well connected and I—'

I pull back from her. 'How bad is this cut? Maybe surgery would be quicker?'

She drops the cotton wool pad onto the saucer. 'You'll live.'

I grunt and suppress a grin. Let's face it, I'm way more experienced at this game than she is. But I must be going soft or something after all, cos I almost feel sorry for her. She's not said a word about what I did to her. Plus, she covered for me with Mum. She didn't have to do that.

I point to the bruise forming on her cheek. 'You okay?'

She puts her hand to her face and nods. 'Right then, I'll sort us out some lunch before you get off, shall I?'

I blink at her, stunned.

'Bolognese okay for you? Keep you going for a bit.' She turns her back to me and starts hauling packages out of the fridge, banging pans.

So that's it then. If I don't tell her, she won't let us stay. And if I do tell her, about the unit and my being there, and the fact that at least two very dodgy men are after us? My brain races to find another option but comes up with zilch.

'Okay,' I say to Jeannie's back.

She turns around, hands me a bag of onions and a knife. 'Peel while you talk,' she says, and starts piling tomatoes into a sieve.

By the time I finish talking, the onions have got my eyes watering like crazy. I tell her everything. Well, not everything. I don't tell her they got me down as a PSK cos what's the point? After the way I just attacked her, it'll only freak her out, and why wouldn't she believe them? Fact is, I don't want her thinking that about me. If she don't know, it's somehow like I'm just normal. A bit screwed up and in a whole heap of trouble, but normal.

She asks questions and I answer them, then she asks something else. She's a natural at this questioning stuff. She would've made a half decent counsellor, only better, cos she don't make me feel like the things I say are being stored in some file somewhere to be used against me later. When she gets to asking about things before the unit, I tell her about the fire, rolling up my sleeve to show her the scarred skin, and I'm thinking about Fat Michael's flaky scalp and raw neck as I do it. I even tell her about Kamal. 'Maybe you read about it. It was in all the papers, more cos of his dad being famous than cos of me.'

I think about what those cops told Mum about me trying to kill Kamal. Maybe that got into the papers too. When Jeannie says she don't remember the story and tells me it would've been around the time she was working abroad, I'm glad. Seems her opinion matters to me. Anyway, I've told her everything now. She'll either help us or shop us. Kick us out or let us stay. Right now, I'm too flaked out to care. It's exhausting, all this talking. Once it's clear that I've finished, she looks me right in the eye. The onions must be getting to her too, cos her eyes are wetter than mine.

'Did you try to kill that boy, David?'

'No.'

She nods and carries on stirring the tomato sauce. 'Why do they believe that you did?'

I shrug. 'They think I'm one of those bad seeds, born bad. Teen mum. Some loser for a dad. Not the best gene pool in the world, is it?'

'Sins of the father? What rot. We're judged by our actions, not our genes. Besides, your grandfather was one of the best.'

'Apart from the little detail of being a drunk driver.'

Jeannie's back stiffens. 'Why are you so angry with him?'

I scowl. 'You sound just like one of my counsellors. And, just so you know, that's not a compliment.'

Her shoulders relax. 'Sorry. My late husband was a psychiatrist. I picked up snippets of the lingo.' She turns to face me. 'I learnt enough about the psychiatric profession to know that what's been happening to you isn't right, David. It's definitely not normal. Your mother should have been kept fully informed about your progress and treatment.'

Here come the questions again. 'Did you have regular reviews? ... Who was representing you? ... See, that's wrong; you should have been nominated somebody to represent your interests. ... Was there an official enquiry into the canal incident? ... Did you go to court? ... No trial of any kind? ... But that makes no sense at all.'

She scrapes the massacred onions into the frying pan and opens her mouth to say something else, but just then Mum reappears wearing this fluffy lemon sweater and tight jeans. Her hair gleams, newly washed. She looks shiny. Clean.

'It's the onions,' I say in answer to the look she gives us. 'You look nice.'

'Thanks.' Her smile is sort of shy.

'You look just like your father,' Jeannie says to Mum. 'You look like him too, David. Same hair. Same chin.'

'He's like him in all sorts of ways,' Mum says, making me do a double take. She's never said that before. 'He's always got his head stuck in some book or other, just like Daddy. And he's a brilliant swimmer too.'

'Are you?' asks Jeannie.

When did Mum even notice my swimming? She never once came and watched when I took my badges. She didn't sew them on my trunks for me. In the end, one of the teachers took pity on me and did it in her lunch break. Mum's always made out like I'm nothing like my grandad.

She's always comparing us and finding me well wanting. When I was little, I used to dream about my real dad coming for me. In my dream, we'd know each other at once cos we'd be mirror images, little and large. Cos if I was nothing like Mum's side of the family, then I had to take after my dad, right?

'Arthur was a county freestyle champion, you know.' Jeannie's voice breaks in on my thoughts. 'He almost made the Olympic squad, but then he met your grandmother and settled down.'

Mum slides back onto the bench and leans her elbows on the table. 'How did you and Daddy meet?'

I swear, if Mum was a cat she'd be purring right now, here in Jeannie's kitchen, talking about her Daddy with someone else who loved him.

'Oh,' Jeannie stirs the pan, 'he was actually dating a friend of mine when I first met him, and anyway, I was married back then. But years later, I bumped into him again.' She smiles at us both. 'Hungry?'

Mum sniffs the air. 'Mm, smells good.'

'Bolognese.' I take the pan across to Mum to show her, and I smell something else. Booze. How could she be so freaking stupid? I turn my back on her and stare out of the kitchen window. Water sweeps across the patio, washing leaves into the gutter and carrying them away. I wish someone'd do that to me: whisk me off to a better life, make me clean. Pea-sized drops of rain hit the panes and bounce off the sill. If Mum don't hold it together, we're going to get very wet.

'Dinner's ready,' Jeannie says, her voice suddenly weary. 'Let's eat. Eating helps me think.'

Amazing thing, the appetite. Not one of us here's got enough energy left to talk but that don't stop us packing away a small feast. Even Mum. I scrape the last remnants of juice off my plate with a slab of bread.

'I need a cigarette.' Mum rummages in her mac pocket and prepares to light up but when Jeannie points towards the conservatory, she shoves the fag back into the carton and stalks off.

The second Mum's out of earshot, Jeannie starts in on me, wanting to know what the hell's going on. Sixteen years ago, she'd been lied to – by social services of all people – and six years ago, Lucy had been lied to about me. What kind of place is the unit anyway? Who's behind it?

'What's it matter?' I shrug. 'We just need to get away. Abroad. France or something.'

Jeannie raises her eyebrows. 'A life on the run? How would that work when you don't have a clue who it is you're running from? Or why?'

'I thought you wanted to help, not criticise,' I snap. But she's right, cos when you run, you get chased. I know that already.

'Lucy's not up to it, David. And anyway, you're going to need an ID card, a passport, an NHS number. Disappearing is complicated. You're not being realistic.'

She's right again, isn't she? France? Sodding stupid idea. I don't even speak French.

'Let's not give up just yet, David. Not until we've looked at all the options available to you.'

I snort. 'Don't make me laugh. Options are for people like you, people with nice big houses, not people like me and Mum. People like us don't get to have options.'

'Right then,' – Jeannie's voice is sharp – 'let's start by navigating our way around that oversized chip on your shoulder, shall we, and see what we're left to work with?' She starts shoving plates into the dishwasher.

I stand up, itching to get moving, to *do* something. I pick up a framed photo of Jeannie. She looks about my age, straight white teeth, apple-shiny cheeks. I stare at my reflection in the toaster: pasty skin, dark circles under my eyes, yellow teeth. I put the photo back and scan the room for others, looking for someone with my hair, my chin. I don't find him.

Outside the window, Mum's head is surrounded by a halo of smoke. What's the betting she's got a bottle on the go out there. What does it matter? Jeannie's right. Again. Mum can't run and I can't leave her, can I? Which leaves me where, exactly?

Lying on a bed, choking on smoke, that's where.

CHAPTER ELEVEN

Once we've cleared the dishes in silence, me and Jeannie sit back down at the table. There's still no sign of Mum coming back in. Jeannie reaches over my head and plucks a carved wooden bear off the shelf behind me. I'm not keen on this whole menagerie thing she's got going on here, but even I appreciate that this bear's beautifully carved. Those could be genuine teeth snarling at me.

'Right then.' Jeannie jiggles the bear. 'Imagine for a minute that you're backpacking through the forest, and you come across the live version. What would you do?'

'Scarper?' I yawn.

'What if this beast could out-run you, out-climb you?'

She hands me the bear and I turn it over in my hands, run my thumbs across the deep ridges of fur. 'Then I'm dead meat, aren't I? That what you want to hear?'

'Go with me on this, David. Please.'

I sigh. 'I could always lamp him one, but my guess is, if I do, he'll have me for lunch.'

Jeannie laughs. 'Right then, so the choice is between flight, which you'll lose, or a fight, which you'll also lose.'

'Look, if you got something to say, just say it will you? I done years of all this scenario shit.'

'What's in your backpack, David?'

I blink, stupid.

Jeannie grins. 'I said you were backpacking through the forest, so you must have a backpack, right?'

She did say that, didn't she? How did I miss it? Okay, she's got my attention.

'So, you're saying I maybe got something like a gun in there, or a net. Or food to distract him with, something like that?'

'What I'm saying is, you can't run, and you can't fight, but maybe you have something we don't know about yet. Something we can use.'

'Something in my backpack?'

'Absolutely.'

'And my backpack is ...?'

Jeannie stretches out a hand and taps my forehead. 'In here.'

I sit back on the bench, my shoulders pressed against the wall, and stare at her. She might be old, this Jeannie, but she's whip-smart, and she's on our side. I'm aware there's this tiny pocket of air inside me, whirling around, and that might sound like a bad thing, right? But it's warm, that pocket. Like hope.

I go to return the bear to the shelf, but she pushes my hand down. 'Keep it. A reminder that you've always got options, David. Always.'

Nobody's given me anything in such a long time, even a stupid ornament, that my eyes sting with tears. I pretend to be totally focused on the bear, running my finger along the ridges of wooden fur until I'm out of danger of crying like a baby.

Jeannie picks up a pad and a pen. 'Right then, shall we start to unpack?'

Here we go. Another interrogation. But this time the questions are for my benefit, not theirs, and that feels totally different.

A short while in and I decide that Jeannie's missed out on her vocation as a cop. It don't take long to figure out that the unit is in a quiet rural area somewhere, away from traffic, away from people. It don't take long to figure out that nobody but patients and staff ever go there. It takes her a fair bit longer to get out of me the few bits of personal stuff I've picked up over the years. Like the fact that Matron's got six cats, all named after film stars from the 1980s. Like the fact that Wilson's got a gambling habit, Miss Beryl's got cancer, and Carson's got an ex-wife eating a hole in his wallet. I never even knew I knew that stuff. All of it goes into the notebook.

A distant part of me registers that Mum's still not back.

'Right, then, the question that keeps coming back to me is this: where is the unit located?'

I shrug, exhausted. 'Could be anywhere. We could only see fields and shit. No other buildings or anything.'

'What about the river you crashed into, what was that like?'

'Wet.'

'Very funny. Salty, fresh, wide, still, fast? Come on, David, it could be important.'

I sigh and sit up straighter. Try to remember. 'Salty. Wide. Pretty fast but not always pulling in the same direction. Dirty brown. Muddy banks.'

'A tidal river then, near the coast.' She writes it into the notebook.

That hadn't even occurred to me. God, she's good, and she shows no sign of finishing.

'What about the roads?'

'The windows were blacked out on the van. Then, when I hitched a ride I had to hole up in the back of the truck so the cameras couldn't … no … wait.' I'm back on the roadside chucking up my condemned man's last meal, traffic whipping by, Rickleson whining. 'We got out at one point. I remember lots of traffic, lorries and cars.'

'How many lanes were there?'

'Four. Two each way, with this barrier thing down the middle.'

'You were on a dual carriageway, then. That really helps.' She scribbles that into the notebook. 'What else?'

I close my eyes and conjure up my list. 'I remember bright blue sky, hedges with prickles, scrubby grass, daisies. One of those big white wind turbines with its blades going round and round. The circle time trees. The warmth of sun on my face.'

'Circle time trees?'

I open my eyes. 'Yeah, they looked like they were having a circle time session up there on the hill, only much friendlier than the ones I'm used to.'

Jeannie pats her pen against the pad. 'And they were at the top of a hill, these trees?'

I nod.

Jeannie slaps the notebook down on the table so hard I jump. 'Come with me.'

She takes my arm and half drags me through the black-and-white hallway and into a sitting room with two brown leather sofas, a coffee table and a grandfather clock tall enough to hide in. Bookshelves line the whole of one wall and Jeannie traces her hands over their spines.

The clock ticks, tocks, ticks ...

'Got it.'

She pulls out a massive book with a glossy cover, titled *Why We Brits Love A Landmark*, and lays it on the coffee table, starts flicking through the pages. She stabs the book with her finger. 'Does this look like your circle-time trees, David?'

I sit down on the sofa and stare at the page, pulling the book closer. My mouth's too dry to answer so I nod. That's them all right. It's weird, but somehow, seeing those trees right there on Jeannie's coffee table makes everything that's happened this past week feel more real.

'They're the 'Nearly Home Trees'. I've been driving past them my whole life. Hang on.' She scrabbles along another shelf and tugs out an atlas. 'Here, just on the Cornwall and Devon border. That's where you pulled over.'

I trace my finger along the thin grey line.

'How long had you been travelling before you pulled over? Ten minutes? An hour? More?'

'Half an hour, maybe a bit less.'

She scribbles in the notebook. 'Were the trees on your side of the road or the other?'

'The other,' I say, the little pocket of hope inside me growing warmer.

'Then you were travelling north.' On the map, she draws a red cross to mark the location where I threw up. 'The unit must be in Cornwall somewhere, about here.' She draws a much bigger circle to the west of the red cross, then sits back and grins. 'Perfect.'

The pocket of air inside me is growing hot now, but that don't change the fact that the circle Jeannie has drawn is huge. How are we going to find one building in all that space?

'What's perfect?' Mum's standing in the doorway with this look on her face that answers my unasked question about what's been keeping her all this while.

'We're piecing together a few facts about where David has been.'

'How does that help?' Mum's voice slurs and the thought flashes through my head that I could cheerfully kill her.

Jeannie closes the atlas and places the landmarks book on top of it, watching Mum all the while. 'Lucy, come and sit over here next to David. Can I fetch you a coffee?'

'You can keep your coffee, ta.' Mum laughs and half falls onto the sofa next to me. She picks up a remote control and the TV bursts into life, the vaguely familiar theme tune to a crap soap. I snatch the control off her and turn down the volume. She drapes an arm around my shoulder and makes like to hug me.

Frustration makes me mean and I stick my face right into hers. 'Get your stinking hands off me.'

Mum flinches. 'Why do you have to spoil everything, Davey?'

'David,' Jeannie says in a low warning tone, and she throws me this look like I'm the one that's out of order here.

I shake Mum's hands off, stagger to my feet and scowl at Jeannie, and the words just fall out of my mouth. 'She's an alky.'

To my surprise, Jeannie takes my place on the sofa and puts her arms around Mum. Hugs her tight and says softly, 'Do you want to tell me about it, Lucy?'

Tears roll down Mum's face and she tucks her head into Jeannie's shoulder and full-on sobs. Jeannie strokes her hair like she's some little girl who's scraped her knees on a slide, not a grown woman who's been boozing it up in the bog.

Jeannie strokes Mum's face with her finger and shakes her head at me. 'Did you really think I hadn't guessed? It's okay, Lucy. Everything's going to be okay.'

I stare at her, sitting there comforting my mother, who's lapping up every minute of it. She's known about Mum's drinking all along then, and she still wants to help us? It dawns on me that she never was going to chuck us out, was she? She only said that to get me to talk. And that means she's managed to pull off in about six hours what a whole string of counsellors failed to do in six years: sucker me into talking. Anger and admiration fight for space in my head.

'What's the point of knowing any of this?' I wave a hand at the atlas, at the landmarks book. 'It don't help us.'

'The point is, we now at least have something to take to the police, something to—'

'No way we're going to the cops.'

'But David—'

'They'll never believe me. They'll take me back there.' Sweat breaks out all over my forehead and I struggle to catch my breath. 'No cops. Promise me. If you don't, we're out of here. Promise me.'

'All right, all right, calm down. But we've got to do something. If we can't go to the police, what do you suggest?'

Not for the first time this week, I'm totally stumped. I throw myself onto the other sofa and fold my arms across my chest. What *do* we do now? I close my eyes, try to think. The room is quiet except for the murmuring of the TV and Mum's fading sniffles. My tired brain is mush, but through the sludge I hear a voice saying '... these psychopaths present a danger to us all and something has to be done about it.'

I grab the remote control and bang my finger on the volume button. On the screen, two people sit in armchairs, placed at an angle to each other. The man is tall, slim, very smart. He's smiling at an equally sharp-looking woman. 'These amendments to the Children's Act aren't about service provision,' he's saying, his tone patient. 'They're about protecting the public. People want to feel safe.'

'Our society is sick,' somebody in the studio audience shouts out, and the camera flicks to a ginger-bearded man wearing one of those black T-shirts we saw earlier at the tube station, white letters emblazoned across the chest: 'Save Our Sick Society – Vote Yes'. He's surrounded by about six others kitted out the same. All around them, the audience fidgets and frowns.

The slim man smiles. It's a straight-up kind of smile, a smile I recognise but can't seem to place. 'Exactly. These amendments will allow us to do our duty.'

'Who's that?' I point at the telly and look at Jeannie, who's watching me closely.

'That's James Treherne.' My face must look blank cos she quickly adds, 'The prime minister?'

'Oh.' I stare back at the telly. 'What's he going on about?'

'He's talking about the changes his government propose to make to the Children's Act next week. What is it, David?'

'Shh.'

'We have a question here from Richard Lampton,' the woman says. The camera scans the seated audience and comes to rest on a suit jacket and moustache somewhere near the back of the studio. 'You have a question for the prime minister?'

'Yes. Thank you.' The man with the moustache clears his throat loudly. 'Good evening, Prime Minister.' He lifts a piece of paper in front of his face; as he reads, his hands shake. 'During his own term in office, your father, Lord Treherne, worked to remove the Treatability Clause from the Mental Health Act, which has now made it legal to lock up adults who haven't yet committed a crime—'

'That's a very simplistic—'

'Your proposals will mean that innocent children can be locked up too. Many accuse you of using your position to further your father's goals. My question is, how much truth is there in the accusation that you are your father's puppet, and that, in fact, Lord Treherne is running this government, not you?'

A loud rumble of voices erupts around the studio and the PM's smile disappears. He fiddles with his cufflink as the audience all start shouting out at once and the woman on stage calls for order. Once everybody settles down, she invites the PM to answer the question.

'Of course that's not true. My government has its own manifesto, its own agenda.' The PM sips a glass of water and takes his time returning it to the table beside him. 'I don't deny that my father and I share some common goals, but we share those same goals with many, many others. I'm sure that Mr Lampton is well aware of this.'

The audience mutters and coughs as the camera switches briefly back to the man with the moustache, who shakes his head but says nothing. The interviewer looks disappointed but thanks the PM and points into the crowd. 'Lady in the front here.'

The camera zones in on a woman with greying hair and tired eyes. 'Prime Minister, how do you morally justify labelling children whose personalities haven't even had the chance to develop yet?'

The interviewer leans forward in her chair and smiles. 'Prime Minister?'

The PM stares right into the lens so it seems like he's looking directly at me. I squirm under his steady gaze. Weird, but it feels like he knows me, like he knows who I am and why I can't be trusted.

'I'll let the facts speak for themselves. The vast majority of reoffenders of serious crime have been diagnosed as having DSPD, a preventable condition.' He pauses to let that sink in. 'And here's another fact. The successful treatment of adults has proved limited. The simple truth is, in order to be effective, intervention must take place earlier.'

'I suppose the question people are asking, Prime Minister, is how much earlier?'

'As early as necessary,' he says, and the camera captures the audience's reaction. The group of black T-shirts nod and clap, while everybody else sits stony-faced.

'By controlling the environment in which these children are reared, we can and will eradicate the development of DSPD.'

The interviewer consults her clipboard. 'DSPD: dangerous and severe personality disorder.' She locks eyes with the PM. 'Isn't that just a made-up term, Prime Minister, invented by the government on the back of a movement led, in fact, by your father, Sir Rory, himself? Isn't it true that even today many psychiatrists and psychologists do not recognise DSPD as a medical term?'

'Every term is made up at some point,' the PM says, his face stiff. 'That's how language develops. Science progresses. Society has to progress alongside it.'

A murmur grumbles through the audience.

'You, man in the second row, red shirt.'

The camera pans in on a face as red as the shirt below it. The audience grows quiet as the man begins to speak. 'If these proposals get passed, how long before our national obsession with everything having to be perfect includes producing the perfect race? How long before we become the new Nazis?' The man's voice has risen to a shout. People in the audience clap, all except the group in the black T-shirts, who shake their heads and scowl. 'My question to you, Prime Minister, is who's watching the watchers?' He points at the PM. 'You? Or your father?'

The camera flicks back to the PM, who's got this frozen smile on his face, his hand on his cufflink, his gaze fixed on the woman sat across from him.

'We seem to be out of time for today,' she says, her face smiling even if her eyes aren't. 'Thank you, Prime Minister, and thank you to everyone in the studio who made this such an interesting discussion. I'm sure the debate will continue to rage on, but for now, from all of us here in London, goodnight.'

Music plays and the camera draws back to show the PM and woman chatting on stage, looking for all the world like two friends in a pub. The audience shake their heads, wave their arms. Some stand up. The black T-shirts sit stock-still, faces grim. Then it's over, and some bloke's voice is sounding all excited about a cookery programme that's about to start.

Jeannie reaches up, takes the remote out of my numb hands and flicks off the TV. A cold shudder vibrates through my whole body. I struggle to make sense of what I just heard but it all blurs together in my head. One thing jumps out at me though. There was no mention of the term PSK on there, although this guy seems to be saying that if, say, I'm dangerous, disordered in the head, they can lock me up forever and there's not a thing I can do about it.

'David?'

'Did you know about that?'

Jeannie grimaces. 'That's why people are marching.'

'Who's marching?'

'Two groups mainly. On the one hand you've got those who don't want dangerous people running around free anymore, which I can understand. On the other hand, there are those – and I'm one of them – who believe these changes to our legal system will smash open Pandora's box, creating a future far more terrifying than any bogeyman could ever be.'

Something finally sinks in. I grip my knees and choose my words carefully. 'So, were those people on the telly saying that, right now, it's not legal to lock kids up for something they might do in the future?'

Jeannie studies my face. 'Not yet, no. But that will all change if this … What is it, David?'

I hesitate. No way I'm confessing to Jeannie that I'm a psychopath, and definitely not to being a PSK, but I got to tell her something.

'That's what they were doing with us,' I say slowly. 'They were always talking about what we might be capable of.' I glance across at Mum, but she's curled up in the foetal position, face screwed up tight, eyes closed. 'None of the talk in there was about what crimes anybody had actually committed. As far as I know, most of those freaks never did anything much other than be freakish. It's all about the future, not the past. Like that James Treherne said, it's about predictability.'

'But the law as it stands doesn't allow ...' Jeannie's voice fades away and her face grows pale. 'Good god, David, if the government is behind what's happened to you, they'll have access to all our records. I tried to foster Lucy. There'll be a trail that could lead them right here.' Her head snaps up. 'We've got to get you both away from here, and fast.'

But before we can do anything, a deafening *bang, bang, bang* echoes off the tiles in the black-and-white hallway and reverberates in my guts.

CHAPTER TWELVE

Jeannie looks shaken for a moment, then she clicks her fingers. 'I forgot about my book group.' She glances at the grandfather clock. 'No, it can't be them. Too early.'

The knocker bangs again and I'm thinking I might've just wet myself when Jeannie springs into action. She shakes Mum to her feet, takes her by the sleeve and shoves us both into the hallway. She fumbles with a key and opens what looks like a cupboard door, but inside there's a small platform and steps that lead down.

The front door shakes as the brass bear bangs and bangs.

'A young friend of mine used to sub-let this cellar,' Jeannie whispers as she pushes the key into the other side of the lock. 'You can secure it from the inside.'

'Is there a back way out?' I hiss.

Jeannie shakes her head. 'Leave it to me. I'll get rid of them. Don't make a sound.'

'No,' Mum pleads when she realises what's happening, but Jeannie yanks the door shut, plunging us into darkness.

I grope for the key and turn it in the lock. It makes this squeak that I'd swear could be heard halfway across London.

'Shh,' Jeannie says. 'Take the key out of the lock. Good. Right then.'

Bang, bang, bang.

I put my arm around Mum, trying to ignore the fact that her whole body is shaking. I can't see where the platform ends and the stairs begin, and the last thing we need is Mum taking a drunken plunge. I lower us both to our knees on the narrow platform. The inhale-exhale of our combined lungs in the black silence of the cellar sounds deafening.

'You got to stay quiet, Mum,' I whisper into the darkness. 'Not a sound, yeah?' I squeeze her hand, but keep my other arm around her shoulder, ready to shut her up if I got to. I press my eye to the keyhole and make out the shape of Jeannie's back as she heads for the front door.

'Okay, okay, I'm coming,' she calls out.

I hear the bolts being drawn back, the chain being slipped off. A handle rattles, a lock clicks.

'Mrs Wicks?'

'Yes.'

'Mrs Jeannie Wicks?'

'That's right.'

A throat clears. There's a pause, then Jeannie's voice again. 'Sorry, I'm not wearing my reading glasses. Could I take a closer look at your card?' Another pause. 'Right then, how can I help you, Chief Inspector? Nothing wrong, I hope? I do try to behave myself as a rule.'

Laughter is followed by snatches of muffled conversation that I can't quite catch. Beneath my arm, Mum's shoulders grow stiff.

Jeannie steps backwards, saying, 'Right then, of course, come in, Officer,' and the air rattles as Carson steps into the hallway, quickly followed by Drummond. 'We can talk in the living room.'

'Very good of you, Mrs Wicks,' Drummond says.

Next to him, Carson smiles his non-smile. 'Nice place you have here.'

A whimper escapes Mum. In a blink, I got my hand over her mouth and I'm breathing into her ear, letting her know it's okay, it's all right, it's just that she got to shut up now, she got to shut up. I feel her go limp so I release my grip on her mouth and put my arm back around her shoulder and whisper, 'Shh, shh,' taking my lead from Jeannie and making it as comforting as I can, like I'm the parent and she's my child and she's just scraped her knees playing on the swings, that's all.

I press my eye to the keyhole again. Jeannie's directing the two men into the sitting room we just vacated and pulling the door shut behind her. The front door is so close, but so is the living room door, and we'd have to walk right past it. There's no chance of Mum managing to pull that off. As I think of Mum, I become aware that my arm is no longer around her shoulders. I grope around in the dark and find her laying near my feet, her knees pulled into her chest, muttering under her breath.

'Shh,' I whisper, and I press my eye back to the keyhole to check the living room door is still closed. 'Mum? You got to be quiet.' I lean down, my face close to hers, and she squeals. Jesus, what does she think I'm going to do? 'Shh, for God's sake, they'll hear you.'

I drop to my knees to shake some sense into her, but she's trembling all over, and I do mean all over: torso, arms, legs, feet. I press my ear to the door and listen; the muffled voices sound conversational enough, and when I hear Jeannie laugh, I turn my attention back to Mum, who's still murmuring, just noises, not real words. She's going to get us all killed. I got to make her quiet. I put my lips to her ear and whisper, 'Mum, if you don't shut up, right now, I'm going to let those men come and get you, you hear? So shut up, yeah? Shut up or they're coming for you.'

It works. She stops whimpering and grows still and silent, and I feel like the biggest shit that ever lived. I check she's breathing. She is, only dead quiet. I hear a noise and press my eye back to the keyhole. The living room door stands open and Drummond's bulk fills the doorway. 'Thanks, Mrs Wicks, but I'm sure I'll find it. Don't trouble yourself. My sergeant here has a few more questions for you.' He steps into the hallway, closes the door with a sharp click, and cocks his head like a dog, listening.

I hold my breath and press my hands softly over Mum's mouth again, but she don't make a sound, don't move a muscle.

Drummond pulls on a pair of black leather gloves then takes out a tissue and rubs the doorknob he's just handled, which is when I'm rock sure that we're in deep trouble. Whatever he's up to, he don't want to leave any traces behind, which tells me he's no cop.

His dark gaze scans the hallway and comes to a stop on the cellar door. I jerk backwards and crouch low, covering Mum's whole body. For once in her life she co-operates and lies good and still.

Footsteps approach the door. I can hear Drummond breathing on the other side. Above my head the doorknob turns and the door shudders in its frame, pushing against the lock. I imagine his black eye staring through the keyhole, his ears pressed against the wood, and I can't shake the feeling that he knows we're here. Maybe he can smell us; maybe he can smell our fear. The door shudders in its frame again and I press my face into Mum's shoulder and bite back the scream bubbling up in my throat. This is it. It's all over for us.

The footsteps move away and the echo of tiles changes to the softer thud of the wooden floorboards in the conservatory.

I swallow, breathe, take hold of Mum's hand and squeeze. She don't squeeze back. I put my eye to the keyhole again and scan the empty hallway while my breathing re-regulates itself. A few minutes later, Drummond walks back into the hallway and pushes open the living room door.

'Mrs Wicks, could you come out here, please?' The edge in his voice is unmistakeable and when Jeannie steps slowly into the hallway with a stiff smile on her face I know she can hear it too.

'Did you find the bathroom, all right?' she says, brightly enough.

'You said you'd spent the day alone, but there are three plates in the dishwasher, three glasses, three sets of cutlery.'

'Oh, that, yes … My sister and her husband popped around for an early lunch. They didn't stay long. Left ages ago. I forgot.'

'Ages ago, you say. What time?'

'Sorry?'

'The pans are still warm, Mrs Wicks.' Drummond smiles a thin smile and I recognise the pleasure he's taking in playing with her cos I seen that same look on Freaky Adam's face a zillion times. 'And I believe, Mrs Wicks, that you were an only child. There's no sister.'

Jeannie grows pale and takes a step backwards, but Carson has come up behind her, blocking her way. It don't take an X-ray machine to see the panic rising inside her. If she loses it now, we're all done for.

'I meant my late husband's sister.' She laughs but it don't sound convincing. 'We're awfully close. More sister than sister-in-law. You know how it is.'

Behind Jeannie's back, Carson slips his own set of gloves out of his jacket pocket and works his hands into them. I want to call out, to warn her, but I can't, cos all I'm thinking is we're trapped in here in the dark, sitting ducks. I should've run, I should've—

Bang, bang, bang.

My eye swivels to take in the front door, which swings open wide. In troop one, two, four … seven women on a noisy wave of laughter, clutching wine bottles, books and soggy umbrellas. And with them is Jack Daniels. The great big hairy mutt strides into the hallway like a bouncer. Drummond takes a step backwards. I never thought I'd say it, but I could kiss that dog. I could give him a smacking great big Frenchy.

The laughter fizzles out as the women notice Drummond and Carson standing there with Jeannie.

'Darling, we didn't know you had company.'

'Male company, what's more. Rather selfish of you, Jeannie.'

'Don't mind us, gentlemen. We'll make ourselves at home while you finish whatever it is you're doing. Unless you'd like to join us? We're always keen to find new members.'

The speaker, a fat woman around Jeannie's age wearing purple jeans and a multi-coloured cape, winks at Jeannie, who musters a smile and mumbles, 'Sorry, ladies, I ...'

'Oh, don't worry about us. We can entertain ourselves, can't we girls? I'll put the kettle on, shall I?'

Drummond looks like he's about to say something when Jack Daniels walks right over to him, stares up into his eyes and lets out a low growl. Drummond's mouth closes, but Jeannie finds her voice.

'These gentlemen were just leaving.' She turns to Drummond and Carson. 'Unless there's anything else I can help you with, officers?'

'Officers? Not been a naughty girl, have you, Jeannie?'

A couple of the women laugh.

Drummond's face is thunderous and I'm betting he'd just love to front it out and massacre the lot of them, right there and then. Carson is grinning, or at least appears to be grinning – who can tell? Drummond scowls at him. Jeannie holds the door wide, inviting them to leave.

Drummond turns his glare on her. 'We know where to find you, Mrs Wicks,' he says once he's managed to edge his way around Jack Daniels, whose eyes track his every move.

'We'll see you again soon, Mrs Wicks,' Carson adds. 'Be sure to take good care of yourself.'

And they're gone.

Jeannie closes the door behind them and releases the catch. She must've flicked it up when she let Carson and Drummond in. Whip-smart. Fecking whip-smart.

The second she's got the door bolted in three separate places, Jeannie leans with her back against it, palms on chest, eyes closed. Her friends are standing there in the hallway, hands on hips, awaiting an explanation, but when Jeannie finally opens her eyes again, she ignores them and rushes over to the cupboard, to us.

'David, open up.'

I retrieve the key and open the door, blinking at Jeannie in the hallway light. Her book group are fanned out behind her, mouths open wide like spectators at a freak show.

'Goodness, David, you're as white as a sheet. Are you all right? Oh God, Lucy?'

Jeannie leans down and turns Mum over so she's facing the ceiling and then I see what she's seeing: white skin, a thick layer of sweat and wide unseeing eyes.

'What the matter with her?' I put my arms under Mum's shoulders and haul her into the hallway.

The fat woman in the purple jeans elbows her way past the others and kneels on the floor next to Mum.

'Florrie's a doctor,' Jeannie says.

Florrie lifts Mum's wrist and feels for her pulse, then places a finger on one side of her neck. Mum don't react, she don't do anything.

'She's just drunk,' I say, but I know that's not it. I seen Mum drunk a zillion times and she's never looked like this.

'She's in shock – catatonic state.' Florrie looks at Jeannie and grimaces. 'We need to get her medical help, and fast.'

And the thing that's freaking me out even more than the blank look in Mum's eyes is the thought that I did this to her, that I'm the one who whispered in her ear that I'd let them come and get her, I'm the one who frightened her so badly she totally lost it. I did that to my own mum. What the hell is wrong with me?

And how the hell are we going to get away from here now, with Drummond and Carson watching the house, just waiting for their chance to come back and grab us?

CHAPTER THIRTEEN

I'm squeezed into this dark space between an out-of-order ticket machine and a drinks dispenser in a relatively unlit corner of Victoria Coach Station. I'm obsessively checking the watch on my wrist – Jeannie's watch, the one she was wearing when she cut my face. Ten minutes to departure. Don't go thinking the watch is stolen, cos I wouldn't do that, not to her. She'd pushed it at me saying, 'Have it, it's yours by rights anyway.' I don't want her thinking I'm a scavenger, but truth is, it's handy to be able to tell the time out here. It's not like it is in the unit, where every minute of the day you're being told what to do and when to do it. Before I got a chance to ask what she meant by 'yours anyway', she was holding out her arms and all her friends were shoving their cash into her palms. Then she was shoving that same cash into my hands. I pat my back pocket. I never been so loaded.

Eight minutes to departure.

The stink of stale pee seeps out of the wall behind me. For the zillionth time my gaze is drawn to the poster on the nearest pillar. 'Our Kids Are Not Monsters. Make your voice heard. Come and march this Tuesday. Their Freedom is Your Freedom'. Somebody's drawn a thick black swastika across it, which gives me this weird feeling in the pit of my stomach. I look away, scan the station.

In bay nine, which is the only one I'm interested in, five people stand in line. At the head of the queue, an elderly couple sit on canvas stools sharing a flask of tea like they're out on a fishing trip or something. The old me would've dismissed them as a potential threat cos of their age, but given the performance I just witnessed from Jennie's book group, I'm not discounting the possibility that they're secret agents with lethal martial arts training and a licence to kill. While I was having a meltdown, and panicking that we were trapped in that house, Jeannie's friends had brewed tea and come up with an escape plan for Mum that involved an ambulance crew, a switch over at the hospital where Florrie works, and a bunch of pensioners ready to scream mugger at the first sight of Drummond or Carson.

Behind the elderly couple, a young mother smokes a fag while tapping a finger at her mobile phone, and I wonder if I did the right thing by refusing to let Florrie sort me out a phone of my own. That way I could've found out what was happening with Mum. The woman in the queue snaps at her over-active toddler while he bounces around the place like a pinball, guzzling a bottle of cola, and I got to remind myself that I didn't refuse the phone cos I don't care about Mum. I just didn't want them having any way of tracking me through technology. Next to the woman, a boy about my age bobs his head to music only he can hear. Now *that* I could've gone for.

A uniformed man, bald and stocky, strides around the darkened coach and presses a switch. A door hisses opens, swallows him and then closes again.

Six minutes to departure.

A sixth person arrives, an elderly woman in a cream leather jacket, towing a suitcase behind her like some mutt on a leash. Which isn't to say I'm not a whole lot fonder of dogs than I was only twenty-four hours ago. Jack Daniels' secret passage through the back of Jeannie's garden and eventually into his own yard became my escape route, and cos Florrie's front door opened onto a totally different street to Jeannie's, it was only a matter of minutes before London swallowed me up. Good old Jack Daniels.

I had to leave Mum behind cos she was still flaked out and no way was she up to fence hopping it out of there. 'Don't worry about your mum,' Florrie had reassured me. 'I'm well used to helping women disappear, even when their partners are policemen or politicians, which is more often than you'd think.' The simple truth is, I can't look after Mum *and* do what I got to do. Jeannie's right. There's nowhere far enough to run if the government is after us. Flight is not an option. Shit, I didn't even dare use any of my cash to check into a hostel last night, just slept in the back of a jeep under a tarpaulin.

Four minutes to departure.

I need to keep my eye on the goal, and I got a goal now, of sorts. The unit is illegal, and I got to find it, prove its existence, then blow the whole thing up. Ideally, I need to do that before the vote next Tuesday, when places just like it will become legal. The problem with that plan is, making the unit public means telling the whole world that I'm a PSK, and spending the rest of my life with people getting that look in their eyes whenever I get too close. I'm not okay with that.

So, Plan B, my plan, is a bit different, and I've kept this bit to myself. I got to know who I am. I got to find out if my original notes are still in the files at the unit, and then figure out where the lies are so I can prove my innocence – if I am, in fact, innocent. I don't feel like a killer. I feel numb. The thought of spending my whole life never knowing either way isn't something I can live with.

So here I am. There's no Plan C.

Three minutes to departure.

The bus quivers to life then the driver reappears and opens the luggage hold. The ancient couple help each other to their feet and expertly fold their stools. The fag-smoking mother scoops up her brat and grips her luggage. Oblivious to the movement around him, iPod Boy taps out a rhythm on his knees. Leather Jacket hauls her suitcase behind her as the queue shambles forward.

Two minutes to departure.

I edge out of my corner, hoodie pulled tight, and stroll across the station and climb aboard, ticket in hand. The driver barely glances at me. I head for the back row where the rear window doubles as the emergency exit.

One minute to departure. My thumb rubs against the edge of the watch where the metal's come away and created a jagged edge. The doors swish shut, there's a series of ear-piercing bleeps as we reverse out of bay nine and I let out a slow breath.

We've gone no more than maybe two or three metres when the bus jerks to a halt, the doors hiss open again, and a new passenger climbs aboard: a woman, youngish, late twenties maybe. Black corkscrew hair bounces off her shoulders as she works her way down the aisle, handbag propped in front of her like a battering ram.

She takes her time, checking out each seat, then stops four rows short of where I'm wedged as far into the corner of the back seat as it's possible to be. She settles into the aisle seat and my antenna kicks back into life. Who in their right mind chooses the aisle seat when a window seat's going begging? You can lean on a window, look out of it, rest your head against it.

But from the aisle seat you can keep a better eye on the other passengers.

The coach finishes its backward crawl and chugs forward, fighting its way through the early morning traffic along the Chelsea Embankment. Outside my window, the Thames churns by, dirty grey in the morning light, and before long we're following signs for the M4 up a concrete ramp and picking up speed.

As we head away from London the view gradually changes from high-rise blocks and concrete cubes to red-brick estates, then to jigsaws of fields and the occasional farmhouse. I can feel Mum getting further and further away as I watch it all whizz by, and still the woman in the aisle seat makes no move towards me. Maybe she's just a normal passenger and I'm just being paranoid. I don't allow my gaze to wander for more than a few seconds at a time from the tartan chairback a few rows ahead of me as the minutes clock up.

At one point we edge past a battered Volkswagen. A girl who can't be more than five years old squashes her nose against her window and sticks out a pink tongue. As we accelerate past, she holds up a small teddy bear and smiles at me. I put my hand in my pocket and feel the shape of Jeannie's wooden bear tucked in there. In the back of a sleek silver Jag, a yellow dog pants against the glass, a woman's arm draped casually around its neck. We push ahead and I see the driver, some smart bloke in dark sunglasses and a bow tie. The worlds these people inhabit are so far removed from mine that I could be watching another life form through a microscope.

Countryside opens out into flat brown plains. We rumble on. Then, just as I'm starting to relax, over the noise of the engine I hear a low buzzing. Three rows ahead of me, the woman leans forward in her seat and mumbles into her mobile, then she's on her feet, hands gripping the empty luggage racks as she sways along the aisle towards me. I pull my hood forward and tuck my chin into my neck until I can just make out her legs. She comes right up close and pauses, and I'm waiting for her to speak, my brain racing to work out what she's likely to say, what I can say back, but then she turns and takes the three steps down to the toilet cubicle. The toilet door clicks shut.

I crane my neck towards the steps and listen. She's talking to someone on the telephone. She got a closer look at me and now she's reporting back. It's only a matter of time before the driver will be forced to pull over, before they come for me, syringes loaded.

I got to get off this bus, but we're hurtling along the middle lane at suicidal speed and being right next to the emergency exit don't help me one bit. I search the bus for something, anything, that might help. Hanging from the back luggage rack there's one of those dustpan and brush sets that the cleaners at the unit use so they don't got to bend over to sweep up. I snatch the brush from its hook and, with shaking hands, slide one end into the toilet door handle and wedge the other into the corner of the top step. It won't hold for long but maybe long enough.

I work my way along the aisle towards the driver, trying to pass the other passengers without sparking anything off. They take no notice of me. The old lady is reading, Headphones Boy is snoring, the couple are doing a crossword, and the little brat giggles and jumps up and down on his mum's lap. I reach the front, grip the ticket shelf. But before I get out a word, the driver, without taking his eyes off the road, taps his fingers against a sign stuck to the plastic partition between us: 'DO NOT SPEAK TO THE DRIVER WHILE BUS IS IN MOTION'.

I tap back at him. 'Pull over. I got to get off.'

The driver keeps his gaze fixed ahead and shakes his head. 'We'll be making a pick-up in forty minutes, son. You can get off then. There's a loo at the back and sick bags in your seat pocket.' He gestures back up the aisle, eyes still on the road.

In front of us, six lanes of traffic hurtle in both directions. We're overtaking a lorry and I don't speak to the driver again right then. I don't want him to lose control of the bus, not like Rickleson did. I'm gripping onto a pole with one hand and the other hand's started shaking, so I shove it into my hoodie pocket and clutch onto the bear. Over the roar of the engine, I hear a clattering start up at the back of the bus. I grip the bear in my pocket and push it through the cloth, pointing it towards the driver.

As soon as we swerve back into the inside lane, I shout, 'Pull the fuck over. I'm not messing.'

That gets his attention.

'Now look, son, get back to your seat or ...' He glances at the barrel shape sticking out from my hoodie pocket. 'Okay, son. Okay. Stay calm. We're on a motorway here. I can't just—'

The clattering's turned into a banging and the young mum leans her head into the aisle, looks at me and quickly withdraws it.

'Stop fucking around and pull over,' I snarl.

The driver flicks on an indicator and squeezes the brakes. In moments, the bus screeches to a halt on the hard shoulder. The doors hiss open. I leap clear.

There's a high bank running alongside the road, and I leap for it, hands and feet scrabbling over loose mud and rocks, slipping down, fumbling up again. Behind me, the doors hiss shut. I reach the top, and over the other side there's a ditch, then a barbed wire fence and then open fields, and in those open fields there's a big brown bull, big enough to flatten a small tower block. Shit, shit, shit, shit, shit.

Behind me, the woman with the dark curls is hammering on the bus doors and shouting at the driver. Beyond them, six lanes of traffic roar by. Across the other side of the motorway, I see a small embankment then a dark forest stretching into the distance. Shit, shit, shit.

Directly ahead of where I'm standing, a black saloon skids to a halt on the hard shoulder and shoots into reverse, wheels spraying gravel.

I skid back down to the tarmac and my feet hit the floor at the same time as the saloon's doors fly open.

I fly too. I fly onto the motorway, and before I know what I'm doing, before I got chance to talk myself out of it, I've already crossed the first two lanes of thundering traffic and jerked to a halt as a campervan hurtles along the fast lane, missing me by centimetres. The force of the backdraught almost knocks me into the path of a Mini barrelling along the middle lane. I dash across the third lane, leap the central barrier and hesitate only for a second before throwing myself into the path of the oncoming rush. Horns blare, the air fills with the hot scent of rubber and somehow I arrive panting but unharmed on the other side.

Six lanes away, Carson and Drummond are playing losers' chicken, guns in hand. I don't got time to gloat, more's the pity. I scale the bank and drop down a nettle-ridden slope and don't look back again until I reach the edge of the forest.

Drummond and Carson are running back towards the black saloon. The black-haired woman is halfway up the embankment holding a pair of binoculars to her face. I close

my fist and salute her with my middle finger. Then I vanish
into the trees, adrenaline pumping.

King of the World.

CHAPTER FOURTEEN

'You'll be David, then.'

The man who says this is at least six foot two, tanned, crinkled skin around deep blue eyes, scruffy blondish hair. About thirty, maybe.

'You Arran?'

I take a good long look but can't decide if it's a nice face or not. Arran takes a good long look right back at me, cocky as you like. I'm desperate to ask him if he's heard from Jeannie, if they're okay, but before I get the chance, he grunts, 'You'd better come, then,' and takes off on his long legs leaving me to either follow him or get lost.

It don't take me long to build up a sweat trying to match Arran's pace as he quick marches me through these country lanes. Twisted hedgerows, dotted with pockets of fiery yellow, line both sides of the road, too high for me to get a handle on where we are. Overhead, birds circle in a clear blue sky.

Despite all the crap I got to deal with, there's this sharp twinge of excitement in my stomach. I know that Cornwall is surrounded by the sea, and my nose is picking up the sharp tang of salt in what little breeze manages to fight its way through the gaps in the hedgerows. I've seen it on the telly, I've read about it in books, but I've never actually been to the seaside in real life. Mum promised me once that she'd take me to the beach, Brighton, but she never did. The thought of Mum makes me ashamed of my excitement. Is she safe? I glare at Arran's back as he marches on ahead.

Around twenty minutes later we veer off the road, clamber over a stone stile and follow a trail of pressed mud up a grassy hillside. No hedges, just green grass and sky. I take a deep breath of air: cold, fresh, and again that hint of salt. When we reach the summit, the ground falls away from our feet, and though Arran don't break stride, I slow to a halt while I take it all in. Towering black cliffs wrap themselves around a curved stretch of golden sand, just like in the movies. The sea dances and glitters and spills white froth onto a beach. The sheer beauty of it makes me gasp.

Arran stops and points. 'Best surf for miles around.' Then he's off again, following a thin, uneven track along the cliff edge, and I'm struggling to keep up with him while trying not to take a tumble, cos right next to where our feet are pounding away, a head-spinning drop ends with sea and sharp rocks.

Arran heads for an isolated block of four concrete flats that juts out from a cliff. A gravelled path winds around the side to an area that contains washing lines and small sheds. Outside steps lead up to the first floor but Arran stops in front of the nearest ground floor flat, lifts the edge of a stone hedgehog, and pulls out a key. I check out the other three flats for signs of life.

'You won't have no truck with them,' Arran says, throwing me a look. 'Second-homers. Londoners. Prefer not to wet their toes till late May. Suits me. Get this place to myself mostly.'

The tiny porch leads straight into a living room where a pair of black curtains, still drawn, covers the whole back wall. What little light seeps through reveals grey slate tiles underfoot, a well-worn sofa and an equally old armchair. A small flat-screen TV sits on a beer crate. A wooden chest holds two empty mugs. The only hints that this might be someone's personal space are a brightly coloured rug by the window and a spindly table that's set out with a chessboard and two chairs. My heart lifts a fraction at the sight of the chessboard. Okay, so it might not be much to work with, but at least it says that me and the frosty Arran got something in common. Which matters, cos he might well turn out to be a jerk but I need him onside.

Arran stomps along a short corridor with four doors leading off it. He opens the last one on the left and it creaks like it's as reluctant as Arran to welcome me in.

'You'll stay in here.'

A metal bunk bed and a plastic clothes rail take up most of the floor space. Two surfboards stand crammed in the gap between headboard and window. My room back at the unit was a palace compared to this hole. I open my mouth to ask if he's heard what's happening with Mum, but Arran raps his knuckles on the door opposite, 'My room. Keep out,' then marches back into the living room and picks up his keys. 'I got to get to work now, in the pub. Be back in a few hours.'

'You're going to work now?'

He narrows his eyes at me. 'You don't need babysitting, do you? Look, I weren't planning on having visitors down, specially not kids who smell like trouble.' He looks me up and down and I bite back the urge to lamp him one. 'Jeannie asked me to sort you out, so I will. But that's all.'

I forget all about lamping him. 'You spoke to Jeannie?'

'To Florrie.'

'Did she say anything? About how they are, where they are?'

'She said to say they're fine.' Arran narrows his eyes again. 'If you're dragging her into something ...' He stabs his finger at my chest and I'm thinking he can read the guilt on my face, cos that's exactly what I'm doing, isn't it?

But they got away, they're safe, that's what matters.

Arran closes his fist, and his arm drops to his side. 'You can watch TV, got a whole heap of DVDs. There's not much food in but I'll bring something back. Florrie says I'm to keep you under the radar, so stay put till we work out what we're gonna tell folk. Got it?'

I sink into the armchair. 'I'm not your sodding prisoner.'

'Maybe not, but this here's a small place. You go poking about and I'll be learning the colour of your underwear from Josie down the Post Office afore I get back. Get my drift?'

He's right, and I'd be a fool not to know it. Round one to Arran.

154

I glance around. 'Got any books I can read?'

'Books?' He sounds surprised, probably cos he thinks I'm some kind of Neanderthal. He points to a small collection of paperbacks on a shelf in the corner: whodunits, puzzles, surf guides. I can see who the Neanderthal around here is. Round two to me, I think.

'I'll be back around eight.'

The front door bangs shut and a key turns in the lock.

First thing I do is check out Arran's bedroom. Next to a large double bed, a red light blinks out of a music system. Clothes hang over a chair back, a blue T-shirt, black jeans, and ... a short rust-coloured skirt. So, Arran's got a girlfriend then. That could complicate things. I notice the seascape hanging over the bed. Something about the style tugs at my memory and I'm back in Jeannie's kitchen, admiring the canvas of the bears. I lift the frame off its hook and hold it in front of me, and immediately I'm drawn into this sweeping stretch of coastline and an ocean so wild I swear it smells salty. There's a signature in the bottom corner that frankly could say anything, but there's no doubt that this is the same artist as the bears one. I put it back. Straight.

Behind the third door off the corridor, I find a bathroom, and behind the fourth I find an artist's studio. Canvases are piled everywhere, hanging on walls, propped on an easel, stacked against table legs. I pick up a sketchbook, one of a dozen or so that sit on a shelf that runs the length of the room. I turn through page after page of coastal and fishing boat scenes outlined in pencil, including one double-page spread with detailed sketches of three bears messing about at a river's edge. I scrutinise the pencilled outlines, trying to come up with a plausible explanation that don't mean that Arran, Neanderthal Arran, created these incredible paintings. It's like finding out that Freaky Adam is a poet. But all the pre-work is here, and the first pages of these notebooks all got Arran's name printed on them.

In the drawer of a wooden desk, I find a laptop. It's ready to go, no password needed. Idiot. Perched on a stool, elbows on the desk, I log on. The default page shows a picture of a crowd, waving banners. The headline shouts 'LONDON SET TO GRIND TO A HALT NEXT WEEK AS THOUSANDS OF PROTESTERS ARE EXPECTED TO MARCH'. I click to enlarge the picture. The nearest placard reads 'Hands Off Our Kids.' The one behind it says, 'Jailing Babies – is this The Future?' Two women hold either end of a white sheet showing a pregnant woman with a red cross slashed across her stomach, and the words 'Not Fit to be Born?' Each letter drips blood into the sheet. The faces in the crowd are mostly scowling. A few of them look like they might be crying.

The article repeats much of what I heard on the TV at Jeannie's. The government wants to start scanning babies and locking up kids, and it seems a whole bunch of people don't like that idea. I thought the government had to do what people wanted. Isn't that what they're there for?

The first words I type into the search bar are 'James Treherne'. Within minutes I learn he went to Oxford and that his father, Rory Treherne, is some sort of lord now but was prime minister himself back in the day. His grandfather was First Lord of the Admiralty. His grandmother was a distant cousin of the queen. In other words, they're a right bunch of toffs. There's a picture of James Treherne as a young boy, maybe five or six, standing between his mum and dad on some yacht. He's waving at the camera. The caption says, 'Rory's Little Protégé.' I grunt. Protégé. Puppet. Much the same thing.

There are loads of articles about the PM's career, how he was groomed for office from the get-go, how he progressed fast through the ranks to become Britain's youngest ever prime minister. There's this photo of him and an older man, him staring blankly into the camera while the older man stares at the back of his head. I don't need the text to tell me the older man is his dad, Rory Treherne, cos you can see it.

I'm just thinking what a spoilt, over-privileged pair they make, when I come across the headline 'KILLER STRIKES AGAIN'. Underneath, it says 'Rachael Treherne, wife of MP Rory Treherne, murdered in her home'. There's a whole heap of articles spilling gross details about how Rachael Treherne was brutally murdered by 'the Equaliser' back in 1998, making her his fifth victim in what ended as a list of nine violent killings before he was caught a year later. Headlines scream about how all the services knew the killer was dysfunctional, but nobody did anything to stop him. I pause to let that sink in, then look again at the picture of James Treherne with his mum, trying to imagine what that must've been like for him, to lose his mother like that. And for his father too, losing his wife like that. Grim or what?

I shudder, then change tack by typing in the words 'dangerous and severe personality disorder'. For the next half an hour the screen spits information at me: DSPD,

ASPD, CD. It takes a while to sort it all out in my head, but what it boils down to is this: if a young kid goes off the rails, they say he's got conduct disorder, (CD). After they're eighteen, a high percentage of kids with CD develop anti-social personality disorder (ASPD). Some of those with ASPD turn out to have dangerous and severe personality disorder (DSPD). Loads of those with DSPD are psychopaths. It's like a giant filter system that squeezes out the really sick ones at the top.

Nowhere do I find any information – nothing at all – on PSKs.

Looking at the other stuff I've found, I'm guessing some of those psychopaths turn out to be potential serial killers. Which puts me at the very top of an extensive list of fuck-ups. I'm about to type in 'psychopath' when the low battery warning flashes up. I shut the laptop down and slide it back into the drawer.

Back in the living room, I yank open the curtains, fling open the patio doors and step out onto a small patio. Chilly evening air, fresh and tangy, blasts my face, and despite all the shit stuff banging around in my head, the view blows me away. A green lawn stretches for about thirty metres to the cliff edge, where it stops dead. From the tiny terrace, I can see the footpath that runs down to the beach, and in the distance beyond that I spot a church tower, several roof-tops, smoking chimneys. But here, there's nothing except me and the air and the grass and the sea. No wonder Arran don't care what his flat looks like on the inside. This is why he lives here.

I stand there until goosebumps finally break out along my arms and drive me back inside, where I slide the doors shut and stretch out on the rug, suddenly exhausted. Filtered through the glass, the warm rays of the setting sun nuzzle my skin, while rolls of clouds unfurl towards me like an invasion of soft white moths and send me tumbling into a deep sleep.

When I wake up, I'm still lying on the rug in front of the patio doors but the view from earlier has been replaced by distant patches of navy on a background of black. I feel as though there's somebody sitting on my chest, making it tight, though even in the pitch darkness I know there's no one there. What was I dreaming about? The memory slides in and out of my grasp: a bear, his big, fat, open gob teeming with spit and yellow teeth, sharp as you like. As my hand gropes for the button that lights my watch, the frayed bit snags my finger. 'Ouch!'

Ten o'clock.

I sit up straight, and the first thought that bugs me is where the hell's my so-called host got to? The second thought is where's my bloody food? Seems like life on the run goes hand in hand with starvation. If someone held a gun to my head and told me I had to find one good thing to say about the unit, it'd be this: you could set your watch by the mealtimes in there. Truth is, they knew better than to let us lot go hungry.

I wander into the kitchen, clock the wooden block of knives on the countertop, the door to the backyard, the key lying on the table. It's light and airy in here, white wood, breakfast bar with two stools, clean cups draining on the sideboard, fridge empty. A glass of water's the best I can do.

It's another half hour before a key jiggles in the lock and Arran comes in on a waft of vindaloo. I'm sat in the armchair pretending to read one of his books, something about this surfer dude who's surfed every beach on every continent and now thinks he's some kind of guru.

'Had to stay for a quick drink with a mate.' Arran kicks the door shut behind him.

Hmm, where've I heard that before?

He disappears into the kitchen. When he reappears and shoves a plate of food at me, I actually whimper with hunger. A fork sticks out of a pile of what could be pork, could be horse, could be dog. I don't care. I'm starving. He fetches another plate for himself, flicks on the TV and flops down on the sofa. I'm pretty sure he still hasn't given me eye contact since he first checked me over back at the bus stop. His rolled-up sleeves reveal wiry arms and a bunch of tattoos and I'm struggling to piece together this Arran with the man who painted those pictures. The burbling telly goes some way to filling the silence and making the atmosphere a fraction less hostile, but only a fraction.

I shovel the curry into my face, all the while faking serious interest in some gardening programme, but out of the corner of my eye I'm watching Arran push his food around and flick his gaze up at me about every ten seconds. When his plate is empty, he puts it aside and the TV goes blank.

'So, what's this all about then?' He tosses the remote control onto the wooden chest. 'You want my help, only fair I should know.'

I shrug. 'Jeannie said you'd be able to put me up for a night and that you know someone who can get the address I need, that's all.'

'What's wrong with Google?'

'You going to help or not?'

'Look, if it were only me involved, I'd do it just because Jeannie asked me to. But getting you that address involves someone else, a friend of mine. You can't just get at a person's medical records. Not unless you work in the field and are prepared to maybe get into a lot of trouble. It's a big ask.'

The only way I have of finding the unit is through finding Miss Beryl, and the only way I have of finding her is through her medical records. I know that she had cancer treatment, and I can take a good stab at her date of birth. That's all I got.

'Don't you think Jeannie understands what she's asking of you and your friend?' I say. 'She strikes me as being pretty damn smart. She wouldn't have sent me here if it wasn't really important, would she?'

Arran glares at me, then sighs. 'Okay, I'll ask them, but their next shift at the hospital isn't till Monday, so you'll have to stay here till then.'

He don't look any more pleased by that idea than I am. I focus on eating.

'We'll need to talk about your story,' he says, and I'm about to ask him what he means exactly when he leaps to his feet and grabs my arm, sending my plate smashing to the floor. Vindaloo spatters across the tiles.

'What the fuck?' I yank my arm back, but he's got a tight grip.

'Where did you get that?' He's tearing Jeannie's watch off my wrist, his face a tangle of bright red snarls.

'Get off.' I swing out a fist and catch him on the side of the head and next thing I know he's got me down on the floor and he's leaning over me, and I can smell booze on his breath. I struggle and thrash, but his long wiry arms are more powerful than you'd think, and he's got me good, both hands pinned to the floor, his knee on my chest.

'Get off me, you fucking alky.'

'You stole this.' Arran lowers his face until his nose is practically touching mine. 'Come on, talk if you know what's good for you.'

'I don't talk to drunks.'

Arran glares at me then suddenly releases my arms and retreats to the other side of the room, and I get the feeling he's putting distance between us cos he don't trust himself not to kill me.

I sit up, rubbing my wrists, brushing my hands over the huge curry stain on the front of my hoodie. 'You're off your head,' I say.

'You tell me how you got this,' he dangles the watch, 'or you can bugger off right now.'

We lock eyes, waiting to see who'll crack first. I don't want to give him anything, to tell him anything I don't got to, but let's face it, I'm not the one who has anything to barter with here.

'Jeannie gave it me,' I say.

'Not that watch she didn't,' he says.

'Yeah, that watch.'

'Liar.'

'Ask her if you don't believe me.'

Arran scowls. 'Florrie said I weren't to contact her, not for any reason.'

I try not to grin. 'Then you got to take my word for it, don't you?'

'I don't have to do anything,' he says, but he's bluffing. He sits down at the chess table and runs his thumb across the face of the watch. 'She wouldn't give this watch to anyone.'

I haul myself back up and into the armchair. He's holding the watch like it offers proof of my guilt, and I think, to hell with rule number one, cos without this bloke on my side, I'm dead meat anyway. We all are.

'She did give it me.' I look him straight in the eye. 'I thought it was odd at the time, but she said it was mine by rights anyway. I don't know what that means but ...' I shrug.

Arran shakes his head. 'It belonged to someone who died, someone very special to her.'

The penny drops and I stare at the watch. 'Arthur Jessop?'

Arran's head jerks up. 'What would you be knowing about Arthur Jessop?'

'He was my grandad,' I snap, and instantly regret it when I see black clouds forming on his face.

That's the problem with words. It's a bit like with the whole unknowing thing – you can't un-say a thing either. Will I never learn?

CHAPTER FIFTEEN

After a breakfast of cold cereal and toast, we walk into the village, where the smell of woodsmoke lingers in the air. I got to hang around like a spare part, half-hidden by Arran's surfboard and cool box, while he shifts crates of beer around and blathers on and on with his boss at the back of the pub. The whole yard stinks like Mum's flat, which don't help my mood any.

I'm itching to get to the beach, my very first beach. If it was up to me, we would've taken the footpath straight down from the flat, but when I suggested it, Arran said no, and I couldn't let him see how desperate I am, could I? So I shrugged, and here we are nearly an hour later, where the sign says 'Beach ¼ mile'. By the time we pick up water, beer, and a giant bag of tortilla chips from the village shop, which is little more than a shed with shelves in, half the morning is gone.

At last, we set off down the road. Along the way, a total of five different locals stop to gossip with Arran, and I bite back my earlier thought that the fewer people who see me, the better. When I'd said that, Arran had shaken his head. 'People come to Cornwall to hide all the time,' he'd said. 'It's like the UK version of the Costa Del Sol. But what they don't get is that the Cornish are dead nosy. Any incomer tries to keep himself to himself is asking for trouble. Best place to hide is in full view.'

He introduces me as his cousin down from London, come to see what real life looks like. I let him do all the talking, and he talks a hell of a lot, which surprises me. Then we round a corner, and my breath catches in my throat.

That thin strip of sand that I'd spied from the clifftop yesterday looks totally different from down here. The beach stretches for miles in every direction. Cave-riddled cliffs tower over our heads. The ocean is this deep emerald green, all except the surf, which is blindingly white. The pounding of water and screeching of gulls fills my head and my lungs, tugs at my guts. Somebody better pinch me and check I'm not dreaming.

We slog along the beach back in the direction of Arran's flat, me lugging the cool box, which bangs against my hip with every step. Who knew sand would be this hard to walk on, even in Diesels? Down by the water, a long-legged woman jogs along the edge of the surf, trailed by two big dogs. A mother and toddler stumble about on some low rocks at the very far end of the beach. Arran heads straight for six blokes sat in front of a small cave.

'Hey.' He plonks himself next to some hairball in a pink T-shirt, laying his surfboard onto the sand next to him. Which means I can't sit there, so I'm left standing here like a lemon with all these faces checking me out. I think about what Arran said, about hiding in full view, and force out a smile. A couple of the guys nod, giving it out friendly enough, so I nod back and drop onto my butt just off to one side of the group. Arran leans across and takes the cool box from me, tosses me a bottle of water then turns back to listen to the hairball, who punctuates every sentence with a long drag on a spliff. I focus on the ground in front of me, letting sand trickle through my fingers like I'm sat in a gigantic sand tray.

Over the next hour or so, more people arrive wielding surfboards and cool boxes. I keep my head low and check out each one. Most of them greet Arran by name, offering high-fives and back-slaps, and not only the blokes either. Out of the corner of my eye I clock the girls, all legs and long hair and white smiles, like people off the telly.

Every now and then someone glances my way, but I got to admit, no one gets in my face, no one tries to make me talk. In fact, no one seems particularly interested in me, which is a good thing, right? After a while, I lie down in the sand and stare up at the sky and tune into the echo of the surf pounding up through the ground, and straight into my heart.

Conversation around the group is mostly about tides, forecasts and wave forms, about tales of wipe-outs, about waves they dream of conquering and waves they've been conquered by. I don't got a clue what they're on about, but it sounds a whole load more interesting than any circle-time session I ever sat through. The suck and hiss of the surf is hypnotic. I kick off my Diesels and socks and wriggle my toes down into wet sand. I'm in heaven, or somewhere that could easily pass for it anyway.

In the early hours of this morning, I'd lain there in my borrowed bedroom with the windows wide open, cradled in the sound of the ocean. Now that I'm down here, right next to the sea, I can hear its rhythm calling to me, can almost feel the cool liquid bending and shifting under my limbs as I thrash it into submission. I pull my feet out from the sand and carve out gritty circles with my big toe. How long is it since I last swam?

'All a bit quiet, like,' a new arrival says to no one in particular. The woman – a few years younger than Arran I'd guess, maybe mid-twenties? – pushes a thick, dark fringe back off her forehead, shields a set of sharp, green eyes, and squints at the horizon. A series of grunts answer her. 'Too flat.' 'A real dumper.' 'Waste of time.' A hopeful voice adds, 'S'posed to be up later though.' She hovers in front of Arran, as though waiting for him to notice her, but Arran is deep in conversation with the hairball, so she comes and sits down next to me, tossing a colourful beach bag on the sand between us.

'Kaye,' she says, and the smile she gives me is wide and warm and brilliant. Or maybe I'm just drunk on the beauty of this place.

'David,' I grunt, my face burning.

Arran raises his head and catches Kaye's eye. He lifts a hand in greeting before turning his attention back to the hairball.

'Nice to meet you, Dai,' says Kaye in that soft lilt that I recognise as Welsh. 'I heard our Art had a visitor down.'

She smells of chewing gum and coconut shampoo, and I'm wondering if that rust-coloured skirt in Arran's bedroom belongs to her. My face grows even hotter, and I focus instead on the sand funnelling through my fingers.

'Here she comes.' Arran gets to his feet, setting off a ripple in the group.

I follow his gaze. The sea has changed. Waves that looked flat when we first got here now snake across the beach, folding with a slap long before they reach shore. All around me, arms and legs struggle into wetsuits.

'Coming in?'

Just for a moment I'm stupid enough to think Arran might be talking to me. I open my gob to answer before I realise he's looking at Kaye. I dig my hands into the sand and concentrate on the horizon. Kaye glances across at me but I make like I don't notice. She smiles up at Arran and shakes her head. 'Think I'll hang out here for a bit, ta.'

Arran shrugs, lifts his board under his arm and runs down to the water.

Kaye pulls a flask out of her bag. 'Tea?'

'No.' I watch the group forge through the waves, every bit of me aware of her, sitting so close, just the two of us left here. 'But thanks,' I add, keeping my eyes on the sea.

She pours herself a cup of stewed brown tea, the kind Mum would approve of. When she finishes drinking, she lifts her face to the sun, eyes closed. She don't seem a bit bothered by me not wanting to talk, and if that's a tactic of hers, then it works.

I crack first and nod towards the black blobs in the sea. 'What are they doing?'

'How d'you mean?'

I sit up. 'Well, they been banging on about waves and stuff all morning, and now they're just sat around on their boards, doing nothing.'

Kaye laughs. 'Oh, that's what's known as waiting out back. It's all part of it.' She shades her eyes with one hand and points with the other. 'See how they're lined up behind where the waves start rising? The idea is to wait there till you see the right wave, then you catch it on its way in, quick smart.'

I squint at the black shapes but don't get what she means.

'You never surfed, Dai? No? Sheesh, you don't know what you're missing.' She grins. 'How about a swim for now instead? You swim?' She reaches behind her, picks up a wetsuit, holds it against my back and flings it down again. 'Too skinny.' She laughs. Her teeth are white and even.

God, how I long to stretch out in the water, to feel it move against my skin, to pound and thrash and kick. But, pathetic though it might be, somehow I feel like accepting would mean conceding round three to Arran. No, scrap that. He already took round three when he pinned me down and made me talk. This would be round four. If he'd wanted me to go into the sea with them, he would've asked, and now I don't feel like I can.

I stare out at the water. He's riding his board across a wave. Both man and board vanish behind a wall of water and then reappear, Arran's head visible, bobbing in the aftermath of the wave. I look away, and find that while I been watching Arran, Kaye's been watching me.

'His bark's worse than his bite, you know.'

'Whose?'

'Your cousin's.'

I scowl at the idea of being related to Arran.

'I'm nipping up to Art's flat a mo',' Kaye says near my ear. 'Won't be long.'

Minutes later she's back, carrying a second wetsuit and a plastic bag. 'Come on, I'll help you get into this oversized condom.' She holds out the wetsuit, but I make no move to take it, so she picks up the sleeve, demonstrates its thickness, then drops it into my lap. I'm opening my mouth to protest when she says, 'Some cracking snorkelling off this beach, mind.'

'Snorkelling?'

Kaye reaches a hand into the plastic bag and pulls out a snorkel and mask. She dangles them in front of my nose like a magician pulling a rabbit out of a hat, and I got this huge grin on my face. Kaye grins right back at me, then we leg it down to the very end of the beach and fall into the sea.

I'm flying, defying gravity, walking on air. A flick of my legs propels me forwards, downwards, up, up, up. Welcome back, King of the World.

The sea is so different to the pool, in a this-knocks-the-spots-off-that sort of way. For a start, the force of the current strokes your skin even through the wetsuit, and I'm already an addict to the sensation. Then there's all the stuff to see: rocks, seaweed, fish, murky fields of plankton, a whole new planet. That other world, with all its filthy lies, can't touch me here.

Kaye turns out to be a pretty good teacher, showing me how to breathe through the snorkel, how to make the most of the airtime it buys you, providing names for everything we see. We stay well clear of the surf and stick to the calmer water in the crook of the bay, working our way slowly along the rocky seabed. A shoal of sharp grey fish flickers in and out of view, dashing between rocks. Long tendrils of sea-anemones perform a Mexican wave in rhythm with the surf. In between dives, we tread water and catch our breath. The freezing temperature numbs my feet and face and all the bits not covered in – what's it called? – neoprene.

Kaye pushes her mask on top of her head. 'Enjoying yourself, Dai?'

No point in even trying to deny it, cos I can't stop grinning.

She cocks her head, sizing me up. 'I want to show you something.'

'What?'

She pulls her mask back on and signals me to copy her. 'Take a deep breath and swim fast, yeah?'

I'm squinting against the sun's glare off the water, and when I turn around, she's gone. I thrash in a circle trying to spot her but there's no trace until I put my mask to the water and peer down. She's maybe three metres below the surface. Filtered sunlight glints off her hair as it fans out around her like some beautiful mermaid, and anyone who's ever read a book knows mermaids might look good but they're bad news.

I pull my head out of the water and look back to shore. We've swum a long way out from the beach, but we're right alongside the rocky bit that fringes the headland. Any problem and I could get ashore easy enough.

The water bubbles and Kaye pops up right in front of me. I pull back and a wave cracks like an egg on the side of my face making me cough and splutter.

She laughs. 'What's the matter?'

'Nothing.'

She studies my face. 'I've been watching you, Dai. You're a good strong swimmer. A natural. You'll be fine, I promise.'

'Fine doing what?'

'Well now, that would spoil my surprise, wouldn't it?' She laughs.

'I'm not big on surprises,' I say.

'You'll like this one,' she says.

Arran and the others are out of the water and back sitting in front of the cave. The toddler I saw earlier is poking a net between the rocks while its mother looks on. Two people sit camped on towels along the shoreline. A gentle breeze skips across the water. Mum's voice comes into my head saying, 'Why do you have to spoil everything, Davey?'

'What do I do?' I pop the snorkel back into my mouth.

'Take a deep breath and follow me, yeah?' Kaye grins, pops her own snorkel in and twists into a dive.

I inhale and follow her under.

We swim low, practically crawling along the sandy sea bottom, moving in a straight line towards the headland. Waves pound overhead and a *thump, thump, thump* pushes against my chest. In front of me, Kaye's feet steadily kick. Walls of rock grow on either side of us and the sea grows colder, darker. My lungs begin to ache, and I glance up to gauge how long it would take to reach the surface, but there is no surface, just rock.

I grab Kaye's ankle and point upwards, my eyes wide, but she just gives me a thumbs-up and points a finger towards what I now see is a tunnel. I look back the way we came. I'll never make it. Kaye moves ahead. I kick hard. There's light ahead of us.

We break the skin of the pool at the same time.

I gasp, my chest pumping fit to burst. Kaye puts her finger to her lips and I follow her raised gaze.

'Wow.'

A dim light, just enough to see by, is finding its way in from somewhere overhead. We're in a deep green pool in the centre of an oval cave bigger than Arran's whole flat. Thick stone ledges spiral up sandy walls, like one of those plastic toys you win in crackers, the kind you got to tilt in order to send a metal ball through a maze.

Kaye pulls herself out of the pool in one swift move and sits on a rocky ledge, shaking out her mask. 'I'm starving.' She rubs her hand absently over her stomach.

I'm way too excited to think about food, too excited to even try to hide it. This cave is so cool. I want to know everything about it. How did she discover it? Who else knows it's here? I haul myself onto the cave floor and wander around, running my palms along the walls, poking my hands into dark corners.

'Smugglers,' Kaye stage-whispers in answer to my questions. 'Pirates and blackguards.'

'Pirates?'

She laughs. 'Well … maybe. But definitely smugglers. They used this cave to store their goods until it was safe to cart them inland. They'd do what's known as sowing the crop – they'd weigh their booty down and push it overboard a little way offshore, near the crab pots. Then a local crabber would chuck in a grappling hook, attach a rope and swim in through the passageway, just like we did, dragging the whole lot in after them.'

Kaye talks on and on and I let her words fill my head, pushing out all thoughts of Mum and Drummond and Carson and the unit until there's nothing inside me but here, nothing but now.

'Anyone ever live in here?'

'Not very practical, seeing as high tide good as fills this place twice a day. If it didn't, I'd live in it myself.' Kaye laughs. She laughs a lot, but I like it cos there's nothing forced or fake or judgemental about it like with some people. 'I call it my little rock womb, because whenever I'm in here I feel as though I'm all tucked up away from the world, safe in the belly of mother earth. That probably sounds daft to you.'

'Nope,' I say. She's just described exactly how I feel in water.

She smiles. 'Art sketched me in here once. I'd never told him how I feel about this place but guess how he drew me? Inside a womb and naked as the day I was born. Talent, that is.'

'Arran's a jerk.' It pops out before I can stop it.

She looks surprised. 'He can be a funny beggar; I'll give you that. Sometimes he finds it hard to let his feelings show. But he's a good man.'

'Huh.' I squat on my haunches, my fingers toying with the snorkel while her eyes burn into me.

'I can see that you're family, you two – no mistaking the resemblance – but how well do you actually know each other?'

I been amazed by how everyone's just accepted Arran's story about us being cousins, but now she's even imagining we look alike? The power of suggestion, eh?

'Our families aren't close,' I say, parroting the script Arran gave me.

'You know about his mam dying though? No?'

Arran's mother is dead? Fear for my own mum threatens to choke me suddenly, and I feel a spark of empathy with Arran. I pretend to concentrate on spitting into my mask to clear it.

'He was only your age. She was an actor, worked in theatres all over Europe, America, Canada. They rarely lived in one place for more than six months at a time. No commitments. Nobody needing them. Nothing to tie them down.'

When she stops talking, the silence that fills the cave feels heavy.

'What happened?' I ask, curious despite not wanting to care.

'Cancer happened. One minute they're living this exciting life full of parties, new people, unfamiliar places, and the next minute she's back here gasping her last. Art won't

176

talk about it, but from what his grandad told me, Art never left his mam's side for months. When she died, he wanted to stay on here, but his grandad was pretty old even then and not up to much, bless him.'

'No father?' I ask, thinking maybe me and Arran got more in common than just a liking for chess.

'There was a dad, obviously, but Art never knew anything about him until his mother was lying on her deathbed, and then he found out that he'd died four years earlier. Art never got chance to know him. Some sort of accident I think; Art doesn't like to talk about that either.' She flicks me a look. 'Must run in the family, this not talking thing. Luckily, his mam had an old theatre friend who she'd always kept in touch with, and she stepped in. She didn't foster Art formally or anything. He was fifteen by then and it seems she'd come up against the authorities when she tried to foster someone else in the past, so she skipped around all that, kept it under the radar. But she made sure he was all right.'

'Was that Jeannie?'

'You know Jeannie then? Isn't she great? Art spent most of his holidays in London with her, but his home has always been here. Can't keep him out of the surf, see.' Kaye smiles. 'He doesn't want to let people in because he doesn't want to get hurt, is all.' She stands up and stretches. 'Tide's coming in. Best get moving.'

I look down. The cave floor is totally covered in water and it's hard to make out the pool we entered by.

'How high up does it come?'

Kaye points to the ledge she's standing on. 'Pretty much up to here.'

I shiver and start to pull my mask over my face.

'No need for that,' Kaye says. 'We're walking out.'

Before I can ask, she hauls herself onto the spiral ledge, walks a full turn of the cave and vanishes into rock. I scramble after her and find a jutted outcrop of rock that conceals an opening. A narrow passage leads away from the sea.

'This way,' she whispers. 'No talking, just in case.'

'In case of what?' I say, and my voice echoes loudly.

'Rockfalls,' she hisses.

That shuts me up.

We climb steadily. The tunnel narrows in places to just half a metre across, but then a dim light grows stronger and we step out into a hollow in the cliff, all bushes and dazzling sunlight. I push aside branches and find myself standing on the very tip of the peninsula. I stare down at the sea, my eyes seeking out the underwater route we'd followed into the cave. The rocky pathway is invisible from up here. All I can see is white froth smashing into black rocks and the expanse of blue beyond.

'If you know what you're looking for, you can work out from the gap in the wash where the sandy trail runs through.'

She's right. In the middle of the chaotic foam and jutting rocks runs a wide ribbon of sandy-bottomed water that melts into the cliff with barely a ripple.

Five minutes later we're sitting on warm sand, sharing a flask of tea and getting stuck into a packet of Hobnobs. Arran and his friends are back in the sea. The mother and child are still on the rocks. It's like we never moved from this spot.

This time I really do need to pinch myself to check I'm not dreaming.

CHAPTER SIXTEEN

The sun dropped below the horizon an hour ago but no one around here's got any intention of calling it a day. When the temperature starts to plummet, a load of us collect up the driftwood that's strewn along the tideline. I help the hairball and another guy to build a fire in the shelter of the cave entrance. I won't tell you the feeling I get from coaxing my first ever proper fire into life cos you'd probably get the wrong idea about me, but anybody says it's not a thrill to watch is lying their arse off. Flames dance and blaze, casting a strange glow over the circle of faces gathered around it. Circle time. That's another life, that is.

I'm sitting next to Kaye, who's leaning into Arran on her other side. He's droning on to his mates about surfing and stuff. I tune him out, I tune all of them out until it's just me and the sand and the fire and the sky.

Two boys and a girl, all around my age, come walking out of the night and drop onto the sand right by me. The boys say, 'Hey,' and look at me like 'so who are you, exactly?' I ignore them and stare into the flames and eventually they wander off, elbowing each other. The girl stays. I sneak a look at her: stocky with shaggy brown hair, wearing rolled-up jeans and a pink woollen jumper. She's got a blanket wrapped around her shoulders, and I don't doubt she needs it cos the jumper she's wearing only reaches to her bellybutton. She holds her arms out to the fire to rub warmth into them, notices me watching and shuffles closer.

'I'm Natalie.'

A smile twitches at the corners of Kaye's mouth. She tucks her face into Arran's shoulder and whispers something. Arran laughs. I squirm. An elbow digs me sharply in my ribs.

'So, what's your name?'

'David,' I mutter, grateful for the darkness.

'Natalie, get over here,' a voice calls up from the beach.

She's so quick I don't see the movement coming but she manages to slide over next to me, so close I can hear her breath going in and out.

'It's only Felix and Billy, clowning around.'

'You've got to see this, Nat,' the voice calls, louder.

Her eyes roll skywards. 'This had better be good.'

She disappears into the night, and I hear voices, then a giggle, then silence. My head fills with a vision of her cropped top and the sliver of belly exposed at the top of her jeans, brown and soft. I feel hot, the kind of heat that comes from the inside, not from the fire in front of me.

'Anyone coming on the march in London on Tuesday?' Kaye's voice breaks into my thoughts. 'Coach goes from Costcutters in St Agnes.'

A few heads nod.

'What time?'

'Four-thirty.'

'Man, that's early,' says the stoned hairball.

'You coming?'

'No, man. I got stuff to do.'

'Like what?'

Someone giggles, but Kaye's not laughing.

'No point sitting around here moaning if you're not willing to stick your neck out to meet your big gob, is it?'

'Marching never did no good. Never will.'

'Try telling the suffragettes that. Or the Black Lives Matter lot. That's just the excuse of the lazy, that is.'

'London don't listen.'

'Then it's up to us to make them,' Kaye snaps.

'How about you, Arran? You going?' one of the younger blokes asks.

'I'm working. 'Sides, I'm not sure how I feel about it all. I mean, who wants dangerous psychos running around loose? Maybe we do need to do something about them.'

And just like that, the outside world crashes in on this one.

My whole body pushes deeper into the sand, begging to be swallowed. The poster at Victoria Coach Station flicks into my head: 'Our Kids Are Not Monsters'. I struggle to keep down the panic. Nobody here knows who I really am, not even Arran.

'This is way more than just something.' Kaye is glaring at Arran. 'It'll be no good whining ten years down the line when the law's been changed out of all recognition and the government can do what the hell it likes. Way too late to stick up for our kids then.'

Arran shrugs. 'I'm not sure, is all. I'm not saying you're wrong or anything.'

'Well good then.'

'Good.'

The group falls silent.

'Man,' the stoned hairball says after a while, 'they going to be locking you up for having a spliff, way things are going.'

'Too right, mate. A spell in some cushy nuthouse might straighten you out.'

'You won't be so smug when they throw your arse in jail for being born dog-ugly, mate.'

Someone giggles and the atmosphere relaxes as everyone breaks off into smaller conversations. The words 'surf' and 'barbecue' and 'party' get bandied around. My guts churn. What would this crowd say if they knew that I'm one of those psychos? What would Arran say?

'David?' Arran holds out a can of lager. 'Just the one'll be all right.'

I shake my head and he shrugs and pushes the can towards Kaye.

'No, ta.'

'Go on, you've hardly had a drop.'

Kaye shakes her head, her shoulders stiff. 'No, ta, I don't want any.'

Arran bends back the ring on a can and froth hisses over his fingers as he sips. 'Forecast's good for tomorrow. You coming in if it is?'

'Maybe.'

Arran's hand pauses halfway to his mouth as he looks sideways at her. 'Maybe what? Maybe yes or maybe no?'

'Maybe probably,' says Kaye. 'I'm going to view that cottage tomorrow, I told you. The rent's good. It's bound to get snapped up.'

'That sounds like fun.' Arran leans back on the sand on one elbow and lets out an exaggerated sigh. 'What's the matter with you, Kaye? It's the weekend. Relax and have a drink for God's sake.' He yanks back the ring on another can and pushes it towards her.

'Leave her alone,' I say.

'You used to know how to have a good time,' Arran says, still holding the can out to Kaye.

I sit up. 'She don't need to drink to have a good time.'

'Are you still here?'

'Stay out of it, David,' Kaye says.

'Bet you think boozing makes you look cool, don't you?'

Arran laughs. 'So, what are you, born again? The anti-alcohol brigade?'

'Yeah, well, wait till you're mopping up her vomit or hauling her out of the gutter or calling an ambulance cos she's fallen downstairs blind drunk. Will you still think it fun then? Still think you're cool?'

Every face around the fire turns to stare at me. The stoned hairball stifles a giggle. Kaye reaches out and touches my arm and it's like an electric shock. I push to my feet and lumber into the darkness, and I don't stop until I reach the sea.

Ice-cold water seeps through my shoes. My trouser legs cling to my ankles.

'That your mother you're talking about?' Arran's voice says at my shoulder.

'Fuck off.'

My face is wet, and I rub my sleeve across it, but roughly, so he won't know I'm crying.

Arran sighs. 'Look, David, we didn't start off right well.'

'Screw you.'

'Okay, my fault. Mostly. But I care about Jeannie. I don't like thinking she's being used, being taken advantage of.'

My head is buzzing, and I don't trust myself to speak. Moonlight traces a silver finger across the surface of the sea, and I concentrate on that until the white noise dies down and I can think again. Arran is still there, standing in the sea right next to me.

'Look, I'm sorry. That watch … it belonged to my father.'

'What?'

'Arthur Jessop was my father.'

I glance down at the watch on my wrist.

'I didn't know who he was until after my mum died, and he was already dead himself by then.' Arran leans his head back and gazes up at the night sky.

I stare at Arran like I'm seeing him for the first time. No wonder he went ballistic. Then I see it, the family connection. Kaye was right all along. It's his mouth, the way it pushes into his cheeks when he looks serious, like now. It dawns on me that Arran was the name Jeannie was about to say when Mum told her she didn't get any inheritance. He's the one Grandad Arthur didn't leave any money to cos he never even got the chance to meet him.

'Your mum,' he says, 'my sister – God, that sounds odd – she's got a serious problem? With the drink, I mean.'

I nod, but I'm only half listening. What does this make Arran to me?

'I'm sorry to hear that,' he says, and he sounds sincere.

So, if Mum is his sister, what does that make me?

'Turns out you're my nephew, David.' Arran grunts, but it sounds more friendly than grumpy. 'Fancy that.'

I can't move. I got a real-life flesh-and-blood relative? An uncle. In the flesh, right here. The feeling that gives me is … weird. Arran might be a bit of a jerk, but suddenly it's not just me and Mum in the world. Suddenly we got family. Now I understand why Jeannie used the word 'perfect' when we found out I needed to come to Cornwall. She knew exactly where to send me. To family, where else?

'Clean slate, yeah?' Arran is saying. 'Start again?'

'Okay,' I say, cos what else can I say?

'Good then,' he slaps my back.

We walk back up the beach, not exactly together but not fighting either. Kaye wraps a thick blanket around my shoulders. One or two of the group throw me a quick smile then carry on chatting like nothing's happened. There's no interrogation, no linking me to that march, no trying to get me to talk about my feelings. I flop onto the sand, and the tension that's been in my shoulders since I arrived starts to loosen.

Does Mum even know that she's got a half-brother? All these years, she needn't have been all on her own. There were people like Jeannie who care about her. People like Arran, who are family. I wonder where she and Jeannie are now?

Natalie reappears and flops down next to me.

'Been collecting razor clams. Brrr.' She empties a handful of long thin shells onto the sand and rubs her hands up and down her legs. 'Lovely barbecued. We'll soon have a feast fit for a king. They call it 'tapas' in Spain. Had it in Benidorm with my nan. Look, still got the tan.' She waves her legs in the air and my stomach does a somersault.

Felix and Billy reappear next, lugging a pot of water and wielding a penknife.

'These'll be great,' one of them says.

I'll take their word for it cos those razor clams stink like old socks.

The three of them get stuck into fussing over the shells while I'm busy being grateful to the universe that none of them were here when I lost it. It's humiliating enough with the oldies. I pull the blanket tighter and lie as close to the fire as I dare. To start with, I'm pretending to sleep just so nobody will bother me, but the thing with pretence is, if you're not incredibly careful it can quickly turn into the real thing.

When I wake up, the thing I see is a pitch-black ceiling overhead, decorated with the brightest stars I ever saw. It takes me a moment to remember where I am, and when I do, I grin up at the night sky.

The fire is still lit, but low, and there's no circle of faces around it. They've all gone off, all except Natalie, who's sitting way too close. When she sees I'm awake, she grins and lies down next to me. I bolt upright and pull my blanket closer, tucking my knees into my chest, trying to put a bit of distance between me and those careless brown legs. But Natalie's legs edge through the sand towards me, getting closer, nearly touching.

'What's your favourite music?' she asks.

'Err …' I rack my brains trying to think of a song or a group I can name but it's years since I thought about that stuff and my mind draws a blank. The only thing in my head is the sound of the sea, sucking the sand, over and over. 'I like all sorts, really.'

'Yeah?' She shifts closer until I can feel her hip bone pressing against the blanket. 'But what do you enjoy best of all? What floats your boat?'

She's playing with me.

Sweat clings to my upper lip. Last time I was even near a girl was way back when I thought girls were a pest, stupid cos they couldn't throw a ball or play computer games beyond level one. Things feel vastly different now.

She laughs, and something tightens in my chest. She's laughing at me.

'What's so funny?'

'Oh, nothing. You. I don't know.' She stares up at the stars. 'You're not like the boys round here. You're different.'

She's watching me watching her, and there's this strange smile playing on her lips. 'Go on then,' she says.

'Go on then what?' I squeak.

'Go on then this,' she says, and she reaches up, puts an arm around my neck, pulls me close and plants her lips on mine.

I'm so shocked I freeze, lips squeezed tight.

She pulls away and gets to her feet, and suddenly I know I want her to stay. I grab her arm.

'Wait.'

'Let go.' She shakes me off and walks away.

All I can do is stare after the faint shadow of her as she recedes into the distance and is swallowed by the night. Did I do something wrong? Of course I did. I grabbed her. Idiot. 'I'm sorry,' I call out into the dark. I tilt back my head and frown. Maybe she's right. Maybe I'm not like other boys. Maybe Wilson's been right all along and there's something seriously wrong with me.

The moon finds its way out from behind the bank of clouds and lights up the beach. I make out Arran and the others down by the water's edge and the faint outline of the path that leads up to Arran's flat. The fire has died down to orange embers.

'You staying around, then?' Natalie is standing six metres or so away, hands on hips, staring at me. A hot flush shoots through me. Does she mean now, like tonight on this beach, or for a few days, or in Cornwall forever? I don't care. I just care that she came back. I nod and hold my breath.

'See you tomorrow night then,' she says, and the moon glances off her wide smile before she turns towards the cliff path and disappears again.

Lying flat on my back, the sand cold and grimy against my neck, I grin up at the night sky. She likes me. She actually likes me.

CHAPTER SEVENTEEN

Yesterday morning I lay in bed listening to the radio as it banged on about how storms were going to lash the Cornish coastline well into evening. A peek out of the window transported me back to early mornings lying in bed in the unit, listening to the seductive patter of rain against my barred window. How I'd longed, back then, to feel the sting of rain on my face. But yesterday, as I watched rain swallow the headland and decimate any hope of hanging out on the beach and maybe bumping into Natalie again, I cursed. So much for the sodding weather forecast.

If I'm honest, the thing that had bothered me even more than not having an excuse to see Natalie again was the idea of being faced with endless hours stuck indoors with only Arran for company, but in the end the day didn't turn out half-bad. Kaye came round, clutching a pack of beer and four cans of coke. The three of us played cards and Pictionary and ate pizza, and Arran laughed more than I would've thought him capable of. A couple of the cracks he made had me belly laughing, and the thought that it might be a family sense of humour thing made me feel a bit odd inside, but in a good way.

After dinner, Kaye fell asleep on the sofa and me and Arran played chess. He slaughtered me, but he wasn't a jerk about it, which came as a double surprise. By the time I got off to bed, leaving the love birds to finish watching the slushy rom-com that Kaye had chosen when she finally woke up, I felt like we'd all been living here together in this flat for forever. Like family.

This morning, Kaye left for work at the hospice and Arran stuck his head around my bedroom door, said, 'Be back late afternoon,' waved a hand and was gone.

The weird thing is, when I get up and realise that for the first time ever I got a whole day ahead of me with nothing timetabled and nobody to tell me what to do with it, I get scared. I'm thinking I don't want to bump into Natalie, cos if we start chatting, she'll start asking me questions, and my mind will be a bit like papier mâché around those legs and I could end up telling her something I shouldn't. And even if it isn't Natalie I bump into, people are best avoided, no matter what Arran's got to say about it. Staying indoors has got to be safer.

I pull out the laptop, pleased to see that it's fully charged, and skim through the news bulletins about tomorrow's march in London, not wanting to contaminate the day any more than I got to.

Then I stupidly tap the word 'psychopath' into the search bar.

When I finish reading, a lot of the stuff in my files makes a sickening kind of sense and the word 'contaminated' don't do full justice to how I feel. About one percent of the male population are psychopaths, which is completely mad, but it seems most psychopaths aren't killers and criminals like you might think. Apparently, a lack of conscience has its uses for things like winning a war or running a boardroom. It means you can focus on your goals without letting morality or mercy get in the way, so loads of those socially functioning psychopaths do pretty well and have important jobs and big houses. They're drawn to power positions, so a fair number of them go into politics too. How they turn out seems to got a lot to do with the 'environment' in which they're raised. If their parents are cruel or dysfunctional, chances are that'll send them off in a warped direction. I think of Mum and can't help wondering how warped she's made me? Warped enough to be a PSK?

I press on and discover that CU, which my file says I got high traits of, stands for Callous and Unemotional. Am I callous and unemotional? I been hiding my feelings for so long, just so they couldn't use them against me, I can't tell any more what's real and what's not. I mean, do I feel stuff the same way other people do? How can anybody know that? Is having a conscience the same thing as sometimes feeling bad about stuff, even stuff that's not your fault? I feel bad about Mum, I feel bad about leaving Oliver all alone in there, I feel bad about a whole heap of things. Does that mean I got a conscience?

And empathy, psychopaths lack empathy. That's key. But I empathised with Miss Beryl when she got the cancer, didn't I? This thought is comforting till I read the next bit about how they're also manipulative and use people for their own ends. I might've felt sorry for Miss Beryl about the cancer, but here I am using her medical records to track her down. Is that what they mean by manipulation?

Psychopaths are also pretty good at denial and self-delusion, and they're very often bullies at school. That explains the obsession with the bullying at school thing in my file, but that wasn't true, was it? And how the hell are you even supposed to know if you're deluded?

I read on and a couple of other things strike me.

The PCL-R form is the form they use to measure psychopathy. Any score over thirty means you're a psychopath. According to my file, I scored 32, which means unless I can prove Wilson's lying about the evidence, then I'm definitely a psycho.

Psychopaths commit acts of violence for a planned purpose, not as the result of a loss of emotional control, which makes sense cos they don't got emotions, do they? I think back to Miss Beryl on that last day, trying to find the underlying cause of why I attacked Freaky Adam, trying to find some way to help me. She wanted to know if my attack was pre-planned, or if I did it cos he got me mad and I lost it. She was trying to defend me, to show the attack was triggered by my emotions, but as usual I wouldn't talk to her. Why didn't I just tell her the truth? All that silence, all that holding back. I've allowed them to fill in the blanks for me and come up with one dog-ugly picture of who I am. All Wilson needed to do was add a few finishing touches to my own masterpiece.

One passage I read makes me shudder, cos it sums Freaky Adam up perfectly: 'The psychopath is a predator and, despite their veneer of charm, people often respond to them by saying, "He made the hairs on the back of my neck stand up".'

I turn the laptop off. Pace the living room. A familiar feeling finds its way up from the place where I keep it buried and gets to spreading right through me until I can't breathe. I lay flat on my back on the colourful rug where the sun is warm through the patio doors. I make myself concentrate on an ink-dot of a fly that's buzzing angrily up and down the glass, desperate to get out but too stupid to find a way. Just breathe, David. You're in Cornwall, hanging out with surfers and cool girls, snorkelling and playing chess and eating good food. There are no vans crashing into rivers, no Drummond sniffing outside my door, no London traffic to negotiate.

So why do I feel more scared today than any other day I remember my whole life?

The answer, when it hits me, hits me hard, cos it goes something like this: for the first time in my life, I got something worth hanging onto.

I stand up and open the patio door and the fly does what it was made to do and flies away. It's nearly midday and yesterday's rain has been burnt away by brilliant sunshine. The warm breeze hums with the distant sounds of surf and gulls, and I'm totally aware that there are no locks on these doors.

An exhilarating three hours later, I tear my salty, scrubbed-clean self away from the beach and head up to the wide, open space along the clifftop. I got to squash down the guilt I feel about having such a blast while Mum is god knows where, cos there's nothing I can do about that right now. Soon I'll be able to help her. But right here, right now, I can see for miles and there's not a soul around, and this feeling in my chest is good and nothing to feel guilty about.

A chunk of rock kicks back from my pounding feet. It rolls and clatters over the edge and drops into waves too far below to see or hear any splash. Unlike only three days ago, I don't flinch at the dizzying drop as I pump my legs hard along the coast path, the wind whipping me awake. Even lying in bed back in the unit, in my secret dreams conjured up like treasures, I never once imagined I could exist in a place like this. Pure. Unspoilt. Free.

A dozen or so gulls unfold from the cliff edge like magicians' doves, cotton-white explosions rising on thermals. Pink heather springs beneath my feet. Beyond the headland, white horses dance against the blue sea. I lift my face into the wind and roar into the sky. There's no going back. Not now. Not ever.

A lone gull shoots up in front of my face, screeching shrilly, apparently as shocked as I am to find my feet so close to the cliff edge. White wings flap then the gull pushes higher and is gone. I stumble back onto the footpath, retracing my steps along the coast, heading for ... I nearly think 'home'.

I'm reaching under the stone hedgehog for the key when the sound of raised voices comes at me from the rear of the flat. My hands grab the porch for balance and I'm scanning for the best direction to leg it – all these freaking footpaths are so exposed – when I hear Arran's voice. Then Kaye's. I edge along the side path towards the kitchen, ears strained for a third voice, or a fourth, for Drummond or Carson, but I only hear Arran and Kaye. Gravel crunches beneath my feet as I draw near the window.

'For God's sake, Kaye, you know I didn't want this.'

'Well, it's not like I did it on purpose.' A short silence, then, 'You think I did, don't you?'

'Well, you of all people should know what you're doing.'

A chair scrapes across the floor.

'No, sorry, look—'

'You arrogant sod.' Glass shatters. 'Get out of my way.'

'Kaye, wait, I didn't mean—'

The front door slams. Arran swears and lets out a low cry. I peer in through the window. He sees me and scowls.

'Where the hell have you been?'

'Out.'

As I enter the kitchen, I got to step over a broken wine glass that's glistening in a pool of red on the floor. Another glass sits on the breakfast bar next to Arran's elbow.

'What were you and Kaye rowing about?'

'None of your sodding business.'

On a pad next to the wine glass, somebody's drawn a pencil sketch of a headland with a figure running along it.

'Were you rowing about me?'

'Contrary to your own popular belief, you are not the centre of the universe, David.' Arran gets off the stool and fetches a dustpan and brush from under the sink. Glass clatters against tile as he sweeps it into the pan, red smears on white.

My relief at not finding Carson and Drummond here is all twisted up with anger at Arran. I want him to punch me so I can have him. I don't care if I lose. 'What, did Kaye tell you to get over yourself or something? And you threw her out. Nice.'

'I didn't throw her out, she—'

'You got no right to talk to her like you do.'

'I said shut it.' He pushes past me and picks up a piece of paper from the countertop.

I so want to hit him. I so want him to hit me. 'Maybe now she'll go and find herself a proper bloke who'll treat her like she deserves,' I shout.

Arran's face grows dark, and I know I hit the spot. He squares up to me, fists clenched. I square up right back, ready for a fight, wanting it … but somehow all my anger slips away. Maybe it's the look in his eyes: crumpled and defeated.

He unclenches his fist and puts the piece of paper on the breakfast bar beside us. His hand is shaking. 'If anyone finds out it was Kaye who gave me this, she'll be landed right in it. So not a word. Got that?'

I unclench my own fist and snatch up the paper, see the address scribbled there. Falmouth.

Kaye is the somebody who had to get Beryl's address for me? I feel sick. I don't want to get Kaye caught up in all this mess. I stare at the piece of paper. It can't be helped. This is why I came here. This is what this whole Cornwall thing was about: finding Miss Beryl, finding the unit, saving Mum. Somehow, I've gone and lost sight of that, and now I don't feel ready.

'So now you can get the hell out of here, can't you?' Arran turns his back on me and walks into the living room.

Game, set and match to Arran.

I stumble into my bedroom and stuff my meagre belongings – a T-shirt, a pair of clean pants – into a plastic bag. I glance around. Nobody would know I was ever here, which is a good thing, right? It don't feel good. On my way back through the kitchen, I slip a knife out of the wooden block, wrap it in a tea towel and stash it in my jacket pocket.

In the living room, Arran is staring at the evening news. I ignore him and head for the door.

'Wait.' Arran stands up and holds out a handful of notes. 'You'll need cash.'

'No thanks.'

'Don't be stupid.'

'Jeannie gave me plenty.'

Arran starts to say something, but whatever it is, he changes his mind and retreats to the sofa clutching the remote control. The buzz of the TV follows me out onto a headland cast in shade.

An hour later, I climb onto a bus heading for Truro, from where I'll pick up a train to Falmouth. According to the map Arran printed off Google for me, finding Miss Beryl's house should be easy enough. The question of what to do once I get there takes me deep into territory I don't want to explore, with or without a map.

For now, all I allow myself to think about is finding her.

CHAPTER EIGHTEEN

Falmouth Docks is the end of the line and I'm the only passenger left on the last train of the evening. The guard gives me a look I don't like as he checks the carriages for sleeping drunks, so I hop out onto the platform and head out of the car park. On the skyline, a giant crane reaches into the night sky and straddles the dark outline of what looks like a battleship. I study my map under a streetlight. Within minutes I'm walking past swanky houses, their gardens dotted with palm trees and giant ferns.

At the crest of a short hill, a frigid blast of sea air hits me with the scent of salt and seaweed. The lights of ships shine yellow just offshore. Wind stings my lips as I cross a road and lean over a metal railing, my eyes adjusting to the darkness, seeking out the sea. Half-hearted waves flop onto a narrow strip of sand with barely a hiss. I turn towards the deserted promenade, consult my map and check off the side streets until I reach Peninsula Close, which is drowning in posh houses, each with a name on the gatepost: Fisherman's Main, Salty-Cove, The Mariners – and then hers, Shore Reach.

Having scanned the tree-lined street for nosy neighbours and found none, I lift the latch and slip into a rambling garden that leads around Miss Beryl's house. It stretches a good hundred metres at the rear, down past a detached double garage that looks easily big enough to live in. There's a light on at an upstairs window. Maybe she's in bed. I check my watch. 10:30 p.m.

Every window catch on the house is fitted with a security device, those ones that look like miniature wheel clamps. Both doors are sturdy and locked. As I circle her house a second time, the upstairs light goes out and the possibility enters my head that she might not be alone. Maybe she's married. Maybe she got ten kids in there. Fact is, I don't know, and that's when it hits home: I thought I knew Miss Beryl, but the truth is, I don't.

I pick my way around to the double garage. The main garage door is locked. There's a smaller door in the wall, opposite the side entrance to the house. That's locked too. A small window at the back juts open, just a touch. It don't take much effort to haul across a bin, clamber up and reach through to release the catch. My hands grip the inside sill until I'm at full stretch, and I drop the last metre to the floor, landing with barely a sound.

Along the wall nearest to me there's a garden bench, a lawnmower, and a barbeque wrapped in a thick waterproof covering. I tug the lawnmower under the rear window and test it. Not perfect, but if I got to get out of here fast, it'll do as a leg up. There's no key for the side door, but that don't matter cos I don't intend going out of here on foot.

There's only one car, which is particularly good news cos it makes it less likely there's a husband hanging around in there somewhere. The other good news is that it's one I recognise from the staff parking lot: navy Volvo, red leather seats, hatchback. I hadn't known it was Miss Beryl's car, but I definitely seen it before when we've been lined up outside during fire alarms. The state of the inside is more what I'd expect from Jeannie's car than Miss Beryl's: boxes of tissues – some empty, some half-full – a couple of tartan blankets, a lump of coats strewn on the back seat, shoes and wellies in the footwells, carrier bags stuffed with god-knows-what crammed into the luggage area. I frown. Miss Beryl's office at the unit is always dead neat. I really don't know her, do I?

I try the car doors. Locked. Damn, I need a Plan B.

The side wall is lined with shelves that hold boxes, files, bags, tools, tins of paint. I pull out my torch and scan the files, but it's all 'Household Bills', 'Insurance', 'Car Tax' and stuff like that. What did I think, that she'd be stupid enough to keep files from the unit in her garage? She might be a closet scruff, Miss Beryl, but she's far from stupid. I got to remember that.

There's a black box fixed to the garage door at top shelf level, and the red flashing light coming out of it tells me the door is automated. On the shelf, there's a stack of old newspapers. I lift off a double-page spread and position it so it looks like the draft from the opening door could've blown it along the shelf. The red light is totally hidden.

I done all I can for now, so I lift the cover off the barbeque, drape it around my shoulders and lie down on the bench, hugging myself for warmth. Okay, so it's not exactly five-star living, but it knocks spots off lying under the trees on Hampstead Heath. The sea laps against the nearby shore and its rhythm lulls me into a restless sleep.

I stir long before dawn, muscles stiff, my bones cold through. My watch shows four o'clock. Outside, the sky looks bruised, patches of purple on black. I check the house for signs of life. Nothing. I take a steamy pee in a bucket, lie back down, and tug my makeshift blanket around my shoulders. Soon I'll need to be ready, but I'm betting it'll be a couple of hours yet before anything kicks off.

Shortly after six, a voice startles me awake. I scramble for the keyhole. The door to the house stands open. A woman, her back towards me, is putting something on the ground. When she straightens up, there's no mistaking that curling hair at the back of her neck, the bits Miss Beryl's always fussing with. Then she turns around and I crouch low. She's less than two metres away from me.

'Fizz, Larios, Sid,' Miss Beryl calls softly. 'Breakfast.'

She's got cats? I know Matron's got cats, but I had no idea that Miss Beryl did. What else don't I know about her?

Inching up to the window, I watch as she whistles through her teeth and calls again. 'Fizz, Sid.' She's wearing a pink woolly dressing gown, patterned with white daisies. From the open door, the smell of oats and sugar taunts me. She looks different here, in her own clothes, in her own home: so vulnerable, so old, so … ill. I remember about the cancer and briefly close my eyes, and when I look again, she's walking back inside, pulling the door shut behind her.

Another hour passes before I hear a door slam shut, footsteps, a key turning in the lock. By the time the side door opens and Miss Beryl walks into the garage, I'm on my knees, ready. The car bleeps as she approaches. Face pressed to the floor, I watch her feet walk up to the driver's door, then disappear as she gets in. The car's engine fires into life.

Seconds pass and I can't breathe. Miss Beryl's window winds down and I'm guessing she's sticking her arm out and trying the remote control from the outside.

Come on. Come on. Come oonnn.

The driver's door reopens and, as soon as Miss Beryl's feet reappear, I reach up and quietly ease the back passenger door ajar, praying the rumble of the engine will cover up any small sounds I make. As her footsteps tap towards the garage door, I slip into the back seat. There's an exclamation from Beryl and a rustle of paper, followed by a long enough racket as the garage door clanks open for me to pull the back door fully shut. The car rocks as Miss Beryl climbs back in and, moments later, the engine purrs and we pull away.

Cramped into a tight ball in the footwell, I tug a tartan blanket over my head and make sure I'm completely covered. It takes everything I got to squash down the voice inside my skull that's screaming at me 'what the hell do you think you're doing?'

I'm going back into the unit, that's what. Not dragged, kicking and screaming. Voluntary. If anything defines insanity, that's got to be it.

Breathe, David, breathe.

For the next hour or so, I lie in the footwell under a tartan blanket that smells of cat. I'd started feeling car-sick the second we left Falmouth, which could be down to the motion of the car, the stink of cat, or just plain fear. The radio isn't helping. Every five minutes a news bulletin kicks in with talk of crowds gathering in London to protest changes to the Children's Act. They expect trouble. James Treherne, the prime minister, is sending in extra police and riot equipment.

I hope Mum's somewhere safe. And Kaye. By now, Kaye will no longer be in quiet, safe Cornwall. She'll be on her way to London, heading for trouble. And me? I'm here in this car also heading for trouble. What do either of us really think we can do to change anything? I bite back the rapidly rising sense of nausea, and comfort myself with the thought that I can still change my mind. I don't got to get out of this car. I can stay here until Miss Beryl finishes her shift and drives me back out again. Nobody need ever know I was here. And Kaye? She can go shopping, have herself a fancy lunch in a city restaurant, then head back home to Cornwall and Arran and the sea. I cling onto that thought as the wheels spin on the tarmac and the stink of cat grows stronger.

The car slows and turns a corner. The road grows bumpier. I remember these bumps from when I arrived and from when I left … was that really only a week ago?

We're nearly there.

Mum's face pops into my head and, as the car slows down, I'm thinking how I'm never going to see her again. What will happen to her? If they catch me, they won't leave her be. If I get caught, she gets caught. There was a time when I would've thought *serves her right*, but that was before I understood why she's such a screw-up, before I saw how vulnerable she is. She did a stupid thing, a bad thing, but she don't deserve to feel shit for the rest of her life cos of it.

Neither do I.

The car must've driven into shade, cos I shiver. It's no good, I got to take a peek. I ease the blanket aside a fraction and peer up out of the window. Tall dark wall. Sky. More wall. The car bumps around the side of a building and draws to a halt.

'Morning Beryl,' a distorted voice crackles. 'Go on through.'

I yank the blanket over my head and hold my breath.

'Thanks, John.'

A metallic creak, an automated sound like Miss Beryl's garage doors, then a juddering as the car edges forward. The gate clanks shut behind us and a moment later the engine stops.

I know where we'll be. We'll be in a compound roughly the size of two football pitches, where the staff park their cars on one side, and we gather on the grass on the other side for roll call every time someone sets off the fire alarm. We'll have driven in through a gate like you'd find on a castle: huge, wooden, curved at the top, banded in black metal, with a miniature people-sized version set into it, bottom left. The walls will be made of thick brick and they'll tower four metres high.

I'm expecting Miss Beryl to get out, but there's no movement in the car. I can hear her breathing, slowly in and slowly out, just like she taught me to do when I feel a panic attack coming. What's she got to panic about? If anybody around here should be panicking, it's me. I'm back inside these walls, and I put myself here. What the holy hell am I playing at? I listen to Miss Beryl breathing, try to match the rhythm with my own breath, feel the panic subside. I can't lose it now. Not here, right on the edge of the dragon's lair.

A few minutes later, the car vibrates with the motion of Miss Beryl getting out. She shuts the door behind her but don't bother locking it. Why would she? Nobody's going to nick her car in here.

Time limps by. I don't dare move. It's as much as I can do to breathe slowly in, slowly out. As the engine cools and the temperature drops, I'm grateful for what little warmth the blanket offers, stinking or not.

Over the next hour, more cars arrive. Tyres crunch on gravel, doors slam, locks hum and beep. Voices come and go. A harsh laugh right next to Miss Beryl's car leaves me shaking.

Then there are no more arrivals, no more voices.

My back aches. Moisture forms on the underside of the blanket, and my face starts to itch like crazy, forcing me to shove the blanket off and gasp for air. Through the car window, all I can see is a brooding grey sky where before it shone blue.

I ease onto my knees and peer through the side window. The compound is deserted. About twenty cars are dotted about the tarmac. The four-metre high walls run along three sides, and the blank face of the unit, several storeys high, forms the fourth. Inset into the middle of the building there's a large metal door, the one we usually come out of when there's a fire alarm. There are two other doors, one each end of the building, but I don't know where they go. There are no windows on this side of the unit.

I crawl onto the seat, stretch my legs and crick my neck. Decision time.

If I go in, there's a chance I'll never come back out. I know how to find the unit now. I should tell Jeannie like we agreed, and let her tell the police. But if I don't find my records, find evidence that Wilson was lying, what then? These people told my own mum that I'm a murderer and she believed them. Do I let the whole world be told that's who I am? Do I spend the rest of my life not knowing? I got to prove that I'm not. I got to prove it to myself. If it exists at all, the proof I need will be hidden deep inside the unit, in its rooms of filing cabinets and computers, and probably in Wilson's office. If the news of this place goes public, they'll destroy the evidence. I got to get to it first.

Now that I made up my mind, my breathing comes easier. The thought of going back inside those inner walls still turns me all queasy inside, but it feels better than the thought of doing nothing. All I got to do now is figure out how to actually get in there. I spent the bus ride to Truro yesterday playing the daily routines and systems around on a loop in my head, searching for weak spots. The exit door in the wall leads into a small porch, then another door. When we come through there for roll call, both doors are propped open, but I reckon if somebody uses their pass to open them now, I can sneak through behind them before the doors get a chance to fully close. If they look back, I'll be toast, but from what I seen of staff moving around inside the unit, they don't tend to. It's risky, but it's all I got.

Now I need somebody to come, so I can check out how long the doors take to shut behind them, then I'll be ready to give it a go.

CHAPTER NINETEEN

It's another half an hour before a vehicle approaches the outside wall. The gate whirs and clunks open. Tyres crunch on gravel. A Land Rover. Open back. Scruffy. Pale blue. The driver's some bloke I don't recognise. He don't look like a doctor, too fit and healthy. Maybe he's a gardener or a handyman. For the first time, it occurs to me there must be a whole heap of people working here that I never met.

The man marches to the big metal door in the centre, swipes his card across the monitor box there and steps inside as the first door opens. He pauses in the porch. The inside door hasn't started opening yet, and by the time it finally starts to swing forward, the outer door is nearly shut. I groan. It hadn't occurred to me there might be a time delay on the damn thing. There's no chance of me sneaking into the building behind the next arrival.

That's Plan A aborted and, for this bit, I got no Plan B.

I'm reeling from disappointment when the side door to the left of the building swings open and a woman backs out, lugging a large black bag in each hand. She pushes the door wide and props it open with one of the bags, then hauls the other bag over to the industrial bins, hoists a lid open and throws the bag up and in. She walks back into the building and, minutes later, reappears carrying a cardboard box. Glass jangles and smashes as she empties it into another bin. She disappears inside again, and a hush falls over the car park. The door is still propped open.

Plan B just got born.

I slither out onto the tarmac and scurry between cars to the open doorway, heart banging in my chest. At the threshold, I pause and look back. Too late to lose my nerve now.

Ahead of me, a hallway splits in three directions. My eyes search for a clue to where each passageway might lead, but the whitewashed walls and blank-faced doors aren't giving anything away.

The stink of over-cooked cabbage hits me. That's something I do recognise. I turn towards the smell. The bin woman is walking towards me, but backwards, dragging another bag. The bag clanks and makes enough of a racket to cover the sound of my feet as I leap into the middle corridor and out of sight. I run, snatching at every passing door handle, every one of them locked. By the time I reach a crossroads, the rattling of cans has been joined by voices.

I plunge down a flight of stairs straight into an obstacle course: a ladder propped against the wall, pots of paint stacked up, plastic buckets strewn across my path. Tunnels stretch in four directions. The floor is bare concrete, the walls raw plaster. I pick the left tunnel and don't slow down, don't stop dodging, leaping, turning corners until I can no longer hear voices and I'm completely lost.

I keep moving cos what else is there? Soon I'm pounding carpet covered in translucent plastic, which crunches and crackles beneath my feet. The walls are freshly painted and lined with doors, each one a different shade of blue or green and with a porthole set into its upper half. I stop running, double over and fight for breath. How far have I come? This place is miles bigger than I ever suspected.

I peer through the nearest porthole and see a whitewashed cell and a stack of unopened cardboard boxes with labels showing a bed, a desk, a chair. The next room is the same, and the next. I shudder. The unit is gearing up to expand. Kaye was right to go to London. The law can't make this okay. Oliver's face pops into my head, followed by the habitual twinge of guilt, which I shake off cos it's not like I left him behind on purpose. From somewhere deep inside me a voice whispers, 'Yes, but you're back now.'

I start to run again.

At the next junction, I turn into yet another corridor, this one with scuffed walls and stained carpet. The lingering smell of paint is gone. At the end of this corridor, a steel door blocks my way. No handle. No keyhole. An electronic lock hugs the wall at head height.

Two other doors flank this one. I try the door on my right. Locked. I try the handle on the left, and it gives so suddenly that I fall headlong through the gap. I steady my footing, step inside, and try to push the door shut behind me. The tatty linoleum underfoot has rucked up and jammed the door partway open, but I wrestle it shut. I'm in a spacious cupboard, lined floor-to-ceiling with shelves full of plastic packs of bog rolls, paper towels, a mishmash of cleaning materials and row upon row of plastic bottles. There's enough light coming in through a high window to read names on labels: Solvitol, Dethlac, Raid. The names don't mean anything to me but the skull and crossbones symbols are clear enough.

The window is ajar. The catch looks broken. I haul a metal trolley loaded with cleaning equipment across to the shelf and scramble up, but the window's much too small to crawl through. Anyway, it leads to an internal courtyard about three metres square, surrounded by impossibly high blank walls. I climb back down, my eyes searching the shelves, desperate for something, anything. A jacket hangs on a door hook. A fumble in its pockets produces a pack of B&H and a green plastic lighter. I pocket the lighter and keep searching. No cash. No passkey. Zilch.

I'm racking my brains for ideas when I hear whistling, then footsteps. I press myself behind the door and slip the knife from Arran's kitchen out of my pocket.

The handle turns and the door pushes inward.

'How many bloody times?' mutters a man's voice.

The linoleum has rucked up again, jamming the door at somewhere around forty-five degrees. Fat fingers grab the handle on both sides and jerk back and forth. The door flies open, hits a jutting shelf, and stops a few centimetres short of smashing into my face. I grip the knife and hold my breath.

The overhead light flicks on and hands reach for the trolley. There's a struggle to close the door but the linoleum is well jammed under there now.

'Sod it,' the voice mutters.

The light flicks off. Wheels squeak. Through the gap between the hinges, I watch a figure dressed in white swipe a card across the electronic lock. The man from the Land Rover. The steel door slowly swings open. The man saunters through, humming loudly. The metal door starts its slow swing back.

It's now or never.

I bolt out of the cupboard and just make it through the gap. I find myself totally exposed in the middle of a long, white corridor. If the cleaner looks back now there's no hiding and no getting away.

But he don't look back, and soon he turns a corner and vanishes, leaving me standing there, clutching the knife and listening to the sound of my own ragged breathing.

A wide set of steps lead upwards, and I take them two at a time and find myself in a corridor that looks familiar. The carpet here has traces of mould along its edges and my heart beats faster as I realise that at last, I know where I am. That's when it really sinks in that I'm back. I pocket the knife, swallow down the panic rising inside me, and take a deep breath in, a slow breath out.

This corridor leads to the swimming pool. I check my watch: 11:08 a.m. My group's got swimming from 11 to 12. The one thing you can rely on in the unit is the routine. It never varies.

At last, I got an idea.

For six years, the swimming pool was the only place I ever felt sane, and even in these circumstances I feel I ought to get some emotional tug out of being here, but the stench of chlorine feels sickly after the clean air of the beach.

Slatted wooden benches are strewn with bundles of clothes, some neatly stacked, others flung in random heaps. Yells and the sound of splashing echo through the tunnel that leads through to the pool. For six years I stripped and changed my clothes at this corner of bench, hemmed in by lockers, as far away from the other boys as it was possible to get. Sometimes I let Oliver squeeze in and share my bit of bench, but often not. A pair of red trousers and a blue T-shirt now claim my corner spot. I don't recognise them. New boy? My gaze travels on until it lands on Fat Michael's neat pile of clothes.

When I edge open the bathroom door, as expected there's no steam, no naked bodies, no yelling and shoving. There's nobody skiving the swim by pretending they need the loo either. Aware that anyone could walk in at any moment, I slip into the end bog and slide its flimsy bolt across. Somebody hasn't bother to flush. Out of habit, my hand reaches up for the dangling chain, but I come to my senses just in time; these old cisterns make a racket to wake the dead. I lower the toilet seat and wriggle into Fat Michael's checked shirt and deerstalker hat, yanking the ear flaps over my face and trying not to think of this same cloth rubbing against Fat Michael's flaky skin. I hunch my shoulders and scrutinise my reflection in the steel-panelled door. Not bad. If I keep my head down and my mouth shut, nobody'll suspect a thing.

I'm halfway back across the changing rooms when a voice stops me dead.

'Hey, pizza face. How'd you get out here before me? I got permission to use the loo, not you.'

I hunch my shoulders and clench my fists, ready for the first blow. A hand grabs my arm and spins me around. 'You!'

It's not like I haven't fantasised about what I'd like to do to Freaky Adam, the thousand unusual ways I could pay him back for every vicious trick he's pulled, but right here, right now, I don't care about any of that. All that matters is shutting him up.

My fist slams into his face, sending him sprawling to the floor. I leap on top, clawing for his mouth, trying to smother it before he can yell for help, but his skin, still wet from the pool, slides out of my grasp. My balance goes and suddenly I'm the one on the floor and his hands are squeezing my neck. I scratch, draw blood, but he don't let up. My hand gropes towards my pocket for the knife but his weight is on me and I can't reach. Spit gurgles in my throat. I can't breathe. Freaky Adam's teeth are bared, his eyes screwed tight, his hands squeezing, squeezing.

Crack.

The sound is distant, like something happening in another world, another time. In this place, in this time, I'm drifting, sinking.

Crack.

Clearer. Louder.

The hands around my throat go slack. Air explodes into my lungs, and I splutter and choke. Above me, Freaky

Adam's head droops forwards like he's leaning in for a kiss. I dredge up the last of my strength and roll sideways.

Freaky Adam's head hits the floor.

Oliver is standing over us, clutching a slat of wood like it's a cricket bat. A huge grin splits his pale face in half. Blood smears his nose and mouth and he's looking at me like I'm a film star who's just walked into McDonald's or something.

'That old nosebleed trick still working then?' I scramble to my feet, rubbing my throat. 'No wonder your timings are shit.'

His grin grows wider. 'Sir's sent me back to the residential zone, told me to sort myself out for fuck's sake.' He hops from foot to foot. 'How did …? Where did you …?'

Guilt washes through me. Even ignoring the self-induced nosebleed, the consequences of me not being here to protect him are written all over his neck and face, and I've barely given my only friend a passing thought.

'Shh. Do you want me to get caught?'

'Caught? You mean—'

'Shut up.'

I poke Freaky Adam with my toe. He's out cold.

'Why are you wearing—'

'Later. I promise. Right now, we got to move him.'

Without hesitation, Oliver pushes the flop of fringe off his face then leans down and grabs one of Freaky Adam's hands. Together we drag him into the bathroom, across the urinal floor, and prop him against a toilet. My belt secures his wrists to the cistern. Oliver finds a towel and designs a makeshift gag.

We stand back to admire our handiwork.

'Is he, you know, dead?'

Freaky Adam's face is deathly pale and suddenly I don't feel so smug. If he's dead, that really would make me and Oliver murderers. I dig Freaky Adam in the ribs. My finger leaves an indent on the pale flesh. Placing a finger around his flabby wrist, I check for a pulse and find one.

'No.'

'What if he, you know, wakes up?'

'We got to hope he don't.'

Oliver reaches past me, grabs both sides of the makeshift gag, pulls forwards and slams back. A red smudge appears on the white tiles behind Freaky Adam's head, clots in his hair. I swear I'm about to protest when I notice the multi-layers of bruises on Oliver's face and neck.

'Just to be on the safe side,' he grins.

I shrug and leave Oliver in the cubicle, telling him to lock the door from the inside, then slide underneath. I pretend not to hear the quick succession of whumps as a fist lands in flesh. That's not cos I'm a sicko or a PSK or anything. It's cos Freaky Adam deserves everything he gets.

When Oliver comes crawling under the door, grinning and panting, I throw some loo roll and his clothes at him. 'Clean your face up and get dressed.'

To enter the residential zone, we got to get through security. Sweat trickles down my face, my scalp hot under the furry hat. I jam my hands deep into Fat Michael's pockets and resist the urge to scratch. Once inside the residential zone, there'll be few enough checkpoints, cos they like to sell us the illusion of freedom. What there will be instead are cameras, everywhere. I think of Arran, growing up free, touring America with his mother, and for a second I regret the way we left it. I might never see him or Kaye again, and they'll never know how much it meant to me, being part of their life even for a tiny bit. It's the only time I ever felt clean.

I bury the thought, stow it away in a mental vault. I'll sort it out later – if there is a later. For now, I bend my head low and keep in step with Oliver.

We reach the entrance and I hear the faint whirr of a lens pushing in for a close-up.

'Michael's feeling sick,' Oliver says to the camera. 'Sir said we could cut our swim short.'

The camera whirrs again and I clutch my stomach as though it aches. A soft click and the door swings open.

The walls gleam with that familiar institutional white, but here in our home area, the white is broken up by gaudy displays of artwork, stories, poems. Display boards sag under the weight of framed pictures of boys undertaking projects in science and geography. Glossy achievement charts boast about progress. And, most sickening of all, photographs record us 'having a good time' at the pool, in the exercise yard, sowing seeds and tending plants in the garden area. And here's a photograph of me, standing chest-high in water, swimming goggles pushed on top of my head. Blank eyes stare into the camera. I hardly recognise myself. The boy in that photograph looks frozen on the inside.

'What's wrong?'

'Nothing. Listen, Oliver, I got to get to Wilson's office to look for something, something that could help me, could help us.'

Oliver frowns, then his face brightens. 'We could go to the therapy suites. Me and Michael are booked in for the next session. I'm with Matron and Michael's with Dr Carl. That'll take us right next to Wilson's room. He's been off sick all week.'

He beams his little-boy smile, and I could almost hug him.

CHAPTER TWENTY

We've reached the heart of the unit. An electronic lock controls access into the therapy suite, which is made up of meeting rooms where all the counselling sessions go on. At the back of each meeting room, another locked door leads into each counsellor's private office. Although I never personally been through there, I hear each counsellor's office has got a further security door that leads to the staff zone. The division between staff and patient zones is sacrosanct, and to my knowledge no boy has ever made it beyond the meeting rooms.

Oliver nudges me.

Matron is approaching, her blonde ponytail swinging as she teeters, heavily laden with folders and books. I hunch my shoulders, Fat Michael-style, and pretend to study a photograph on the wall, a group of sullen boys playing football in the exercise yard.

'Oliver, so sorry, am I late?'

'No Miss. I'm, you know, early.'

Matron comes to a halt just behind me. 'I'm not quite set up yet. Would you mind waiting out here a bit longer?'

'Course not, Miss,' Oliver says, and I think we're going to be all right but then he goes on, 'We, you know, didn't want to hang around in the zone.' His tone implies there's been trouble, and if Matron wasn't stood right there, I'd kick him.

I sense her gaze on my neck. 'Are you all right, Michael?'

Reaching under my hat to scratch, I grunt and shrug my shoulders, squint harder at the photograph. For a moment, it's like time stops still, then Matron sighs and behind me a door opens, then closes.

A hand tugs at my sleeve. 'She's gone.'

Before I get chance to congratulate myself on choosing a disguise that actually works, the door right in front of me opens and Miss Beryl starts to walk through it. I duck and spin around, but she's already clocked my face.

'David!'

I spin back around and shove her into her room, my hand over her mouth. Oliver follows me in, shuts the door and pins her arms behind her. I pull the knife out of my pocket and wave it around to punctuate my words. 'Not … a … fucking … sound. Got it?'

At the sight of the knife, Oliver grins and Miss Beryl's training kicks in. She stops struggling and visibly relaxes as she slips her bland counsellor face on, masking any fear and whatever else I saw in her eyes a moment ago.

My hands are shaking. The familiar smell of her perfume confuses me. Up close, she looks even more drawn and weak.

'Not so tight,' I say to Oliver, who scowls at me but allows her arms to drop a few centimetres lower. 'I'm going to take my hand away, Miss, but if you make a sound, it'll be the last one you ever make. Got it?'

She nods and I remove my hand from her mouth.

'You startled me, David,' she says, her voice calm. 'What are you doing here? Why are you wearing Michael's clothes?'

'I'll ask the questions today, Miss.'

'Yeah,' Oliver pipes up, 'we'll tell *you* when you can talk.'

The only way I was ever getting out of the unit alive was if nobody knew I'd even been in here. Sneak in, sneak out. That was my plan. Now what? Unable to think, I need to act, so I haul a leather chair out from behind Miss Beryl's desk and plonk it down in the middle of the room. 'Sit.'

Oliver lets go of her arms, and she obeys me and sits, which comes as a relief. The chair expels a soft whoosh of air as she lowers herself onto it. My eyes are drawn to the row of pills on her desk.

'How is it?' I ask. 'The … you know.'

'Cancer. You can say it, David.'

'Cancer?' Oliver's eyes grow wide.

'Shut up,' I say.

He dips his head and busies himself rummaging through Miss Beryl's desk, yanking drawers open.

Miss Beryl cocks her head at me. 'You didn't tell him?'

'I promised, didn't I?'

She gets this weird expression on her face. 'Thank you.'

I shrug. She's doing that bonding thing and we don't got time for this shit, but I don't know what to do next either, so I mumble, 'S'okay.'

'Seeing as you ask, it's not so good. The cancer.'

'You look all right to me,' I lie.

'Yes, well, it's not the outside that's the problem.' She attempts a smile. 'You know, when I heard about the crash, it seemed impossible you could have survived, and yet I've had this feeling all week … What are you doing here, David? Why did you come back?'

'Why d'you think?'

She considers me for a moment. 'Revenge?'

'Is that what you really believe, Miss?'

'No.' Her eyes search my face. 'No, I don't think it is.'

'But you do believe I'm a psychopath? A serial killer?'

She opens her mouth. Closes it again.

'I know all about the PSK thing, Miss, and I know that what you're doing here is illegal, so there's no point lying.'

Somewhere behind her counsellor's mask, her eyes register surprise.

'You've been busy, David.'

'What did I do, Miss? What did I do that made it okay to lock me up?'

'You didn't *do* anything.' She shakes her head at me like I'm being a bit dim. 'That's not how this works.'

'So how does it work? Don't fuck with me, Miss. I got nothing to lose here, and I'll know if you're lying.'

'Fair enough.' Miss Beryl clears her throat, stares at the ceiling, then at her knees, then finally lifts her gaze to meet mine. 'Sounds like you've figured a lot of this out already, David, but, well, okay.' She clears her throat again and nods, as much to herself as to me. 'We've been able to ... to diagnose psychopathy for a long time now.' She gives me an apologetic smile. 'The problem is, only a tiny minority of psychopaths are also PSKs, and in the past we've had to wait for them to kill before we could do anything about it. And that's obviously too late for the innocent victims.'

'You're saying you can tell now, without waiting?'

She nods. 'We can predict which ones will become serial killers. It's a combination of an MRI scan and a diagnosis using the Homicidal Triad, together with family history.'

Oliver looks up from where he's punching papers with a stapler on Miss Beryl's desk. 'The homicidal what?'

'Triad. It means three-pronged. In this case, late bed-wetting, bit of a loner, interested in arson. I'm simplifying here, but by using these tools we can find our PSKs *before* they inflict terrible damage, and, in the main, we can prevent them from ever acting out.'

'You saying you can fix them?'

She smiles. 'That's the whole point, David. The most important letter in PSK is the letter P for potential. This isn't about who you are, it's about who you will become if you aren't pointed in another direction. It's not your history, it's your future.'

The air in the room feels hot, sticky. 'Rubbish. No one can know the future.' I yank Fat Michael's hat off my head and fling it to the floor.

'Oh, but in this case we *can*. We can predict with one hundred percent accuracy who will develop into a PSK. In the vast majority of cases, this programme can prevent a PSK from ever developing into a killer and we can watch them closely to make sure that remains the case. They can go on with their lives without wrecking the lives of so many others. That's what makes the programme so exciting.' She gives him a sad smile. 'You needed help, David. That's why you came to us.'

I been watching her face closely while she tells me all this, and she's telling what she believes to be the truth. Her truth. She really thinks she been saving us this whole time.

'What about those who fail the programme?'

She pauses. 'I'm trying to explain—'

'I failed, didn't I?'

Her face hardens. 'I tried everything in my power to help you, David. Everything.'

'Is that how you justify it to yourself? Is that how you sleep at night? They tried to kill me.'

'Nonsense. You would have been taken care of, but you wouldn't have been allowed to act out your fantasies in the wider community. I'm sorry, David. It's not your fault, but how is it right to the families of your future victims to let their suffering happen when we could prevent it?'

'And what if you're wrong?'

'Look, there's always going to be the small possibility that in the future, a released patient could undergo triggers that sets them back onto the wrong path. But in the rare case where that might happen, we know them and we'll recall them quickly, so the programme will still have prevented huge numbers of terrible crimes from being committed.' Her mouth sets in a straight line. 'But we're not wrong about who is or isn't a PSK in the first place. It's the accuracy of our diagnosis that allows me to sleep at night. This is my life's work, David. There's no bycatch factor.'

'Bycatch?'

She has the good grace to blush as she explains to me how bycatch is a fisherman's term for the creatures you net by mistake when you're trawling for something else. Every psychological test known to man has a quota of false positives in its result – the inevitable bycatch – except, according to Beryl, the one for PSKs. This test is one hundred percent accurate, and I failed it so I needed to be brought into the unit. That's why she can sleep at night.

'Are you okay?' Oliver says to me, and I jump cos I've sort of forgotten he's here. 'You look, you know, funny.'

I blink and shake the buzzing out of my head. Oliver is perched on a stool behind Miss Beryl's desk, thumbing through a stack of papers, tossing each one to the floor once he's scanned it.

I look at Miss Beryl. I got to find a way to shake her out of her religious belief in this place.

'Okay,' I try. 'Let's say I buy into the idea that you're right to lock us up in here in the first place, cos you're only trying to save us from ourselves, whatever. But what if the programme, the way you figure out who's no longer a *potential*, has been corrupted?'

Her face creases with sympathy. 'I'm sorry, David. I've been through your files with a fine-tooth comb. All the evidence is there.'

'What if I told you that my files are full of lies, that Wilson has been making stuff up about me?'

A flicker of doubt passes across her face.

I turn to Oliver. 'Listen. Leave that. I need you to tell Miss Beryl the truth about something, okay?'

He puts down the pile of papers he's rifling through. 'Sure.'

'Right, so, do you remember when you got your head shoved down the bog? Yeah? Okay, tell Miss Beryl who did it. Go on, you can tell her the absolute truth.'

Oliver looks at Miss Beryl with his huge eyes. 'Freaky Adam,' he says.

Miss Beryl frowns, and I'm right on it.

'I've seen my notes, Miss. No, listen, it don't matter how. In them, Wilson says I confessed it was me who did that, but I didn't do it, and I didn't confess to doing it. Why would I? Wilson lied.'

Oliver beams at me but Miss Beryl looks doubtful, so I press on. 'When it happened, I was in the pool, with Carson. You were off on holiday, remember, but you'd arranged extra evening sessions for me while you were away.'

'But the assault on Oliver took place during morning showers,' she says.

'That's a lie.'

We both look to Oliver, who says, 'It was, you know, around teatime.'

'See. He got targeted cos I wasn't around to protect him. You can check. He spent the night in CSU. There's bound to be records.'

Silence stretches between us for what seems an age. Miss Beryl's eyes are lined with dark shadows. 'Why would Mr Wilson lie about a thing like that, David?'

'I don't know. That's why I came back; to prove he's been lying, cos there are other lies in the files I saw too.'

'Such as?'

'What does it say in there about Kamal Chakrabarti, Miss? That's right, nothing. You've never heard of him, have you? But when I got brought in here, they told my mum it was cos I'd drowned this boy from my school, Kamal Chakrabarti.' I pause. 'They didn't say they thought I'd turn out to be a killer, they said I already was one. They started lying about me before I even came in here. Somebody's set me up and Wilson is part of it.'

'Oh, now you're really letting your imagination—'

'I been asking myself why, and the truth is, I don't got a clue. I just know that they're lying about me. I know they're trying to make me out to be something I'm not.'

'Look, David—'

'If you're so sure you're right, Miss, why not put it to the test? I don't know why Wilson set me up, but if there are copies of my files still here, I'll prove to you that he did.'

I take a step forward, lay the knife on the desk within her reach and step back again, my hands out, palms up.

'If it turns out I'm wrong, well, then you get to hand me over with a clear conscience. You'll have my blessing to sleep at night. What you got to lose?'

She stares at me for the longest time, then shakes her head. 'I can't believe I'm agreeing to this.'

'Are you saying you'll help me?'

She pauses. 'I've been worried about Mark Wilson for a while now. There's something going on with him; he's jittery, evasive. I'd made up my mind today to flag up a formal concern, not something one likes to do to a fellow professional.' She nods her head. 'Yes, I'm saying I'll help you.'

Air escapes my lungs so fast my knees buckle.

'I've given my life to this project, David, and I don't have all that long left. If there's something wrong, I want to know about it.' She picks up the knife. 'But if I find out you're lying, you'll get no more help from me. Understood?'

'Understood.'

CHAPTER TWENTY-ONE

Miss Beryl's been gone forever. She said it'd only take her five minutes to grab Wilson's files and bring them back here. I'm probably a fool to trust her, but truth is, I'm a sitting duck. There's nothing to stop her turning me in, and nothing I can do about it if she does. My fingers trace the shape of the bear in my pocket. Whatever Jeannie might got to say about it, options are for other people, not the likes of me.

'How long now?' Oliver asks.

I check my watch again. 'Twelve minutes.'

He opens the outer door and scans the corridor. 'Come on.'

I hesitate, grab Fat Michael's hat, then follow him out.

We scurry past three rooms to reach Wilson's office. A green light shines above the door, which tells me it's unlocked. I pull up short. No way Miss Beryl would risk someone walking in on her rooting through Wilson's drawers. She would've locked it behind her. Oliver forges on ahead and enters the room, and before I can decide whether to hide or bolt, his grinning face pokes out of Wilson's doorway.

'Come on.'

A distant bell rings out, marking the end of the swimming session. Any minute now, Fat Michael will discover his clothes missing, which might or might not be taken seriously. How long before they find Freaky Adam? That's when all hell will break loose. I follow Oliver through the door and groan as it clicks shut behind me.

My gaze sweeps the circle of plastic chairs and comes to rest on the ball sitting on Wilson's black leather throne. I pick up the speakeasy and run my finger along a repair in its stitching. A flush of terror passes through me. I'm back inside these walls and I came here of my own free will. My head spins and I grab Wilson's chairback to stop myself falling.

'Look.' Oliver's voice cracks like a whip through the buzz building up in my brain. His eyes are like gobstoppers and he's clutching something in his hand. Something flat.

'Let me see that.' I snatch the object off him. There's a miniature photo of Miss Beryl set in a plastic key fob.

'It's a, you know, real key.' Oliver's grin splits his face. In the unit, it's every boy's dream to get their hands on a passkey.

'It's Miss Beryl's.' I look around like she might still be there. 'She must've dropped it.'

'Try it on this door.' Oliver points to Wilson's private office.

'Something's happened to her. Maybe someone caught her going through Wilson's stuff.' I hold up the passkey and examine it, questions fizzing through my brain. 'I bet she left that door open, like a signal to say something's wrong. I bet she dropped the key on purpose.'

Oliver grabs the passkey out of my hand and swipes it through the lock. The door to Wilson's office slides open.

The room is sparsely furnished in cheerless shades of brown: a battered wooden desk, a worn leather chair, a computer, a couple of metal shelves holding a few dusty textbooks and a pot of hair cream. Gross. The only bit of colour in the room is the screensaver, a bubbling mountain stream. I imagine Wilson sitting in this little cell of an office, dreaming about being somewhere else.

The drawers hold nothing but empty mint wrappers and a screwed-up cigarette carton. A waft of peppermint fills my nostrils and my head spins again. This time I grab the desk for balance, which disturbs the computer monitor. The screensaver vanishes and is replaced by a blank green screen with an open square window in one corner. A flicker of movement catches my eye. I hit the full-screen symbol. A fuzzy fish-eye view of a corridor pops up. Two figures are walking away from the camera.

I'd know Wilson's shiny bald head anywhere. He's not off sick. He's right here, with Miss Beryl walking ahead of him, glancing back, saying something. He shoves her onward. The two figures disappear around a corner.

I grab the key back off Oliver and rush to the outer door, swipe the lock, then hesitate. Once we go through this door, we'll be in the staff zone and no amount of disguise or bullshit will save us.

'You don't got to come,' I say to Oliver. 'Freaky Adam don't know who hit him. If you go back now, nobody'll know a thing about it.'

'Are you kidding?' Oliver snatches the passkey out of my hand. 'This is the most fun I've had in, you know, forever.' He grins, marches out into the empty corridor and fist-pumps the air.

'Shh,' I say, and we both strain to listen. Somewhere to our left, a door clicks shut. 'Quick.'

We sprint down the passageway but soon pull up short, our way blocked by a steel door. Oliver produces Miss Beryl's passkey with a flourish, and sure enough it performs its magic. We move on through and another bell signals the start of the next session. Registers will be checked, names will be called, Oliver's and Freaky Adam's absences will be noted. A search will be carried out.

We edge forward, past a set of stairs leading down to my left.

'Where are we?' Oliver whispers, his breath warm on my ear.

'Shh.'

A faint noise floats up the open stairway. A door closing? I grab Oliver's arm and descend into a cold corridor that stinks of airless rooms and wet plaster. Plastic crackles underfoot. Bare light bulbs shed a sickly glow over half-finished walls and unpainted skirting boards. We're back in the hidden parts of the unit.

Every door is locked. We pass more of those little cells I saw earlier, and Oliver stays so close to me we're in danger of tripping. I stick out my elbows and try to push him off, but he stays closer than a shadow.

At the next junction we stop.

'Listen.'

In the distance, somebody cries out. We strain our ears but the silence resumes. We continue walking until we come to a set of double doors, where we press our faces to the small windows set into their upper halves.

Ladders, paint, and scaffolding lie in pockets of clutter around a cavernous room. Stacks of bricks are piled up in patches as though they've collapsed there. A collection of fire hydrants and casings of alarm boxes lie thrown together like casualties of war, wire spilling out of their guts.

In the middle of the room, Miss Beryl is perched on a low stack of cement sacks, head bowed. Wilson is pacing in front of her, facing Miss Beryl, his back to us. I edge the handle down and ease the door ajar. A good few metres inside the room, a de-humidifier is thrumming away, good and loud, which easily covers any noise my feet make as I slip into the room and crawl behind the nearest stack of bricks.

Gaps between the bricks form perfect spyholes. I check to make sure Wilson's still got his back to the door, then I turn around, intending to signal Oliver to follow me, but Oliver is already lying at my feet, eyes wide. I put a finger to my lips and mime a 'shh'.

'Tell me where he is,' Wilson says right into Miss Beryl's face. 'Come on. Now. Before they get here.'

Oliver grips my arm tight and mouths, 'Who?'

I shake my head at him just as Miss Beryl echoes his question back at us.

'Before who gets here? Mark? Who did you call? Who's coming? Talk to me, Mark.'

I recognise what she's doing, taking over the conversation. One minute he's asking her to tell him something and the next she's asking him to tell her something. She been doing that to me for years. Problem is, Wilson's a trained counsellor himself, and he's having none of it.

'Nice try. Tell me where he is, or stay quiet and we'll let them get it out of you instead. See if you're so full of it then, hmm?' He pushes away from her and paces up and down, passing so close to where me and Oliver are crouched that I can smell his sweat, can hear the rasp in his chest as he lights a cigarette and inhales. His shirt is crumpled and stained, his shoulders hunched, his skin dull. All his cock-of-the-walk energy has drained away. He looks at his watch, then at the door.

'Surely we can sort this out before things get out of hand?' Miss Beryl struggles to her feet and the effort shows on her face. It's like she's suddenly turned into a really old woman.

'Sit down,' Wilson snaps.

When she don't do as she's told, he strides across the room and shoves her back onto the bags of cement. I grope in my pocket for the knife. Empty. Damn it, I gave it to Miss Beryl. Stupid, stupid, stupid.

Oliver is clinging to my sleeve now, clearly not finding this fun anymore. 'Let go,' I hiss, trying to prise his fingers off me. If I can get a bit closer, take Wilson by surprise, I got a chance. I need to do it now, before whoever is coming gets here, but Oliver won't let go.

'What's going on?' Miss Beryl says. 'Just tell me. Mark?'

Wilson shakes his head. 'They're not going to let the likes of David Jessop screw it all up now, not when we're so close.'

He's standing directly ahead of me, the perfect chance to take him, but at the sound of my name, I freeze on the spot.

'You've been lying about your sessions with David. Falsifying your notes. Haven't you, Mark? Why would you do that?' Miss Beryl's eyes widen. 'Did we make some sort of mistake with David's diagnosis? Is that what you're covering up? Look, whatever this is, I'm sure we can clear it up if you just—'

Wilson laughs, a loud bark of a laugh. 'Mistakes? Oh, Beryl, you really are precious.'

'Look, Mark, I know the main functions of the system are foolproof – identifying the PSKs, filtering out those who intervention fails with – but not if somebody tampers with them. Have you tampered with the filtering system, Mark?'

Wilson sighs. 'Keep up, Beryl. Nothing's foolproof. They haven't perfected the research into identifying PSKs. This *is* the research, warts and all. You're a scientist, you know that every test has false positives, hmm? If they could get your lot to believe we had an infallible method of identifying these kids, just because you want it to be true, they knew they wouldn't have any trouble selling that idea to

Joe Public. We've got about four bycatch in our current intake, fifteen percent. About average.'

Miss Beryl goes pale. Her voice is a strangled whisper when she says, 'Four bycatch?'

He almost looks like he pities her. 'Yes, bycatch, false positives, call them what you like.'

My brain scrabbles to keep up. Is he saying there are four innocent boys in here?

Miss Beryl looks like she might faint. 'You're saying David really could be innocent?'

'You're missing the point,' Wilson sneers. 'They're all innocent, hmm? That hasn't stopped you from being a part of having them locked up though, has it?' He laughs. 'Don't worry. Your precious David isn't bycatch. He's something else altogether. You really have no idea who you're messing with, do you?'

The words 'David isn't bycatch' roll around and around on a loop in my head, blocking out the rest of what they're saying. When I manage to tune back in, Wilson is speaking.

'... units just like this one are being prepared all across the country.'

'But why? PSKs are so rare. There are only—'

'PSKs are just the start. You have to look at the bigger picture. Once they have the power to weed out problem children there'll be no stopping them. Intervention's the first step. As soon as people accept that principle, the next step will be to prevent undesirables from getting born in the first place. After that, they'll expand into other areas of life.'

'But that's not what we're about here, Mark. We—'

'Oh, for fuck's sake, wake up. That's exactly what we're about. Controlled breeding. Think about it. No more juvenile delinquents. No more fucked up kids growing up to commit burglary, rape, murder. It's a brave new world, Beryl, and you've played your part in creating it.'

'But what you're describing, that's—'

'It's the future,' he says. 'You can't stop it.'

I picture Kaye, marching in London, and my breath catches. What chance has she got? What chance has any of us got?

'You're a fool, Beryl,' Wilson says. 'A small-minded fool. Tell me where David is, hmm? I know you've seen him.' He pushes his face right into hers. 'Tell me, or you'll be sorry.'

'Never.'

Miss Beryl makes a sudden run for the door. Wilson leaps and grabs her. I shove Oliver's hands away and am halfway to my feet when the double doors crash open and Drummond comes striding into the room, Carson jangling at his heels.

Oliver yanks my shirt, and my jellied legs collapse me back to the floor. I choke down the scream building inside me. I'm too late, I've left it too late.

'Thank god,' Miss Beryl cries.

'Carson,' Wilson says, releasing his grip on Miss Beryl and sending her stumbling into Drummond's chest.

Drummond plants his free hand on Miss Beryl's arm and walks her in reverse until she's back sitting on the cement sacks.

Wilson stares at Drummond. 'Who's this?' he asks Carson.

Drummond's thin lips twist into a smile, and he takes a briefcase off Carson and lays it at Miss Beryl's feet. 'I'm the man who's going to sort this fucking mess out for you,' he says to Wilson as he smooths his hand across the lid of the case.

Seeing the briefcase reminds me that I still don't got any evidence. I got nothing. And now Drummond and Carson are here, and I'm trapped, and Miss Beryl is in serious danger, and the future is coming and there's nothing I can do about any of it. It's as much as I can manage to not throw up.

'I'm Mark Wilson. It was me who caught her and brought her down here.' He hovers at Drummond's shoulder. 'She's seen David. She won't tell me where he is, but I know her, and I know she's seen him.'

'Don't worry.' Drummond pops the catches on the briefcase. 'She'll talk.'

CHAPTER TWENTY-TWO

Drummond stubs out his cigar and stands in front of Miss Beryl with this big, sick grin on his face. She stares at the briefcase like it's a bomb, and from this angle I can't see what's inside, so it might be. Deep in my gut I'm wondering if they've found Mum, found Jeannie, found Arran and Kaye. Has Drummond made *them* talk.

'What's he going to do?' Oliver whispers in my ear.

I slap a hand over his mouth. If Drummond realises we're here, only a metre away …

'I caught her going through my files,' Wilson whines. 'She's helping him. I'd bet my life on it.'

'You just did,' Drummond says, which shuts Wilson up.

'Carson?' Miss Beryl calls out. 'Carson, what are you doing? We're friends, aren't we? Please, Mark's lost it. He's—'

'Cut the crap,' Drummond says.

Carson looks like he's about to say something, but Drummond throws him a look. Carson scowls and shuts his mouth, fiddles with some kind of earpiece he's wearing. He keeps his gaze off Miss Beryl.

Drummond keeps his eyes fixed on her. 'Where's the Jessop boy?'

Miss Beryl looks again at Carson, but he refuses to catch her eye. She gives up and turns back to Drummond. 'I don't know where he is, how could I? If I did know, why wouldn't I tell you? Out there, he's a threat to every one of us. Be realistic.'

'But you're not a realist, are you, Beryl? You're a moralist, an idealist.'

'She's lying. Aren't you Beryl, hmm?'

'Shut it, Wilson.' Drummond throws Wilson a look then crouches down, reaches into the briefcase and withdraws a long black truncheon, the kind an old-fashioned policeman in a black-and-white movie might carry.

Oliver's breath grows hot under my palm as he wriggles. I grip onto him tighter, partly to keep him quiet, partly cos I need to cling onto something, someone, and right now he's all I got.

'This is a simple tool; a bit like you, Beryl.' Drummond circles her, tracing the truncheon along her neck. 'But even the simplest instrument can be effective in the right hands. You will tell me what I want to know.'

'This is crazy.' The fear in Miss Beryl's voice makes my stomach clench.

'Well, we're in the right place for crazy.' Drummond laughs and brings the truncheon to a rest across her throat.

'Carson, please ...'

Carson ignores her and fiddles with his earpiece. 'The march has turned into a full-scale riot,' he informs Drummond. 'Twenty-five protesters dead in Hyde Park.'

'That's twenty-five fewer snowflakes to worry about,' Drummond laughs.

My breath feels thick as I struggle to hold off a rising panic. Please, please don't let one of them be Kaye.

'You're all heart, Drummond.' Carson's eyes flash. 'My sister's no snowflake and she's gone on that march.'

'More fool you for letting her.' Drummond points at the earpiece. 'Take that thing out.'

Carson stares at Drummond, who glares right back until Carson yanks the earpiece out and lets it dangle on his shoulder. 'You're the boss.'

'Glad you realise that.' Drummond sighs. 'Okay, Beryl, to business.' He lifts her chin back with the truncheon and leans right into her face. 'First of all, one of our digital trackers triggered unusual activity on your medical records yesterday. We don't know who yet – don't worry, we'll find out soon enough – but somebody who works in the maternity ward of all places, opened your medical records. Not planning on getting pregnant at your age, are you? No, thought not. Then today, Wilson here tells me he found you in his room going through Jessop's files. And, on top of all that, somebody's taken a piss in a bucket in your garage. Now, I find all this very interesting, don't you?'

Bile forms in the back of my throat. They know. They *know*.

'I told you,' Wilson says, triumphant. 'I told you she was up to something.'

'And I told you to shut up.'

'That's why I brought her down here, why I—'

Drummond swings the truncheon wide, and Wilson's nose explodes in a cloud of red as his feet leave the floor. Miss Beryl screams. I clamp my hand even tighter across Oliver's mouth and hold on fast.

Drummond tuts as Carson hauls the shocked and bloody Wilson to his feet. Blood streams out of Wilson's mouth and nose as he splutters, coughs, sways. Carson hands him a crisp white handkerchief. Within seconds, red soaks right through it and pours down his chin, his neck, his shirt. Wilson shakes his head and blood splashes the floor.

'Stay still.' Carson dabs a second handkerchief at Wilson's chin.

'I've lost a tooth.' Wilson probes his mouth, his voice shrill. 'I've lost two teeth.'

Drummond shrugs. 'I told you to keep your mouth shut.'

Wilson stares bug-eyed at Drummond, and for a moment I almost feel sorry for him. Almost.

Drummond wipes his truncheon with a tissue and frowns. 'Did anybody see you bring her down here? Anything we should worry about?'

'No. No. I was careful. No one saw a thing.'

'Good.'

'So can I go now?' Hope shines in Wilson's eyes, grotesque against the backdrop of smeared blood. 'I don't want to be here when you' – he glances at Miss Beryl – 'do what you need to do.'

'Sensitive. Nice.' Carson pushes the saturated hanky into Wilson's hand.

'Can't think what else we need you for,' Drummond says. He smiles a thin-lipped smile that seems to be aimed more at Carson than Wilson.

Carson gestures at Wilson to take off his shirt. 'Can't have you going out of here looking like that can we?'

Wilson tears off his bloodied shirt and flings it aside.

The next few seconds happen so smoothly my brain don't grasp straight away what's going on. Wilson is spitting on a tissue and scrubbing blood from his face. Carson's shedding his own jumper as though intending to offer it as a replacement, all the while giving it out friendly enough with that smile that's not a smile. Wilson strains a smile back at him. Everybody's smiling, except Miss Beryl, who looks like she might be praying. Carson stretches out the arm he's got the jumper in and hooks it around Wilson's shoulders. A gun appears out of nowhere. Carson places the muzzle on the side of Wilson's head, shoves the jumper over it, and pulls the trigger.

The explosion is shockingly quiet.

Wilson slides down Carson's chest and lands in a heap at his feet. Carson lifts his legs free and drops the bloody jumper to the floor, a look of distaste on his face. Miss Beryl starts to sob.

Oliver wriggles, slippery as a fish beneath my clammy hands. Carson tucks his gun into the back of his trousers.

'Now, if there are no more interruptions ...' Drummond turns his attention back to Miss Beryl.

I don't do anything. I can't. It's like I've stopped functioning, stopped breathing, stopped feeling, stopped thinking. I can't tear my eyes off Wilson's body with its mannequin-like limbs sticking out at angles. But I'm watching it in the same way I'd watch a movie, knowing it's not real. The smile on Wilson's lips looks frozen and fake, but his blood looks real enough, and when the metallic, tight smell of it reaches me, I gag. A physical reaction, not an emotional one. I don't think I got any emotions left. I'm cold as ice.

A warm wetness seeps into the chill of my knees and brings me back to earth. I look down. Oliver is lying in a pool of his own piss, staring at Wilson. I try to cover his eyes, but he pushes my hands away.

Neither of the men so much as glance at the corpse. They got all their focus on Miss Beryl, who looks fit to faint. And while they're watching Miss Beryl, they got their backs to the door.

I drag Oliver's head around and force his gaze towards the collection of fire extinguishers heaped against the wall. If we can set off the alarm then maybe, just maybe, someone will come. I can't believe that Matron, with her Pollyanna blonde ponytail, is any more a part of this than Miss Beryl is. It was important to Drummond that nobody else saw Wilson bring Miss Beryl down here, so there will be others who don't got a clue what's really going on.

I point to the extinguishers and mimic striking a match, then I reach into my pocket and produce the green plastic lighter. I press both the lighter and Miss Beryl's passkey into Oliver's hands. His white knuckles fold around them. I point to the extinguishers again and then to the door.

Oliver, the unit's resident expert on fire-starting, shakes his head, nostrils flaring, eyes over-bright against sheet-white cheeks. As the dehumidifier breaks into a protracted and loud humming, I put my mouth to his ear and whisper, 'Let's you and me bring it all down, yeah?'

Oliver clasps and unclasps the lighter in his hand, then wipes his knuckles across his snot-smudged face, turns onto his hands and knees, and crawls towards the exit. Without a ripple, he slips out of the room.

Miss Beryl screams, a piercing shriek that sounds like it's being ripped right out of her guts.

I push to my feet and step out from behind my sanctuary of bricks.

'You wanted me, I'm here. Leave her alone.'

I get my wish, as two black guns swing in my direction.

Drummond grins, and through a hazy fug I see Miss Beryl shake her head and sob. That's when it sinks in – Miss Beryl's trump card was the fact that she knew where I was hiding, and now I've gone and revealed her hand.

Drummond flicks his tongue across his lower lip and looks at me like I'm a tasty new snack he's always wanted to try.

Miss Beryl's skirt is hitched up around her hips, revealing thighs covered in raised red welts. Terror – the real, sweaty, what-the-fuck-have-I-done sort of terror – bubbles up in my throat and threatens to choke me. I swallow hard.

Drummond gestures to Carson, who works his way around the room, checking behind every brick, every sack. 'Clear,' he says, before coming to stand behind Miss Beryl.

Drummond yanks the deerstalker hat off my head. Without it, I feel naked and exposed. 'Welcome to the party, David Jessop.' He grins. 'Shall we dance?'

The truncheon arcs and catches my shoulder, and as I stagger backwards, flailing for balance, I swear I see Carson start towards Drummond then stop himself. Hot pain shoots down my arm, and despite my best intentions, I let out a howl. Carson's face is blank as he stares at me, and I think I must've imagined his reaction a moment ago.

Drummond chuckles and rubs his thumb up and down the truncheon. 'Well, much as I'd like to stay and play, David, time's getting on, so let's get down to business. I want to know where you've been, who you've spoken to, and how you got back in here. And you're going to tell me.'

I stiffen my shoulders and thrust my chin out. Drummond shakes his head as though disappointed in me. Then he turns towards Miss Beryl and signals to Carson, who pins her arms behind her back. She squeals and thrashes, her eyes wide with terror.

'Wait,' I cry. 'I'll tell you everything.' Carson releases Miss Beryl and steps back.

Drummond taps the truncheon against his palm and grins. 'Let's start with some names, shall we?'

Names? My mouth won't work. Whose name should I give him? Mum's, Jeannie's, Arran's, Kaye's? My eyes flick to Wilson's bloody corpse. I'd be signing their death warrant.

'I thought you wanted to co-operate, David,' Drummond says.

I look at Miss Beryl. She looks straight back at me, and something happens in her eyes. She shakes her head, a tiny fraction but it's enough. I hear her. No matter what I tell them, we're both dead meat.

Drummond sighs and raises the truncheon above Miss Beryl's head, looking almost bored. I lunge at him, ready to rip his throat out, to claw his eyes from their sockets, but before I even get close, the truncheon changes direction and smashes into my left ear, sending me skidding face first in a cloud of dust. I scramble to my feet, head pulsating, vision blurred.

'Let me help you out,' Drummond says, calm as you like. 'I already know about your mother, about Mrs Wicks in London, and of course Florence Nightingale here. What I want to know is, who else have you spoken to? Who else have you got involved?'

I choke back the thought that I can't save Mum, I can't save Jeannie; nothing I can do now can help them. It's only a matter of time before he finds Kaye, then Arran, and there's nothing I can do about that either. Nothing I can do to stop any of this.

'Screw you,' I say.

The truncheon smashes into my chest so hard my feet lift off the floor. I lie on my back, coughing blood.

'Get up.'

My legs won't co-operate.

Carson bends down to haul me up, and as his head comes in close, he whispers, 'Stop winding him up, will you?'

and the way he says it comes across like he's on my side, but that don't make sense. When I finally manage to refocus, I wish I hadn't, I wish I'd stayed on the floor and let the bastards beat me to death. Drummond has abandoned the truncheon and is pointing a gun at Miss Beryl.

'You disappoint me, David. I thought you cared about her. Then again, your kind never really care about anyone, do they?'

Even here, even now, the irony of that coming from Drummond don't escape me. If I had any strength left in my legs I'd lunge at him, but I don't, and he knows it.

'Tell me who else helped you, and I'll let Beryl live. She lives or she dies. You decide, David. What's it to be?'

Miss Beryl's gaze is locked onto mine. Drummond and Carson fade into the background as I focus only on her face. Her skin is ashen, but her eyes are calm, at peace almost. All at once I know why. No matter what happens here, she hasn't got long to live. She's ready to let go.

'I'm not a PSK, am I, Miss?'

Her eyes fill up. 'I'm sorry, David,' she says.

I smile at her and she smiles back. We both nod. There's only one way to play this.

'Screw you,' I say again to Drummond, though my eyes don't leave Miss Beryl's face.

At the first shot, I feel rather than hear the scream leave my throat. A ring of blood spreads through the front of Miss Beryl's shirt and suddenly Carson is behind me, his fingers squeezing the back of my neck. Consciousness slips from my grasp.

When I come round, I'm propped against the pile of cement sacks, my hands tied behind my back. Miss Beryl is lying on her front at my feet. I close my eyes. My limbs refuse to move. Fat fingers pry my eyelids open and Drummond peers in at me.

'We're wasting time.' Carson's voice echoes in my head.

'Back off,' Drummond snarls at Carson, then he looms closer and the spicy stink of his aftershave invades my nostrils. His face is splayed like a reflection on the back of a spoon. His voice bounces around the cavernous spaces in my head.

'You can tell me now, David, or you can tell me later, but you *will* tell me. Now would be more convenient, less … painful.'

Given that my mouth resembles the inside of a cereal box, I muster up an impressive amount of phlegm, and spit. Pink saliva glistens on the bridge of Drummond's nose. His eyes lose all sense of depth and become swirling bottomless holes, sucking me in.

A high-pitched wail shakes the air and jerks me out of my daze.

Drummond's head snaps back.

'Fire alarm,' Carson yells above the racket, and only then do I recognise the other smell lingering in my nostrils. Soft, grey billows of smoke are wafting under the door. I bite back a grin. Oliver did it. Good for him. Too late though. Too late for Miss Beryl. Too late for me. Too late for all of us.

'There're no sprinklers down here yet,' Carson bellows at Drummond. 'All this paraphernalia lying around, this place'll go up in seconds. Let's get out of here.'

Carson goes to grab my arm but Drummond shoves him away.

'He's had his chance.' He aims the gun at my head.

'No need for that. We can take him with us.'

'Out of my way.'

They're shouting to be heard over the clanging of the alarm. I squeeze my eyes shut, feeling oddly detached. It's like I been waiting for this moment for a long time, and now it's finally come. All these people getting hurt cos of me. I can't stop any of it but at least I don't got to help things along. Not even Drummond can make a dead boy talk.

I recognise the sharp *thunk* of air as the silencer kicks in, feel a shock, and everything goes blank. All my clamouring thoughts are wiped clean from my mind, leaving a cool, calm space. The alarm is still going but I can't hear it. Or I can, but at the same time there's this silence in my head. I stop breathing. Start again. Crack open an eye.

Drummond is kneeling in front of me, his gun dangling at his side, his lips twisted into a mawkish grin. He tilts sideways and lands in a puff of dust. Carson leans down to pick up the fallen gun.

I feel like the world just slipped to one side and I can't find my balance.

Carson shrugs. 'You said it, Drummond: we're all expendable.'

He slips a knife out of his boot and steps towards me. I shrink back, squealing. He reaches behind me and hacks through the rope that binds my hands, then stands and turns to go, popping his earpiece back into place.

'Wait. What just happened?'

Carson turns and cocks his head at me. 'Just doing my job, David.' He glances down at Drummond's body. 'Nice when duty and pleasure come together like that.'

I feel his breath on my cheek as he comes over and leans in close. 'But let's be clear about something. If you ever crop up in my life again, I *will* kill you.' He places a hand on my shoulder and squeezes. 'Got that?'

'You're letting me live? Why?'

'What's the matter? Don't you want to?' He brings a hand up to his earpiece and grimaces. 'It's all over.'

'What is?'

'The march. Waste of time anyway. They're packing up. Going home.' He nods at a layer of smoke hanging centimetres below the ceiling. 'If I were you, David Jessop, I'd do the same.' He glances at Drummond again. 'I just killed one of our own. I've got my own hide to worry about now.'

There's a faint rattle and he's gone, and the world slips back into place, leaving me space drunk. I stare at the three bodies laid out around me like some scene from a horror film. I turn Miss Beryl over. Her cold stare sends me reeling backwards.

The sharp pain hits me at the same time as the heat. A red stain spreads across my waist. Drummond must've got off a shot after all. I check myself out. The bullet hit me just above my hip. It burns like hell. I clutch my hand to the wound. Smoke sneaks around the doorframe and crawls along the walls.

Choking on pain and rage, I grab Fat Michael's hat from where it lies in the dust, jam it against my nose and mouth, and lurch towards the same exit Carson took.

CHAPTER TWENTY-THREE

By the time I tumble out into the corridor, Carson is long gone. The shriek of the fire alarm is even louder out here and vibrates in my chest. I tug the flaps of Fat Michael's hat around my ears to cushion the racket, then plough forward.

The corridor twists and turns. I stagger along, unsteady on my feet, bashing into the sides whenever I try to speed up. I settle for a slow jog, then run smack into a dead-end. A security door blocks my escape. I grope in my pocket for Miss Beryl's passkey. Shit, I gave it to Oliver.

I crouch on the floor, below the smoke, but why bother? I got lucky all those years ago when I set my sheet on fire and crawled into bed with Mum, but there's no neighbour to call for help now, no big and brave firefighter to carry me to safety.

The fire alarm stops. Silence.

That should be a good thing, right? But it's not, cos now I'm laying here in this black silence, suffocating. My heart beats so fast I swear it'll explode. What little breath I can catch comes fast and shallow and noisy. My skin sweats, yet I'm freezing.

A sob chokes me. Given a choice, I'd rather be shot than die like this. What Jeannie said about always having options comes back to me. I laugh into the void, cos I still get to choose how to die, don't I? Do I lie here until the flames get me, or do I let the smoke finish me off first? I groan and curl up tighter, which makes me think of Mum in the graveyard, stroking my hair. They say your life flashes in front of your eyes, don't they? Mine don't take long. Mum, our flat, King of the World, the unit, Drummond, Carson, Cornwall, Arran, the sea, Kaye marching against the future, Natalie's legs wriggling in the sand.

I'm starting to lift the hat off my face, to let the smoke in, when it hits me. The march has failed. If I die here, then everything Wilson talked about will come true. The law will be changed. The future will win. There's only one person who can stop that. Me. I got to live to tell the world what's going on here.

I clamber to my feet. Sway. Grab the door handle to steady myself. And it turns. I fall into the next corridor on a wave of smoke, and even as I fall, I'm thinking 'electricity.' Nothing in this place works without it. No electricity, no locks.

I kick the door shut, wave away the smoke that's followed me through, and fill my lungs with clean air.

I'm alive.

I stumble forwards, find a staircase leading upwards and haul myself up it. At the top I turn right and forge onwards. After what feels like forever but is probably only minutes, I see something lying on the floor ahead – a pair of swimming goggles. Still wet. I push on around the corner and then I see it. The door to the pool. A whimper of relief escapes me cos I now know where I am.

As I'm passing the door to the pool, I hear a muffled scream. I pause. Carry on. Stop. What if nobody has found Freaky Adam? What if he's still in there, tied up? Ahead of me I see smoke just starting to crawl along the ceiling. Leaving him there like that is as good as murder. I edge forward, then stop again. If the situation was reversed, there's no way he'd go back for me.

The smoke is getting thicker. My throat scratches as I swallow. The pain in my side is growing sort of numb. I got to get out of here, while I still can. I edge forward again.

Shit, shit, shit. If I leave him there, it proves they're right about me. I'll be a murderer. Oliver too. Especially Oliver.

In the bathroom, daylight filters in through narrow windows and I'm grateful to be out of the blackness. The moans are coming from the end cubicle. It's Freaky Adam all right. It takes three hard kicks to get in. By then, the freak's moaning has escalated into a muffled screeching. The gag is still in place, and above it, his eyes blaze with fury. I yank the towel out of his mouth.

'Oh, you are so, so dead, you and that freaky boyfriend of yours. Just you—'

I shove the gag back in and quick-slap Freaky Adam's head against the cistern, Oliver style, until he stops struggling and his head flops forward.

Even in here, smoke is building up against the ceiling. I soak a towel in the sink and wrap it around Freaky Adam's head, then grab another for my own face so I can pull Fat Michael's hat back onto my head for disguise. I tuck the sides of my towel into the ear flaps, then manoeuvre Freaky Adam over my shoulder. He weighs a ton. Pain shoots through my belly in protest, but my legs, though wobbly, hold firm.

Back in the now smoke-filled corridor, a wave of heat hits me. Flames have started to lick the walls, and overhead I hear a whoosh, followed by a shower of water that fills the corridor and saturates my grateful body. I push on, one hand on the wall to guide me, one hand gripping onto Adam. Chunks of falling plaster catch at my feet and turn the floor slippery. From somewhere close by, a boom of shouts draws me onward into a corridor filled with smoke but dry underfoot. Up ahead, daylight filters through the thickening haze. Grey, people-shaped shadows move across a junction, the pounding of their feet sporadic and muffled.

Minutes later, I follow two boys out into the compound in which Miss Beryl parked her car only hours ago. I picture her body engulfed in flames, and I hobble out into the light and dump Freaky Adam onto the gravel. Sharp, clean air burns my lungs. I double over and retch.

Feet rush past behind me. Gravel crunches. A scattergun of voices. Two men lift Adam up and drag him across to the field, where people are crawling over every blade of grass. Patients and staff are milling about. I never seen it like this before. Chaotic. Intimate somehow. Several boys are running wildly around, yelling and waving their arms. A week ago, I would've been thrilled at this unexpected and violent break in the monotonous routine that passes for life in the unit. Matron waves a clipboard in the air and calls for order. Some hope.

I spit out the last traces of vomit and look around. I know it's selfish, and I know she's back in there, dead cos of me, but what I'm thinking is that without Miss Beryl to drive me out of here, I'm totally trapped, and if I don't get out, the unit will expand and there'll be nobody to stop them.

'Michael.' Dr Carl is standing about ten metres away.

It takes me a moment to remember about the hat. Dr Carl points to where the boys are being corralled. I raise a hand like I'm just coming, then bend into the wall and pretend to retch again.

He takes a step towards me, but then a fight breaks out over on the field. 'Get a move on,' he yells, and he runs towards the brawling boys.

I squeeze my eyes shut. I fucked up. Miss Beryl is dead, and I'm trapped back in here. I'll never see Mum again, never swim in the sea, never hang out on the beach with Arran and Kaye. I take a deep breath, exhale, inhale. I got to get a grip, got to calm down, got to think …

Hot breath brushes my neck and I jump high enough to break records.

A voice giggles in my ear, 'I did it.'

I spin around to find Oliver, grinning like a right nutter, waving his arm to take in the chaos.

'I did all this,' he says.

'For God's sake.' I grab his arm and yank it down to his side. 'Are you trying to get me caught?'

'That cupboard was full of stuff, just like you said. I made two—'

'Shut up. Look, I got to get to Miss Beryl's car, over there. Maybe I can hide, wait till things quiet down.'

Oliver's eyes shine. 'I'll come with you.'

'No.'

The hurt in his eyes is like a slap.

'I mean, they'll know if you're missing. I can … I can come back for you … later.'

'But—'

'Hey.' Fat Michael is standing on the field, hatless and pointing at us. 'Hey, you.'

Dr Carl turns to look at where Fat Michael is pointing, and does a double take. A handful of boys swing their gaze back and forth between me and the real, hatless Fat Michael. The silence gradually head-hops as more boys catch on. In the end, only Matron is moving, calling out names and waiting for answers that don't come, until eventually even she clicks that something's up. Her voice tails off. Every pair of eyes in the compound's got their gaze set on me.

'Run.' Oliver pushes me but I just stand here like a dummy. Out of the corner of my eye, I clock Dr Carl and five orderlies walking towards me.

'What's the matter with you? Run.' Oliver shakes my arm. 'Run, David. Run.'

To my left lies the outer wall with its four metres of brickwork. A dozen or so vehicles are still dotted about the car park in front of it. To my right lies the field of boys, where Dr Carl and the orderlies have formed a line and are advancing. In front of me there's Oliver, pleading with me to try, at least try. The orderlies stop a stone's throw away from us. I still can't move. It's like I'm super-glued to the spot.

Oliver rushes at the orderlies, his skinny legs pounding, fists flying. A scream comes out of his mouth that might be 'Geronimo!'

The nearest orderly quickly and easily pins him to the floor and holds him there.

Oliver's feet kick, kick, kick. A string of swear words spills out of his mouth. And I'm thinking, if a little squirt like Oliver can fight to the last then so can I, cos I still got options, don't I? They can do what they like to me, but there's no rule says I got to go quietly.

My feet come back to life and I pelt towards the car park. I bounce around Miss Beryl's car and screech to a halt facing them, hands splayed on the bonnet, ready to dart in either direction. Dr Carl gestures right and left, and the orderlies fan out to form a semi-circle. He signals again and they advance, coming at me from three sides. The fourth side is blocked by the exit wall and those castle-like gates, built originally to keep enemies out, but just as good at keeping prisoners in.

I back up, dodging from car to car, sucking myself deeper into their trap. When there's no more cars, I clamber along the wall, skidding and scraping along its brickwork until I reach the smaller gate set into the body of the big one. I press my back to it and face my enemies.

Dr Carl crooks his finger and four men move forwards, apparently in no hurry to finish this game. They creep closer and closer, and a word leaps into my brain:

Electricity!

I feel for the handle behind me and shove. The gate opens, and I'm flying across open moorland on feet cushioned by air. As I float away, away, away, I hear sirens riding the airwaves towards me and see blue lights flashing in the distance, coming this way. Huge brown birds screech skywards, disturbed by the racket. I run and run, and when my legs won't carry me any further, I drop to my knees and crawl. When even that hurts too much, I stop and look back.

The orderlies have drawn to a halt about a pool's length behind me. They're staring at the approaching posse and looking to Dr Carl for guidance. Dr Carl hesitates, then turns and runs – not after me, away from me. Away from the approaching vehicles. A nanosecond later, four white-coated shapes are pounding at Dr Carl's heels.

Matron appears at the gate, too far away for me to make out the look on her face, but I can imagine it. She slams the gate shut just as the first police car screeches to a halt outside the walls. The unit once again becomes a dull building that wouldn't make you think twice if not for the plume of black smoke reaching skywards from its heart.

The racing vehicles look like toy cars, not quite real. The bobbing white shapes of the scarpering orderlies could be rabbits running scared. The moor stretches out in every direction. Three fire engines roar past, closely followed by two police cars. Despite the deafening wail of their sirens, I feel all alone. Empty.

'David.'

I gaze up into the sun and my head spins. The voice comes again, closer, louder.

'David.'

I struggle to my feet and sway like a drunk. I got to be hallucinating.

Arran, long loose limbs, is running towards me, an arm raised in greeting. A police car screeches to a halt on the road ahead of where Arran stops and faces me. It can't be him. I'm dreaming.

'Are you all right?' Arran spins me full circle like I'm a surfboard he's inspecting for possible damage.

'The future,' I croak.

'You're hurt.'

I lift my hand from where it's clutching my side and hold it in front of my face. Wet. Red. I turn my palm to show Arran. My feet shift backwards. With an odd sense of dropping into a void, something inside me lets go and I spin.

A pair of arms appear under my back and lower me to the ground. Arran's head floats on the surface of my underwater world. A blurred police helmet hangs over Arran's shoulder.

Then there's nothing but black.

CHAPTER TWENTY-FOUR

Hot light sears my eyes shut again. Something soft and warm presses down on my elbow. I want to recoil from the contact but my arm seems to be made of lead, and when I try to thrash out, it barely moves. The warm patch grows warmer.

'Dai, can you hear me? You're in hospital.'

Kaye? I try to move my lips but everything spirals, then goes black.

My eyelids blink open and three creased faces come into focus around my hospital bed: Kaye, Arran, Jeannie. I attempt to sit up, to search out Mum's face, but it would take a crane to lift my head off this pillow.

'Mum?'

'We're taking good care of her, I promise.' Jeannie's voice. 'Be patient. Right now, you need to rest.'

'Miss Beryl?' I mutter.

Then I remember.

Black.

Kaye is leaning over me, glancing from my face to a machine that *ping-ping*s near my ear. 'He's awake,' she says over her shoulder.

Arran's head appears, then Jeannie's doctor friend, Florrie. I wish Jack Daniels was here.

'David?'

'Dai?'

What do they want? Why can't they leave me alone? The room pongs of hygienic surfaces and dirty bodies.

'Get lost,' I murmur.

'He's doing fine,' Florrie says.

Black.

The following morning, only Jeannie's face greets my sticky gaze.

'Arran and Kaye stayed here all night. They've gone home to wash, have something to eat. I'll call them, tell them you're—'

'No.' I run my foul-tasting tongue across my lips: dry, flaky.

'If that's what you want. There's no rush. The doctor said with rest you'll be fine. The bullet missed all the essential organs.'

I stare at the ceiling, try to grasp hold of the thoughts that float around the edges of my mind like stray balloons. Every time my hand stretches towards their trailing strings, a gust of wind snatches them out of reach.

'Mum?' I whisper through a throat dry as burnt toast.

Jeannie puts her hand at the back of my head, lifts me forward and tilts a straw into my mouth. I sip, then flop back onto the pillow like I've swum the channel.

'She's not great right now, David, but she's being taken excellent care of and she's going to be just fine. It'll take time, that's all.'

I nod, then wince with the pain that even that tiny movement sends shooting through me.

'Don't worry about your mum for now. Concentrate on getting yourself better. I'll take good care of her, trust me.'

'And Oliver?'

'Try not to think about all this now.' Jeannie offers me the straw again.

I push the straw away. I know he's not right in the head, Oliver, but I can't just abandon him again. 'Where is he?' I croak.

'There were twenty-six boys in there, David, and they were preparing for a lot more.'

'I promised I'd go back for him.'

Jeannie places the plastic cup and straw onto the bedside cabinet, apparently a task she needs to concentrate all her attention on. 'You have to realise … for some of them, home just isn't somewhere they can go back to.'

'Where is he?' My voice cracks.

'You're not to upset yourself.'

I manoeuvre my elbows higher up the bed and force my head off the pillow. 'Tell me,' I mutter through the pain.

'All right.' Jeannie presses me back into a lying position. 'Oliver is in a clinic up in Manchester. For now, there's no choice.'

I sag back onto the pillow and drag an arm over my face. Another institution. He'll hate that.

'It's only temporary.' Jeannie lays her hand on top of mine.

I clench my fist but don't snatch my arm away. She means well, I know.

'As soon as it can be arranged, all the boys who can't go home will go to proper families.'

I struggle to sit up again. 'What about the transfers?' Even as my lips form the question, my cynical self wonders why it matters. But a thought has ballooned into my head and won't be shaken off. At least some of the boys who failed the programme might be bycatch, and that's got to matter, don't it?

A coughing fit racks my chest. Jeannie gently forces me back onto the pillows. 'Thanks to you, David, the proposed amendments to the Children's Act are dead in the water. They'll never get them through Parliament now, and those twenty-six boys have a real chance in life.'

She's avoiding my question. 'But the others?'

'There's so little to go on.' She shakes her head. 'We're all so proud of you. Everybody has been saying how …'

I zone her out.

Black.

Something cold rubs against my forehead. A cloth, wet. My eyes open. The cloth lifts.

Arran steps back and says, 'You need to eat.'

'Can't.'

272

Arran bullies me through half a bowl of bland chicken soup. He uses a blue checked tea towel to mop up the spillage, and there's plenty of it. It's like I'm a baby again. Helpless. Hopeless.

'How did you find me?' My voice still sounds croaky, but better.

'The morning after you took off, Jeannie phoned. When I told her I'd let you go off by yourself … Well, she weren't happy.' Arran fidgets with the tea towel in his lap. 'Not one of my proudest moments. And then she explained what was going on. Why didn't you tell me? I might have been more … Anyhow, I remembered the address I'd given you, so I headed over to Falmouth.

'When I got there, I bumped into two men coming out of the woman's gate. I didn't like the look of them, so I kept on walking, casual like, and as I was passing, one of them got a phone call and I heard him tell his mate that she'd been caught trawling through some documents. I guessed they were talking about the woman you'd gone looking for, so I followed them. When I saw the smoke, I phoned Jeannie, told her what was happening. She made sure it got treated like a full-scale riot.'

I want to listen but my eyes close and the steady *ping-ping* of the machine carries me back to sleep.

By the next morning, my stomach is aching from hunger and the machine next to my bed is gone. A nurse arrives, offering a bowl of sweet porridge, sugar frosted across its surface. I spoon it down and she wipes my chin and leaves.

Kaye materialises in the open doorway and hovers on the threshold. 'All right to come in, Dai?'

Truth is, I want to be left alone, but Kaye perches on the stiff leather chair next to my bed and smiles.

'How are you feeling? Better?'

'Getting there.'

'Good.' She smiles, and it's such a warm smile. 'They reckon you'll be discharged later today. Jeannie's arranged to take you up to her place in London, for now, and me and Art have to head into town this afternoon so—'

'Don't let me stop you.'

The last time I'd seen Arran and Kaye, they'd known nothing about me, not about who I really am, and that had felt good. Clean. Now that they know, seems they can't wait to get away from me.

Kaye's face turns serious. 'Are you angry with me, Dai?'

'Why would I be? None of this is your fault.'

'No, but—'

'So, you can get back on with your life then, can't you? Forget all about this.'

'That's what we wanted to talk to you about.' Kaye glances at the open door. 'I should wait for Art.'

'If you're worried about being alone with me, you don't got to stay.'

'Worried?' She looks genuinely puzzled. 'It's not that, it's just …' She lays her hand on a tiny bulge in her stomach and her face lights up. 'You don't know about this one, yet, do you?'

An image of Kaye in the cave flashes into my head – her little rock womb. 'You're pregnant?'

'That's what me and Art were rowing about. It's all right; we both just needed time to calm down, get our heads around things, especially Art. I'd known for days.'

'Congratulations.' I hesitate. 'I'm sorry, Kaye.'

'For what?'

'For involving you, for putting you in danger. I didn't think—'

'You've nothing to be sorry for.'

Her smile looks genuine, and I relax a little. I don't want to be angry at Kaye. I meant what I said. None of this is her fault. I just don't want them to leave me. Especially now. And I *am* sorry. Every waking moment.

'Me and Art, we've been talking.' She laughs. 'Endlessly.'

'About me?'

'Well, yes. But not just you.' She lays her hand on my arm. 'Everything that's happened, it's made Art think about how Jeannie was there for him when he really needed someone, how she looked out for him. And she's not even related to him, whereas you're his nephew. Blood. And now, he's about to be a dad and everything … Well, we – both of us – want to ask you something.' She pauses and glances again at the door. 'I should wait for … Well, okay … we were wondering, me and Art – and you don't have to decide right now – but, well, we'd like you to come and live with us. Here, in Cornwall.'

I must've misheard her.

She's leaning towards the bed, her elbows on her knees, hands knitted together on her belly, brows pulled into a sharp, concentrated frown. She must mean come for a holiday. Or come until I'm well enough to go into care. Or something.

'I don't think so,' I say, though I don't know why, or what I mean by it. The words just come out.

Live with Kaye and Arran? In Cornwall? By the sea? Or live in London. With my mother. She needs me, don't she? I shake my head. No, she don't. She needs Jeannie, not me.

Kaye sees me shake my head and rushes on. 'Like I said, you don't have to decide right now. Jeannie is happy for you to stay on with her, if you prefer. But your mother isn't going to be properly well for a long time, and I know you're nearly sixteen, but even so, everybody needs a family. We want to be yours, us and your little cousin here. But it's your choice.'

'My choice?' I echo, dumbly.

She's offering me a clean slate, a family, a home by the sea. And I get to choose?

'You'll have to stay with Jeannie for a bit, just till you get better. That'll give us time to get the cottage ready. You can decide then, when everything's ready. Maybe you can come down and visit first, see if you like our new place.'

An uncle. A cousin. A family.

'Look, we'll try to hurry things up in town. I'm sure Art will want to speak to you before you get off to London. We'll see you later, okay?'

It's too much. I turn away, faking tiredness, and Kaye slopes off.

By the time Jeannie arrives, carting an armful of clothes and a mug of lukewarm tea, my head's clearer and buzzing with questions. How come Mum never knew about her brother? How come Arran didn't know who his father was until his mum died? How come Jeannie knew all this stuff? And why keep it a secret?

'It wasn't my secret to share,' Jeannie explains. 'Arran's mother was my oldest friend. It was through her I first met your grandfather. She'd been dating him in a casual, uncommitted kind of way, which was the only way she ever dated anybody. Arthur had been widowed for a year by then, and with Lucy still so young, he wasn't looking for a relationship as such either.'

'I thought you said *you* were his girlfriend.'

'I was. Later. My friend went off touring, America mostly. Next time I met her she was trailing a two-year old son. She made me swear never to tell Arthur he was the father because she knew he'd want to be involved and that would be the end of her freedom. It seemed an easy enough promise to make because he'd moved to another area by then and I thought I'd never see him again. Then I bumped into him at my am-dram club twelve years later and I knew it was love. He felt the same.' She blushes. 'I was widowed by then, but there was this awful secret I'd kept from him about Arran. It was complicated, but we knew we wanted to make a life together.

'I knew I had to tell him he had a son, but first I wanted to talk to my friend, forewarn her, but I was having problems tracking her down, so eventually I told him anyway. This was just before we headed off to the Lakes. He was so upset and couldn't wait to meet Arran, but it was Lucy's birthday, so we went ahead with the holiday. And then ...'

'Then he went and crashed his car.'

'I wish I hadn't told him about his son. Maybe that, on top of what happened to his little girl, was just too much for him to bear.' Jeannie sighs. 'But what's done is done, we can only move forward. After my friend died, I told Arran about Lucy. He wanted to find her, wanted to meet his sister, but we had no idea where she was and eventually, we gave up.' She squeezes my arm. 'But that's all in the past. What's important is now, and the future. Look, try to get a bit more sleep while you can. We should be able to get on the road soon.'

I'm getting a headache, so she leaves me to sleep, which I do, fitfully, full of frantic dreams of bears and caves and high, high walls.

When I next emerge from my underworld, Arran and Kaye loom into view.

'Hey, sleepyhead,' Kaye says.

'Hey, nephew,' Arran grins. 'Glad we caught you before you got off.'

'Did you mean it?' I say.

Arran lifts his eyebrows at Kaye. 'Course we meant it. You're family. Soon as you're out of here, we'll get everything wrapped up. You can stay at Jeannie's till you're back on your feet.' He hesitates. 'But we'll come up and see you later this week, spend some time with Lucy, visit her at that rehab centre.'

Kaye picks up my hand and presses it between both of hers, her palms warm against my cold one, and I find I don't mind. Not one bit.

'So,' she says, 'you will come back then?'

CHAPTER TWENTY-FIVE

The copper – long face, legs thin as a stick insect's – lowers himself into the armchair. I'm slumped on the makeshift day-bed Jeannie's made up for me on the sofa. I tug the cotton duvet higher up my chest, which is tricky, cos Jack Daniels is camped on the other end of it.

'Unfortunately,' the cop says, 'the fire destroyed all the paperwork, all the computers. Without that evidence, there's little chance those at the very top will ever reach court.'

Behind him, a log fire crackles and spits in the grate, but that's not why my face is hot. I went back into the unit to get my files, to prove Wilson was lying about me. Now I'll never know the full story, and that's my own fault. As usual. It was me who told Oliver to start that fire. Then again, the truth's not likely to be anything good, is it? All I can do is hang onto the thought of what Miss Beryl said, about P being the most important letter in PSK. I might have been born with some seriously shitty potential but, even though I can't prove it, at least I know that Wilson set me up, that I didn't fail the programme. Which means I got the potential to be whatever I want, don't it? I push the quilt aside, drag it back. I'm hot. I'm cold. Jack Daniels throws me a filthy look.

Jeannie comes in carrying a tray with a jug of water and three full glasses.

The cop takes one, and nods his thanks. 'As for your friend, Carson, he's gone to ground so thoroughly I doubt he'll ever surface again; at least not in any recognisable form.'

'He's no friend of mine,' I say, and what Carson said nags at me again. Duty? Doing his job? Why was it his job to kill Drummond? No matter what angle I come at it from, it don't make sense.

'And the people behind it all?' Jeannie asks.

'We have our suspicions.' He looks as though he's about to say something else but pauses.

'Don't worry, Officer,' Jeannie smiles sweetly, 'I'm aware that Drummond had some … for the sake of discretion shall we call them … very powerful connections in our government.'

The cop's eyebrows hit the ceiling. 'How did you come by that information?'

'My late husband was *very* well connected,' she says, managing to layer in an air of grandeur as she says it. 'I trust the force will be fully following up on all lines of enquiry, regardless of how powerful those involved might be?'

The cop clears his throat. 'I assure you we will. We are.'

'Good. I'll be following your progress with great interest. What else do we know about Drummond?'

The cop leans towards Jeannie like he's conferring with a colleague. 'You might be aware of this already, but he was

Lord Treherne's bodyguard until about sixteen years ago, and then he went off radar. There's been no trace of him until now.'

'Yes, I was cognisant of that.' Jeannie smiles, and I got to admire the way she pulled that information out of him. He isn't even aware that she did it. 'And Carson?'

'Carson's a ghost. On paper, he doesn't exist. Smells of MI5 to me.' The cop sees my face and adds, 'Don't worry, David, you've got nothing to fear.'

Nothing to fear? Try telling that to the nights I spend tossing and turning. If I'm not bycatch, then I'm not totally innocent, am I? The doctors at the hospital seem convinced that I am, but at the back of my head there's this little voice asking whether I only saved Freaky Adam to prove I'm not a killer, which isn't the same as not actually being one, is it?

'Parliament is in uproar,' the cop goes on. 'Even without any solid evidence, the prime minister has no choice but to resign. He'll no doubt lie low somewhere, wait for the storm to pass, but there's no coming back from this.'

Despite my anger, I can't help feeling a twinge of sympathy for James Treherne. All this time I been lying around in hospital, then on this sofa, I been thinking about it; losing his mother the way he did, it's no wonder he was obsessed with the whole serial killer thing. Not that that makes what he's done okay, but still …

'It's his father, Sir Rory, who should be held to account,' Jeannie says. 'I don't doubt he's the one pulling the strings.'

I don't doubt it either, but then, if I was married and came home to find my wife's bloody corpse lying in my bed,

I might feel the same way about stopping it from happening again.

'No comment.' The cop grimaces then turns to me. 'By exposing the unit, you've pulled off what hundreds of thousands of protesters couldn't. You should be proud of yourself, David.' He pockets his notebook and stands.

'And Oliver,' I say.

'And young Oliver,' he agrees.

'What will happen to him?'

'They've found him a proper home, with a good family. He'll be okay.'

'Can I see him?'

'Not until our inquiries are finished.' He sticks out a hand, grips mine and shakes. 'Take care of yourself, David. And try to stay out of trouble.' He winks.

As Jeannie sees him out, I stroke Jack Daniel's ears. I hope Oliver is allowed a dog in that new family of his.

Before the week is out, the cop's predictions all come true and I'm wishing I'd asked him for the lottery numbers.

The bill is shelved, indefinitely.

The prime minister hands in his resignation and is reported to be hiding out in some London club where no one can get to him.

The press can't dig up enough scandal, and even though they got nothing concrete to say, they get through a sink full of ink saying it.

Jeannie keeps her curtains shut and her phone off the hook and two more weeks pass before I can visit Mum. Sitting up on her stiff white bed in the rehab centre, she says she understands my decision, that it's okay. Maybe when she gets better ...

Jeannie tells me I always got a place here with her, but really, I know she wants Mum, not me. And with all these reporters camped out on the doorstep, fact is, being here's not been all that great. It's my birthday in a few weeks and, okay, it might be pathetic to be getting excited about such things at sixteen, but this could be the first time I get to actually celebrate the event. Kaye's been dropping hints about a course of scuba diving lessons.

I've made my choice, it's the right one, and now I can't wait to get on with it. The sooner I get down to Cornwall, the better. Just a few things to tidy up first.

Sweat dampens my T-shirt, though the weather is now cool and breezy despite a morning of rain that's left everything smelling of mildew. Over on the car park, a couple of pigeons squabble over an empty crisp packet. At the foot of the stairs to Mum's flat, a sheet of newspaper flaps and snatches at my feet. I head up to the fourth floor. The door has a cat flap in it. She got herself a cat? She never said. I jiggle my key in the lock, and steel myself. The door gives out a classic horror-film creak as it swings open onto a narrow, dark passage with peeling wallpaper and nicotine-yellow paintwork.

The frozen block of dread I been carrying around for days melts away. My old home looks sad and pathetic but there's nothing to be scared of. The air is rancid with something I don't recognise and don't want to investigate. I think of Cornwall, of its sharp air and steep cliffs and underground secrets, and the cottage that Kaye and Arran are getting ready. 'We'll make your room real pretty,' Kaye had teased. 'Pink floral borders, fluffy pillows, a ton of cuddly toys. Jeannie tells me you're partial to teddy bears?' I'd punched her in the arm and grinned.

Long-forgotten habit makes me gather up the mountain of junk mail and toss it onto the rickety hall table. In the living room, nothing's changed: same furniture, same décor, just older, dirtier. I move on through to the kitchen and trip over a bundle of grubby clothes. The stack of dirty dishes has become home to two black cockroaches, which scuttle in circles at the disturbance and burrow deeper into the gaps. I frown at a box of cat food, its cardboard ripped and torn, dried nuggets spilled across the grimy countertop. No sign yet of a cat. The air in here feels cold and damp. I remember that.

She must've found it hard after I went. I try to picture her, night after night, all alone, but the images that come are too miserable to dwell on. No point in lingering. Just collect her stuff, as promised, and get out of here.

When I first visited her in the rehab centre, she lay propped up on pillows, pale as a ghost. Jeannie had offered to buy her anything she needs, but Mum told me she wants familiar things around her. She tried to explain how, when she eventually came to, she'd found herself in a strange place surrounded by strange people who've got a strange way of doing things. She wants her own stuff there, so she remembers who she is, and I get that. So here I am.

It's impossible to resist a quick peek at my old bedroom. I halt in the open doorway, not knowing what to make of what I see. I expected to find my old room turned into some sort of dumping ground for newspapers and empty bottles and whatever other crap she couldn't be bothered taking down to the bins. But the bedroom in front of me is pristine, not a wrinkle out of place. My pyjamas are folded on the pillow. The bed's made up with my Superman quilt cover. I lift a corner of the quilt and sniff. Clean.

All my things – a creased set of Pokémon cards, a broken Nintendo Switch, an old Transformer with its grey plastic showing through chipped red and yellow paintwork – are arranged in a neat circle on top of my dresser next to a framed photograph. I pick the picture up and stare at it. There I am, around three or four years old, my eyes bright, my teeth white, my hair wild. My foot is perched on top of a football, one muddy, scraped knee pushing up towards the camera. I look happy.

I yank open the wardrobe and, yep, here are all my clothes, the blue Olympics T-shirt, my tatty black hoodie, my worn trainers. Not a speck of dust. My nose picks up the faint scent of polish. The only unclean thing in the room sits on the windowsill next to the bed: a mug, half-full of brown liquid with soft green mould forming perfect circles on the surface.

I perch on the edge of the bed. She must've been in here just weeks ago, drinking tea, and doing … what? Going through my stuff? Thinking about me? At the graveyard she'd sworn she'd never stopped missing me, but I hadn't believed her, and now here's this room, like some kind of shrine.

I stand up. No point in going back over any of this. No point. I've made my decision and it's not cos I'm still angry at her or anything. It's just that … this is my chance to grab a real life for myself. I can be happy living on Cornwall's north coast, I know I can. Arran might rub me up the wrong way sometimes, but his presence makes me feel safe. Kaye makes me feel likeable, lovable even. And I don't need to worry about either of them cos they don't need me to take care of them. Then there's my unborn cousin: a clean slate, my chance to be part of a real family, no baggage.

But if I'm being honest, the real deal-breaker is the fact I'll be living by the sea. Just thinking about that makes my chest feel funny – in a good way. I don't got the words to explain it, but I know I'm meant to live by the sea. I never been surer about anything in my life.

Mum's got to stay in London; she needs to be fixed and for that she needs Jeannie, not me. When she gets better maybe she can come. Jeannie too. Anything's possible, isn't it? I wipe my sleeve across my eyes; I'm turning into a regular cry-baby.

I cross to Mum's bedroom, keen now to get on with it and get out of there. When I push the door wide, a black shape shoots out and whizzes past me. I press my hand to my chest until my heart rate slows back to something approaching normal. That'll be the cat then. I'm thinking that I'm glad she got herself a cat for company, something to cuddle when she got lonely, but then it sinks in. Nobody's been back here for weeks and not once did Mum mention any cat. The poor thing's been left all alone in here, frightened, totally deserted. I know she's been ill and that, but she didn't even think to tell us. Jeannie could've come and got it.

Her bedroom is dark and smells grim. I flick the light switch but nothing happens. Lecky's cut off again. I feel my way across to the window and yank the black velvet material aside. The windowpanes are so filthy that daylight don't exactly flood the room, but at least it illuminates its darkest corners.

I pull a bin liner out of my back pocket, yank open a dresser drawer and cram the contents in. Her wardrobe yawns empty except for five discarded hangers and some mismatched shoes stuffed into an Asda carrier bag in one corner. But on a low stool, a pile of semi-clean clothes teeters, and I sweep these into the sack, then bag the small, framed photograph of my grandad that she keeps beside her bed. For good measure, I add an ornamental clay cat she keeps as a reminder of her mother.

The neglected flesh-and-blood cat mewls hysterically in the background, shaking me free of my earlier guilt. Cornwall is the right thing to do. On a kitchen shelf I find an unopened tin of cat food. The cat swallows every scrap and promptly vomits. I don't bother to mop up; it's not like we're ever coming back here. I fling a towel around the cat and wrap its legs tight, trapping its claws. It hisses and flays and spits at me as I make my way back outside. As the door shuts behind me, I feel the backdraught from my old life brush along my spine.

Jeannie is sitting in her car waiting for me, her face anxious. She ignores my warnings and opens the towel. When she sees the cat, thin and scrawny, its eyes wide with fear but bold with hunger, she wails, 'Oh, you poor thing,' and takes the cat into her arms and shushes it quiet. In no time it's curled up in a ball fast asleep in her lap. How did she do that? A minute ago, that thing was all set to tear my eyes out.

'There's a box back there with some tools in it,' she tells me in a soft whisper. 'If you empty it out, we can put him in there for now.'

As I pull the box onto my lap, I remember another box. While Jeannie uses the towel to fashion a soft bed, I stare out of the window at my old stamping ground, where it's possible that my childhood treasures might still lie buried.

'Won't be long,' I say, climbing back out.

Ignoring Jeannie's protests, I set off for the woods.

Minutes later I'm pushing my way through the overgrown holly that serves as three of the four walls that make up my special place. The trunk of a yew tree forms the fourth, and its bowing branches create a rough roof. My hands dig on autopilot, knocking aside small rocks and scraping away layers of dirt until I uncover a sizeable hole.

My box is gone.

The only real surprise is my disappointment. What did I expect around here? What does it matter anyway? I'm getting up to go when a hand draws back a branch and a head materialises in the gap. Old Brockerton elbows his way into the small clearing, a yellowed snout pushing into view between his ankles.

The snout growls and I clench my fists.

'Saw you,' old Brockerton gasps, 'from the car park … Thought I'd missed you … So slow.' He bends double and coughs. 'Chest,' he says, thumping the accused region. 'No good.'

Bertie sniffs around my ankles and licks at my socks, his tatty tail beating the air.

'Been looking out for you … since …' Old Brockerton waves a hand vaguely in the direction of the park and I nod to let him know I understand. Though I don't, not really. What's his problem? What business is it of his whether I come or go? I'm not a little kid anymore. I won't be bullied.

'What do you want?' I say, my voice cold.

He points at the empty hole near my feet and coughs. 'Tried to stop them. Bloody kids.'

I shrug. 'Don't matter.'

'Lucy … she's all right?'

'Not really.'

'She coming back?'

I shake my head and his face falls. 'Then you'd better … have this.' He shoves his hands deep into the pockets of his thick coat and withdraws a small metal box. A box I don't recognise.

'What is it?'

'Lucy's.' He holds the box out to me. 'Said if anything happened to … give it to you.' He bends over in a fit that leaves him purple and sort of shocked looking. When he raises his head again, spittle clings to the corners of his mouth and seeps into the grooves around it.

I take the box off him and lead him out of the woods and around the side of the tower block. I recall belting down the hill while he tried to flag me down. Poor sod can barely breathe, and I went and forced him into a jog.

'Sit on the step here. Get your breath back.'

Old Brockerton turns thick, watery eyes up at me and points at the box that I'm turning over in my hands. There's this tiny padlock on it, nothing that'd keep more than a sparrow out, but still. 'She kept it at my place.' He manages a weak smile. 'Give it to her?'

'Course.'

Old Brockerton coughs hard into the back of his hand and wipes his knuckles across his lips. 'Don't end up like ... my son. Died ... because of me ... I was ... like Lucy.'

Shame washes through me. Old Brockerton had a son who died? It's never occurred to me that he might have his own grief, his own story.

'I'm sorry,' I say. I seem to be saying that a lot lately. 'Look, I got to go.' I turn and walk a few paces, but the wheezing and spluttering turns into a full-blown coughing fit and I go back and take hold of his arm. 'Come on, let's get you home safe first, Mr Brockerton. Call you a doctor.'

He refuses the doctor, but I make sure he gets inside, and I fetch him some water in a none-too-clean mug. I'll get Jeannie to call someone anyway. From the state of the flat, he could do with some other help too. I remember how Mum would always be popping down to see him, making sure he was okay. She'd been a friend to him. He'll miss having her around.

When we say goodbye, we both know it's for the last time.

CHAPTER TWENTY-SIX

Outside my train window, trees dance in a high wind as the miles flash by. I steal glances at my fellow passengers. In front of me, a pair of nuns covered head to toe in black-and-white habits share a magazine and whisper to each other. The seat behind me is empty. Across the aisle, a middle-aged man in a striped suit bites into a burger that smells so meaty I curse myself for refusing Jeannie's offer of a packed lunch.

I force my mind off my stomach and pull Mum's metal box out of my rucksack. Questions about the box have crept into my dreams all week. Why leave it at old Brockerton's place? Why the padlock? Why tell him to pass it on to me if something happened to her?

I know I told old Brockerton I'd give the box back to Mum, and I will, but not yet. When I took her clothes into the rehab centre yesterday, she'd wanted to know if I had anything else for her. I'd shrugged, 'Like what?' and she'd seemed happy with that. She's getting better at last, slow bit by slow bit, and no way I'm giving her anything that might freak her out again. I need to see what's in there first, just to check it out. And cos I know, no matter which way I spin it, it's Mum's box, not mine, I wanted to open it when I was by myself, without Jeannie around to maybe talk me out of it. So I waited, until now.

A quick twist with a screwdriver and the lock pings onto the table. I slip it into my pocket before anybody sees, then lift the lid.

Newspaper clippings. Boring stuff. Political.

Hang on. Political? That don't square with what I know about Mum at all.

On the other hand, I didn't know she kept a secret box in old Brockerton's flat, did I? I didn't know she had a cat. I didn't know that Jeannie even existed. It occurs to me that maybe there's more to Mum than just the bits I know about. But really, *politics?*

I glance through the pieces. There are clippings about leadership elections, by-elections, general elections, going back years. One's about the opening of a children's centre in Hackney. In the margin, someone (Mum?) has scribbled 'D.O.B. 17.09.91???' I run the date over and over in my head, but it means nothing. Another clipping shows the Docklands and a new ship being launched. I riffle through, and my breath catches in my throat when I see it: the article about Kamal drowning and me trying to save him takes up the entire bottom half of the front page of the *London Evening Standard*. Mum's cut out the entire page. There's this great big picture of me. Grinning. Young. Unknowing.

My hands shake as I stare at the photograph, trying to see what lies behind the eyes. Was I a PSK even then? Was the instinct to kill growing in me, getting ready to take me over? My face looks so innocent. The article bangs on about what a hero I was, what a fine example of youth. The guy who wrote that article didn't care that my mum was a drunk, that I didn't have a dad, that we were dirt poor. The guy who wrote that article thought I was good. There's a long quote from Kamal's famous footballer dad, saying how grateful he was that I tried. Could they both be so totally wrong?

Something's bugging me. I scan the page again and there it is. In the top section of the paper, above the article about me, there's another picture. It's a bit blurred but I recognise him all right. James Treherne, prime minister until a few days ago. He was the health minister back then; it says so right under his picture. The article's about how he plans to revamp the Mental Health Service, drag it into the twenty-first century. My gaze flicks from the images of his face to mine, and back again. This can't be a coincidence, can it? There he is, there I am, and only days later I'm being dragged off to the unit, a secret part of the very health service he's in charge of. Put that together with the fact that his own mother was murdered by a serial killer, and the chances of coincidence are just too vast to dismiss. But none of that explains why the hell Mum would've hidden this article in a box all those years ago.

The train is slowing down. Outside my window, a long platform emerges and a tinny voice booms overhead 'Exeter St David's. The train on platform ...' I stuff the clippings back into the box, fling on my rucksack and shuffle to the door in need of air.

For the first time in weeks, the wind packs a chill that cuts straight through my jacket. I jump down onto the platform, take in great gulps of fuel-packed air, and barge through a huddle of students who are busy boarding. My legs carry me blindly up and down the length of the platform before the guard starts yelling for everyone to stand clear and I got to clamber back on board. I collapse onto the nearest seat and root in my rucksack for the box. I stare and stare at the page with my story on it. There's something else bugging me but I can't quite grasp it.

I spring to my feet and work my way along the aisle, my mind buzzing like a hornet's nest but coming up with zilch. The next carriage hosts the buffet bar. I had planned to grab a hot drink and something to eat – a burger or ten – but my appetite's deserted me. I push on through.

I squeeze inside a vacant toilet, slam on the lock and stare at myself in the mirror. I need to calm down. The unit has gone. It's over. I can mess up the rest of my life trying to work it out, or I can let the past go. The ground underfoot judders as we trundle along the track, the rhythmic hum of the engine soothing.

I screw the newspaper article into a ball, step on the bin pedal and prepare to toss it in. Time to move on. My future lies ahead of me and for once it looks good. Really good.

But something is still bugging me, and I release the pedal. The bin clangs shut.

Somebody tries the door. Grumbles. I shove the article back in the box, throw water on my face and glance at my grandad's watch, a reminder that the past is still with me.

I'll be there in a couple of hours. Arran and Kaye will know what to do about the box. I shrug my rucksack back onto my shoulder and return to my seat.

For the rest of the journey, my head swims with thoughts of what Arran and Kaye might say when I show them the box. Will they think I should've destroyed it, or that I should hold onto it and give it back to Mum when she's all better? It feels good knowing I got people I can talk to about this stuff. Not counsellors, wanting to pick my head apart, but family, wanting to help me.

I'm so wrapped up in all this, I don't register the tannoy when it announces that the next station is Newquay, and I'm watching the departing passengers march past my window when I spot the Newquay sign on the wall right in front of me. Grabbing my rucksack, I scramble along the aisle, jump down onto the platform and scan the faces, seeking out Arran or Kaye. I double-check the station name. Newquay. Right place. I check my watch. Right time. They're late. Great.

The train gears up and clanks out of the station. In a burst of chatter and clatter, the other passengers and those who came to greet them disappear through the bollards and out to the car park. An old man humps his suitcase along the platform, its wheels *clack-clack-clacking* along. In the car park behind the station, cars bump across potholed tarmac and the noise of their engines fades to silence as they disappear. The train guard slips through a door and I'm alone in the hollow hush of the empty platform, the saddo that no one cares about. Same old, same old. You'd think I'd be immune by now, but disappointment stabs my chest.

Wind sweeps along the platform. I shiver, zip up my jacket, fling my rucksack over my shoulder and march out to the deserted car park. Now what? I pull out my flash new mobile. Battery dead. Great. I go old school and dig out the *What's Up Cornwall?* guidebook. Kaye gave me this book to persuade me that Cornwall is a great place to live. And it worked, but not cos I thumbed through its coloured photographs and mini fact-files and fell in love with the idea of Cornwall. I'd already done that. It worked cos her giving it to me proved she really did want me to come, that she wasn't just saying it. Or so I thought. I sneer at my own gullibility. If I'm so bloody popular, where's my welcoming committee?

But the guidebook at least has a map of the area, so I start walking. There's still work being done on the chimney in the new cottage, so for the next week we'll be at Arran's flat, huddled darkly under its rocky backdrop. By the time I reach the coast path, daylight's given way to navy skies, and the wind bares its teeth.

Before my finger hits the bell, the door swings open and Kaye stands in the entrance. She looks … what? Apologetic? Embarrassed? Ashamed?

'Forget, did you?' I push past her into the living room. Shrug off my rucksack. Go to speak, then stop.

This is all wrong. Arran is tied to a chair. His eyes are shut. Blood dribbles from a cut on his head. I turn to Kaye. Her face is pale, contorted.

'What the—'

Crack. Wood on bone. Splinters of pain explode in my head.

As I go down, I glimpse a face at Kaye's shoulder.

CHAPTER TWENTY-SEVEN

At first, I can't open my eyes. A sharp pain pulsates through my skull. I groan. On the third attempt, my eyelids part. Light spills in. The room spins and I retch. Nothing comes up. I force myself to focus. Gradually, the blurred edges straighten out. The room takes shape.

Arran is still out cold. Kaye is tied to a chair. I'm slumped on the floor against a cold radiator. Thin rope binds my wrists to the pipes.

Behind me, I hear ragged breath. A face hovers into view. Cold blue eyes. I shake my head to clear my thoughts. I know that face. The eyes, the shape of the nose, the thrust of the chin. My brain races to match it to a memory. I'm back in Arran's flat, the night I first arrived here, on the internet, looking at a picture of the future PM as a little boy. On a yacht. With his mum and ... his dad. What the hell is he doing here? No. It can't be him. It can't.

But it is.

Rory Treherne, father of James Treherne, stares at me, then turns and walks out of Arran's patio doors.

'Dai? Are you all right?' Tears stain Kaye's cheeks and swell her eyes.

I shake my head. Mistake. The room lurches and a trickle of blood runs from my nose into my mouth, metallic and sweet. 'Do you know who that is?' I hiss.

'Yes, it's—'

Rory stomps back in, carrying something. He grunts, puts the object down and slides the door shut behind him. I twist my hands against the rope and scour a layer of skin off my wrists. I welcome the pain. It helps me focus, helps me contain the rage building inside.

Rory comes around the sofa. A gun dangles from his hand.

'Please,' Kaye begs. 'Art's hurt. We need to get him to a hospital.'

He shakes his head and actually sounds regretful when he says, 'That won't be possible.'

I rack my brains for what I know about Lord Rory Treherne. Husband of a young mother murdered by a serial killer. Puppet master of the disgraced prime minister.

'Let them go,' I say. 'This is about the work at the unit, isn't it? They got nothing to do with any of that.'

He rams the gun barrel into my cheek, steel so cold it burns. I know better than to let him smell my fear, so I thrust my chin towards the barrel and glare at him.

The skin around his blue eyes crinkles. 'I have to admire your fighting spirit, David,' he says, then sighs and picks up the object he brought in. Metal. Square.

Kaye squeals as he opens a cap at the front of the can, and the stench of petrol pollutes my nose and stings my eyes. All pretence of calm deserts me for a moment and I heave and thrash against the rope, cry out as it cuts into my wrists and snags on the jagged edge of my watch.

'Please,' Kaye sobs. 'I'm pregnant.'

For a millisecond, he pauses, but then petrol glugs out of the can as he sloshes liquid over the sofa, the armchair, the packing boxes lined up against the wall. There's something about the way he moves. What? I can't pinpoint it.

'Why are you doing this?' I ask. 'What's in it for you?' Behind my back, I wriggle my arms and drag the rope back and forth against the sharp edge of my watch. 'It's too late to change anything now. The unit is gone.'

'You think I don't know that?' His icy gaze sweeps my face, but his hands keep on sloshing petrol around. 'Three decades working to get those monsters off the streets, all undone by some fucking kid.'

'Is that what this is? Revenge, cos I stopped you and your stupid son playing at being gods?' Behind my back, my hands move up and down as I saw and saw at the rope. Got to keep him talking.

He clenches his jaw and surveys the trails of fuel he's laid. 'Drummond was right; we should have killed you and your mother in the first place.' He lifts the can and saturates the curtains.

I blink. What has my mother got to do with the unit being closed down? My feet slip and slide on the wet tiles as

I pedal the floor, trying to back away from the splashes of petrol. My throat feels raw.

'Don't you see it, Dai?' Kaye says.

'See what?'

Rory glares at me and I glare right back. And then I do see it, cos it's not just *his* face I'm looking at, or even just his son's face.

It's my face too.

All the blood drains out of my head. The room wobbles. Snatches of thought race through my mind. I'm nearly sixteen. Mum was nearly sixteen when she slept with that boy. That newspaper. My face on one half of the page, James Treherne's face on the other. How didn't I see it?

'So ...' the pieces finally slot together, 'you been covering up for your son all this time. That's what this whole thing's been about?'

For a moment he looks ... what? Regretful? Confused? He pauses and locks his gaze onto mine.

'James threatened to hand himself in to the police if I touched either of you.' He shakes his head. 'My son was always weak. Drummond took care of the father, then he kept the girl out of harm's way. That should have been the end of it.'

I stare at him open-mouthed. 'You murdered my grandfather?' As I say the words out loud, it sinks in that this man in front of me is also my grandfather.

He thrusts out his chest and stabs the air with his finger. 'I did what had to be done.' He looks down at the can in his other hand. 'We were well on the way to stopping those monsters once and for all, but then there you are, on the front page, your picture right next to his.' He punctuates each sentence with a thrust of the can that sploshes petrol over the curtains. 'You're on Twitter. You're on TV. You're in a fucking football stadium for Christ's sake.'

Petrol fumes scorch my throat. I spit, then catch my breath as it dawns on me that I was never in the unit cos they thought I was a potential serial killer. They never did believe I'd killed Kamal. The whole thing was one stinking big lie from the start. I'm not even bycatch, not even a mistake.

'So, you had me hidden away in the unit?'

He turns to face me, shrugs. 'I had no choice. That reporter you spoke to got curious about your background, then spotted the likeness between you and James. Did some digging. Son-of-a-bitch thought he could blackmail me.'

He steps back and shakes petrol over my clothes, my hair, my shoes. The stench burns into my nostrils. My eyes blink and sting. I gag, kick, squeal. Kaye screams and the sound of it fills my head. He drops the can, opens the matchbox, easily sidesteps my thrashing feet. My head is a whirling froth of rage and impotence. Behind my back, my wrists sting and bleed. I fight to control my breathing, to calm down. If I don't pull it together, we're all dead. I got to slow him down.

He takes out a match.

'So why kill me now, when it's all over? It don't make sense.'

There's a sharp stink of sulphur as the man, who biology tells me is my grandfather, strikes the match and looks me square in the eye.

'My family's political path is damaged, but we'll recover in time – we always do – but you just won't stay hidden, will you, David Jessop?' A tiny flame flickers in his hand. 'People have died. James won't confess now; he won't do twenty years for you. This finishes right here, right now.'

I thrash and kick and pull against my ropes but there's nothing I can do. I can't run. I can't fight … Jeannie's words echo in my head. *What's in your backpack, David?* My gaze travels to where my rucksack stands propped against the door, Mum's box tucked somewhere inside it. Finally, the penny drops. I throw my head back and laugh as convincingly as I can muster.

It works. He pauses, frowns.

Once I've got his attention, I say slowly, clearly, 'If you kill me, your son won't be the only one going to jail.' I manage a wide grin. 'Mum knew. She knew all along.'

His hand pauses in mid-air and I fix my gaze on the burning match. 'Yeah, that's right. You thought she didn't have a clue, but she's known for years who my father was. She's got this box. An insurance policy, she calls it. News clippings of elections and stuff. James Treherne's entire career. His date of birth. My date of birth. That piece in the *London Evening Standard*, the one with me and him on the same page. It's all in there.'

'You're lying.'

'My father's date of birth is 17.09.91. That's right, isn't it? Oh, and I nearly forgot,' I force another grin, 'she put a lock of my hair in too, crawling with DNA. Kill me and the police will find it, then the whole world will know your dirty little secret.'

He bares his teeth and pushes his face into mine. 'Where is it?'

'She posted it. For safe keeping.' I tilt my chin at Arran. 'You want to know where it is, you got to ask him.'

He swings around to face Arran. Kaye shakes her head at me, her eyes huge. I ignore her. Miss Beryl got killed cos I revealed that her hand was empty. If Arran knows something this psycho needs to know, then he got to bring him around, don't he? He'll need Arran alive, and I need to buy more time.

Rory lifts the match to his lips and blows. I flinch as he grabs my T-shirt by the neck and wrenches. 'Don't play games with me, David.'

'I'm not.'

He releases me and turns on Arran. Shakes him. Slaps him. Arran's head lolls from side to side. On the second slap, he lets out a low moan. His eyes flutter open, roll white, close again.

Rory turns to Kaye. 'Where do you keep the brandy?'

I work the rope back and forth against my watch. *Come on.* My wrists burn.

Kaye's voice comes out shaky. 'Whisky. In the kitchen.'

He storms out and kitchen cupboards slam, bang.

I fling myself forward. Yank. Strain. Yank. The rope snaps. My arms fly out to my sides. My knuckles scrape the wall. Stabs of pain as blood rushes back into my fingers.

I crawl to Kaye's side.

'Go,' she hisses. 'Run.'

I tear at her ropes, but the knots are rock hard. A loud smash from the kitchen. A string of curses.

'Get help, Dai. It's our only chance.'

'I can't leave you.'

A bottle clinks against glass. Footsteps. 'He's coming. Go.'

Arran stirs and groans. 'I'll come back,' I whisper.

And I run. Out into the night, where the sky glimmers with just enough stars to outline the tongue of headland. The wind in my back pushes me along as thorns scratch and grab at my legs like sharp claws. It's like my body don't even belong to me. In the dark, I miss the path, but my feet don't miss a beat. The only sounds are of waves smashing onto rocks and the *thump, thump, thump* of my heart. There are no other lights on in the block of flats and no time to reach the village to fetch help.

I stop and look back. An ear-splitting roar as Rory bursts from the lighted doorway.

I make no attempt to hide. Wait for him to come closer. Make sure he sees me. Then I push on at a jog, too far ahead to make an easy target, but close enough to draw him onwards. I sense rather than hear him lumbering behind me, and I'm grateful that he's old and out of condition. If he still had a Drummond or a Carson to call on to do his dirty work, I'd be toast.

At the tip of the headland, I skid to a halt. Only the sea and the night and the stars lie ahead. Waves thunder into the foot of the cliff. A blanket of white froth. Through the middle, a black snake of calm water.

I wait for him to catch up.

He stops a few metres short of me. Stands there, hands on knees, panting. He waves the gun and beckons me to come towards him.

I stare across the strip of heather that separates us. I know what he's thinking. He's thinking I painted myself into a corner. He's thinking I got no choice. But I just about had it with not having choices. 'Screw you,' I yell into the wind, then I turn and run, and I keep on running even as the ground beneath me disappears and my legs pedal thin air, and I'm falling, falling, ears full of thunder.

A splash.

A shock of cold.

Dark.

Wet.

I kick to the surface. Take a deep breath. A wave lifts me and throws me at the rocks.

I dive, thrash and claw, down, down, down, deep and dark, until I'm fingering soft sand and the current draws me through the channel in the rock.

Moments later, I lie gasping like a landed fish on the floor of the cave. My shoes are gone, my knees bleeding. On numb hands and feet, I scramble up the rocky ledge, through the tunnel, and back out into the night.

I scan the headland, but from here there's no sign of him. He'll be heading back to the flat, trying to wake Arran. I fly up the coast path, ignoring the sharp stones, the frigid air, the thorns, and praying, praying, that this time I haven't blown it. My bare feet race across the patch of grass in front of Arran's flat. I grope under the stone hedgehog and slide the key silently into the lock, blood thumping in my ears, hands shaking. I ease the door ajar and force myself to peer inside.

Kaye is lying on the floor, legs sprawled, arms still tied to the chair behind her. Her eyes widen when she sees me. I put a finger to my lips.

Halfway between us, Rory stands with his back to me, blocking my view of Arran, fist drawn back. 'Where is it?'

My knees wobble with relief when Arran answers, his voice weak, but clear. 'Let her go … I'll tell you.'

Rory's fist crashes down and Arran cries out.

Like a feral cat, I leap, nails drawn. Rory piles forward under my weight. Arran's chair topples and splinters and all three of us crash into a heap. The gun clatters against the skirting board. My nails dig into flesh, tear at cloth and skin. Below me, Rory bucks and heaves towards the gun. A hand reaches back and grabs, and chunks of my hair are ripped out of my scalp. Fire burns through me and I scream and lose my grip for a second. His hand is centimetres from the gun. I grab onto his neck and my mouth finds flesh and I sink my teeth in and taste blood. He howls and rolls over onto his back, away from the gun.

My hands find a spot around his throat and squeeze, not caring about the fists that are pummelling into me or the body that's twisting around beneath me. Not caring about anything except the need to end this, to save them. My foot finds the gun and kicks it away as the face below me turns red, then purple, then white. Razor-blue eyes bulge in their sockets. Almost there. Almost done. Rory's eyelids droop and his limbs stop thrashing. Just a little bit longer and it'll be over. Dribble seeps out of the sides of his mouth.

I release my grip, let my hands go slack. I can't do it. I can't kill him. I can't.

I roll off his limp body and crawl to my knees. When I raise my head, I catch a movement in the corner of my eye. He's making a lunge for the gun. I lunge too, get there first, leap back and point it at him.

He's on his feet, swaying. 'You haven't got the guts. Weak, just like your father.' He makes a move forward.

'Stop.' My hands shake.

He gestures for the gun and takes another step closer. 'Give that to me.'

I step back, and there's someone behind me. Arran. On his feet, hands reaching for the gun. I let him take it and he points it at Rory.

'Stay right there or I'll shoot,' Arran says, and there's no doubting that he means it.

Rory stops and looks from me to Arran and back again. He bends down and picks up the can of petrol from where it lies against the skirting board.

'Drop it,' Arran barks.

Rory ignores him and keeps his gaze fixed on me. 'I hope you can live with yourself, David. All those killers you've set free. All their future victims. That's on you.'

'What?'

'She was beautiful, my wife, and what that monster did to her, what others like him will do ... Their blood is on your hands now.'

My mind scrambles to understand what he's saying. He's saying that even though I'm not a killer, I got to take the blame for those who are, that it's all still my fault. Well fuck that.

'You're the one standing there with a can of petrol in your hands,' I snap. 'You're the one trying to kill two people that never did anything to anybody.'

He looks at the can, coughs a laugh, 'Touché,' then splashes fuel all over his shoes, his trousers. He drops the can at his feet and reaches for the box of matches. Pulls one out.

'Put that down,' Arran warns.

He shakes his head. 'We each of us have to do what we have to do. Remember that, David.'

'Stop.' I start towards him. 'It's over.'

His grin is oddly sorrowful as he raises his hand to strike the match.

Arran's teeth are clenched, his eyes blank, as he levels the gun and fires. *Thunk. Thunk. Thunk.*

CHAPTER TWENTY-EIGHT

I bang the stop button on my wristwatch and estimate the distance to the shore. My lungs are aching, but I beat my best time so I'm happy. I spit out salt and tread water in a rhythm of deep breathing that echoes the waves and takes me back to this morning's counselling session.

Dr Lindon couldn't be more different to the doctors at the unit. For one thing, I'm her client, not her patient. For another, the sessions with her actually help. I been thinking a lot about stuff I never dared think about before, and facing my fear is making me stronger.

Turning onto my front I slip into an easy, slow crawl, letting water funnel between my fingers, ticklish and soothing. At the edge of the bay, I tread water and squint across at Arran, who holds up an arm, waves, then heads home, clutching his surfboard. He's off to meet Kaye over in Truro, to look for wallpaper and stuff for the nursery. They asked if I wanted to go with them but, much as I can't wait for the baby to come – that's going to be the best

Christmas pressie ever – I'm not into the whole cot and mobiles thing. Not yet, anyway. Kaye says she's found a place that sells pickled walnuts and she's promised to pick a jar up, just for me.

Arran says he's at peace with having done what needed to be done, that he's glad it was him, not me. Cos he's never felt like a murderer, has he? He knows he did the right thing, whereas I would've doubted myself forever and I got enough to work through as it is. Like the fact I been wrong all my life about Grandad Arthur: all that anger and hatred towards him when all he did was die cos he loved Mum so much.

We went up to see Mum last week, all three of us: me, Arran and Kaye. She looks so much better. I gave her back her box and she wasn't mad at me, not one bit.

'My insurance policy.' She smiled. 'I guess it worked, didn't it?'

She'd found out about my dad when I was seven and she saw him on the telly. That night in the Lakes, she might've gone on to get drunk as the night wore on, but she was sober when she first laid eyes on him. Seeing him there on the news, in his power suit, driving around in his chauffeur driven car had terrified her. She never told a soul. All that time they thought she was just some drunk numskull who knew nothing, and all along she was watching them right back. Full of surprises, my mum.

Today's session with Dr Lindon was tough, but I'm sixteen now and should be able to take it. Cos as Dr Lindon says, it's all about choices, isn't it? Some stuff we don't get a say in, like who our family is or how we're raised. But none of that matters if we choose one path over another, one way of being over another way of being. Despite a very dodgy gene pool on the paternal side, I'm not a killer. Never was, never will be. Rory made his choices and I've made mine. Genes got nothing to do with it.

As for my father, today Dr Lindon wanted to talk about my feelings towards James Treherne, feelings I still keep tucked away in a grubby corner of my mind, lumpy and quiet and covered in a dust sheet. At night, when I allow myself to let go and dream, unseen hands lift the cloth, exposing a dark shape here, a spiky presence there. But, until today, I never whipped the sheet clean off and stared at what lies beneath.

I been treading water for too long and my whole body shivers as I drag my mind back to the task ahead. If I'm going to stand a chance in next month's county trials, I got to shave at least two seconds off my time for tomorrow's training session at the pool in Truro. My arms slice through short, choppy waves, and I tilt my body left and right until it's no longer possible to distinguish between the rise and fall of my chest and the lift and lull of the sea.

An hour later, I'm lying flat on my back on hot sand, daring to dream. I do that now, in life-after-the-unit – I dare to dream.

The first sign anything's wrong comes in the shape of a man wearing a black suit, glimpsed out of the corner of my eye, despite the fact that he's standing in cliff-shadow to one side of the path. Another dark shape flanks the path on its opposite side. Overhead, a gull screeches and I sit up and scan the sand. The only ways off this beach are either up that path (not a chance) or through the cave. Or – a third way comes to me in a flash – I could swim for it and pray some passing fisherman picks me up.

The possibilities are bouncing circles in my head when another figure appears on the path and heads towards me, bold as you like. I jump to my feet. How long will it take me to reach the sea? Twenty seconds? Thirty?

My feet refuse to budge.

The figure looms closer and I feel as though I'm being sucked down into wet sand.

'Hello, David.'

James Treherne, PM-that-was, stops right in front of me. His face sweats above a blue shirt and tie tucked into a pair of jeans that are way too hot for the day. There's a brown paper parcel tucked under his arm.

My knees turn to liquid. They're never going to leave me alone, are they? I drop to the sand.

'May I?'

It takes me a moment to realise he's asking permission to join me. It's a politician's request. Before I can say 'no', he's already sitting on the sand next to me, yanking his tie loose. He lays the brown paper parcel between us and gazes out to sea, eyes puffy and fluid, mouth drawn down.

'I'm leaving, David. Leaving the country.'

'Don't let me stop you.'

'These past few months have been hell.'

I stare at him, speechless. He can't be expecting sympathy, surely? He's been booted out of office and I'm glad. If Mum chose to charge him with statutory rape, he'd be off to jail right now instead of preparing to skip abroad before anyone can charge him with anything solid. But she don't want to. All she cares about is being safe. She's healing, slowly. She don't want to go back into the past.

Me? I been in the news way too much already, so I explained to the cops how I wrecked Rory Treherne's political dreams, so he went off his rocker and tried to kill me. Revenge, simple as. Which means James Treherne is getting off lightly.

'What do you want?' I ask the man who is, as fact would have it, my father.

'I wanted to give you this.' Paper crackles as he taps the parcel and pushes it towards me. 'Just take a look. Please.'

First I eye the parcel, then his face. There's something fluid about his skin. It's like a thousand tiny muscles are twitching away under the surface. It dawns on me that I'm not the only one who's nervous, and I catch myself actually feeling sorry for him. I sigh. I'm getting way too soft.

I peel back layers of paper until I'm holding a rough canvas photograph album, its edges serrated and yellowed. He nods at me to open it. Laying its spine along my right palm, I lift the front cover.

Inside, there's this picture of a toddler pushing a ball around a garden. The toddler's bright eyes, caught on camera, make me gasp with recognition. James reaches over and taps the toddler's mud-stained knees and scattered hair. 'Me, when I was three.'

Seeing my father, I see myself: mirror images, little and large. Nothing could've prepared me for this breathless ache in my chest. He traces his finger across to a woman, standing in the doorway.

'And that's my mother, your grandmother. I wish we both could have known her.'

My hands are shaking, and he reaches across me and turns more pages, exposing picture after picture of the boy who grew to be my father.

'This is your history, David. I wanted you to know who you are.'

'I already know who I am,' I say quietly.

He fixes his gaze back on the horizon as he undoes the top two buttons on his shirt and tugs his tie looser. Sweat trickles down his neck. 'Of course. I just meant, where you came from.'

Eventually, I close the album and rest it on my knees. He's staring at me with this intense look on his face.

'If you want to tell the world about me, David, I won't deny you.'

My neck stiffens. 'You'll be holed up in Bolivia or somewhere by then.'

'Not if you don't want me to be.'

I shrug. 'Makes no difference to me where you are.'

'I've always tried to protect you,' he says, his voice suddenly urgent. 'Your mother, too. I need you to know that.'

I turn to him, a cold anger forming in my gut. 'You let him bang me up with a bunch of nutters.'

'I kept you alive, I ...' His hands flutter as he searches for the right words. 'You and your mother are the only things I ever dared defy my father over. You don't know what he was like. If I'd pushed it, he would have killed you both.' He fiddles with his cufflink. 'He started grooming me for political brilliance the day I was born. Nothing, certainly not me, was going to get in his way. But I've always protected you, David.'

'Bullshit,' I snarl. 'If that van hadn't crashed, you would've left me to rot in whatever hellhole they were taking me to.'

'I would have found a way to get you out. With the law set to change and our work about to become more public, the unit was no longer a safe hiding place. My father arranged to get you transferred, but Carson was going in with you. He would have—'

'Carson?'

'Yes. I assigned Carson to take care of you until I could find a way to free you.'

The image of Drummond lying face down in the dust flashes into my head. *Nice when duty and pleasure go together like that.* So, Carson really was on my side all along. Put there by my father to protect me. The anger in my gut subsides a fraction, but that don't mean James Treherne is off the hook.

'All you had to do was own up to what you did. Then there would've been no point in him killing us, no point to any of it. Me and my mum would've been safe.'

He sighs heavily. 'I'm not a brave man, David. Not like you. I did what I could.'

His hands fidget and fiddle with his cufflink and I remember what Rory said: 'My son was always weak.'

I become aware of the midday rays burning into my neck. 'Well, it wasn't enough,' I say, and I look directly at him for the first time.

He avoids my gaze and nods. 'Losing the chance to know my son – a son I could have been proud of – is the biggest regret of my life.' He turns his face up to mine, and the need in his eyes comes as a shock. 'If there's any way you could forgive me, let me be a part of your life. Maybe later you will—'

'You're wasting your time,' I tell him. 'You made your choice a long time ago.'

'At least say you'll think about it. I could help you in all sorts of ways. I still have money, connections.'

'What good has any of that wealth and power ever done you? Or your father?' His neck reddens, and I realise that all my anger has evaporated. 'You don't got anything to offer that I want,' I say softly.

I don't want to hurt him. I just want him to go away. He can't help me. He'll have his hands full trying to sort out the messed-up state of his own head, which is even worse than mine if you ask me.

'I'm sorry,' I say (for the last time, I swear).

He turns his face away, straightens his sleeves, taps his cufflinks. Then he reaches into his pocket and proffers a business card, which I ignore, forcing him to lay it on the sand.

'If you change your mind …'

'I won't.'

'You're all the family I have in the world, David.'

I say nothing, and he walks away, his shoulders lower than when he arrived. Two figures melt out of the shadows and the beach once more belongs to the sand and the sea, the cries of the gulls, and the sharp tang of salt. When I feel sure that he's not coming back, I stand up, race into the sea and fling myself into its waiting arms.

Not until I've washed the last traces of the past from my pores, do I clamber out, shove the album into my rucksack, and head up to the village. I'm meeting Natalie for lunch. My mobile beeps. I slide my finger across the screen and check for messages.

Natalie. 'Be there dreckly.'

I smile and pick up my pace. Even though Natalie is always late, I been much too well trained to follow suit. I will be there at least five minutes early, waiting for her. Some behaviours, once learnt, are impossible to change. But not all.

I smile to myself. No, not all.

Acknowledgements

In the long journey that it's taken for this book to find the right publishing home, many people have helped me along the way.

Firstly, my heartfelt thanks go to my mother. Sorry it's taken so long to finally put a book into your hands, Mum, but life's been busy. I'd also like to thank my brother, Stephen Morgan; without his help this book might never have got off the ground. Thanks go to my sister too, Jacquie Beacher, for never asking me what on earth I thought I was doing with my life.

Amongst the writers whose encouragement and support throughout the writing of this book have been invaluable, I'd like to acknowledge Robin Falvey, Millie Light, Derek Thompson, Susie Bower, Jeni Whittaker, Rhodri Powell, Angie Sage, Anne Kennedy, Warren Stephenson, Joanne Worthington, Jeannette Marshall and Sarah Owens for the myriad of ways in which you helped to birth this book into being.

There are many more writing colleagues than I have the space to name, whose friendship, support and much needed humour have been, and still are, hugely appreciated. You know who you are; thank you each and every one of you.

Special acknowledgement has to go to Jane Moss, my partner in *The Writing Retreat*, and all the writers who come and retreat with us. You've been part of my writing family for nearly a decade now and we've shared a lot along the way.

I mustn't forget to thank Falmouth Fire Station, who looked at the crash and fire scenes in this book for me, and shared their knowledge and advice with great generosity.

To Charlie Carroll, Roz Watkins, Kit Fielding, Professor Catherine Leyshon and Dr Amanda Light for taking the time to read and endorse my offering. It's hugely appreciated.

Massive thanks go to my publisher, Hermitage Press, who are working so hard to create a home for Cornwall based writers. To Dr Paul Taylor-McCartney and Sally Hawker for being this book's champions in so many ways, to Sarah Dawes for your copyediting eye, to the talented Laura Clayton for your cover artwork, Oliver J Tooley for his formatting know-how and to Ben and the team at TJ Books for printing such a beautiful book.

And of course, I wouldn't have lasted five minutes following the tough road that is writing without the camaraderie, warmth and love of so many of my friends both in Cornwall and further afield. Again, you know who you are. Big hugs to you all.

Kath Morgan
September 2023

Online Support

www.papyrus-uk.org

www.nhs.uk/mental-health

www.samaritans.org

www.kidscape.org.uk

www.nspcc.org.uk